JACK DAWKINS

*being the further adventures
of the Artful Dodger*

TERRY WARD

Jack Dawkins

Published by The Conrad Press in the United Kingdom 2018

Tel: +44(0)1227 472 874
www.theconradpress.com
info@theconradpress.com

ISBN 978-1-911546-30-6

The Conrad Press logo was designed by Maria Priestley.

Printed and bound in Great Britain by Clays Ltd, St Ives plc

This novel is inspired by the character of Jack Dawkins, the 'Artful Dodger' in Charles Dickens's *Oliver Twist or The Parish Boy's Progress*, first published in volume form in 1838.

This is the last we see of the Artful Dodger in *Oliver Twist*, from the end of Chapter 43.

'Silence there!' cried the jailer.

'What is this?' inquired one of the magistrates.

'A pick-pocketing case, your worship.'

'Has the boy ever been here before?'

'He ought to have been, a many times,' replied the jailer. 'He has been pretty well everywhere else. I know him well, your worship.'

'Oh! you know me, do you?' cried the Artful, making a note of the statement. 'Wery good. That's a case of deformation of character, anyway.'

Here there was another laugh, and another cry of silence.

'Now then, where are the witnesses?' said the clerk.

'Ah! that's right,' added the Dodger. 'Where are they? I should like to see 'em.'

This wish was immediately gratified, for a policeman stepped forward who had seen the prisoner attempt the pocket of an unknown gentleman in a crowd, and indeed take a handkerchief therefrom, which, being a very old one, he deliberately put back again, after trying it on his own countenance. For this reason, he took the Dodger into custody as soon as he could get near him, and the said Dodger, being searched, had upon his person a silver snuff-box, with the owner's name engraved upon the lid. This gentleman had been discovered on reference to the Court Guide, and being then and there present, swore that the snuff-box was his, and that he had missed it on the previous day, the moment he had disengaged himself from the crowd before referred to. He had also remarked a young gentleman in the throng, particularly active in making his way about, and that young gentleman was the prisoner before him.

'Have you anything to ask this witness, boy?' said the magistrate.

'I wouldn't abase myself by descending to hold no conversation with him,' replied the Dodger.

'Have you anything to say at all?'

'Do you hear his worship ask if you've anything to say?' inquired the jailer, nudging the silent Dodger with his elbow.

'I beg your pardon,' said the Dodger, looking up with an air of abstraction. 'Did you redress yourself to me, my man?'

'I never see such an out-and-out young wagabond, your worship,' observed the officer with a grin. 'Do you mean to say anything, you young shaver?'

'No,' replied the Dodger, 'not here, for this ain't the shop for justice: besides which, my attorney is a-breakfasting this morning with the Wice President of the House of Commons; but I shall have something to say elsewhere, and so will he, and so will a wery numerous and 'spectable circle of acquaintance as'll make them beaks wish they'd never been born, or that they'd got their footmen to hang 'em up to their own hat-pegs, afore they let 'em come out this morning to try it on upon me. I'll—'

'There! He's fully committed!' interposed the clerk. 'Take him away.'

'Come on,' said the jailer.

'Oh ah! I'll come on,' replied the Dodger, brushing his hat with the palm of his hand. 'Ah! (to the Bench) it's no use your looking frightened; I won't show you no mercy, not a ha'porth of it. You'll pay for this, my fine fellers. I wouldn't be you for something! I wouldn't go free, now, if you was to fall down on your knees and ask me. Here, carry me off to prison! Take me away!'

With these last words, the Dodger suffered himself to be led off by the collar; threatening, till he got into the yard, to make a parliamentary business of it; and then grinning in the officer's face, with great glee and self-approval.

Having seen him locked up by himself in a little cell, Noah made the best of his way back to where he had left Master Bates. After waiting here some time, he was joined by that young gentleman, who had prudently abstained from showing himself until he had looked carefully abroad from a snug retreat, and ascertained that his new friend had not been followed by any impertinent person.

The two hastened back together, to bear to Mr Fagin the animating news that the Dodger was doing full justice to his bringing-up, and establishing for himself a glorious reputation.

JACK DAWKINS

*being the further adventures
of the Artful Dodger*

PROLOGUE

Jedidiah Fagin had not gone quietly to his death.

On the hour of his execution he was hauled unceremoniously from his cell in Newgate Prison, screaming as loud as his parched throat would permit:

'I don't want to die! Please, it's not time! Not time!'

The turnkeys, dragging his emaciated form along the echoing, stone passageway remained unmoved by his pleas. One of them remarked blithely:

'Not time, Fagin? Nobody 'ere knows what time it is; not since you stole all the clocks and watches in London, they don't. Besides which, a minute or two either way don't make difference; not in eternity it don't.'

The second turnkey was his equal when it came to a lack of compassion. 'Stole all the clocks and watches in London? That's a good 'un, Billy boy. You are a wag an' no mistake!'

Weakened by the condemned man's diet of bread and water, Fagin never stopped weeping, cursing and praying all the way to the Press Yard, a grim space within the prison that sunlight rarely entered, surrounded as it was by towering walls. A brief struggle ensued here as his manacles were removed and his arms pinioned.

The sombre little procession continued on its way, with Fagin's lamentations combining and competing with the intonations of the Ordinary. The worthy priest was praying aloud for Fagin's soul and for those of the two other, rather more stoical men, also being escorted to the Debtors' Door, beyond which stood the gallows. This wooden contraption had the classical façade of the prison as a backdrop. The splendid architecture successfully concealed the horrors that lay behind it, but didn't prevent the escape of an overpowering stench in to the surrounding streets.

On that cold February morning, Fagin's ragged figure was sandwiched between twenty-year-old Richard Moore, convicted of highway robbery, and Hiram Lesky. He was paying the ultimate price for ambitiously attempting to establish his own mint. A very dapper, little man; standing five feet two inches in his stockinged feet, the forger had been arrested after arousing the suspicions of his tailor by paying a bill with a cascade of shiny new florins.

Fagin was the main attraction for the crowd pressing in on the scaffold. Gossip and the sale of an enormous number of handbills providing lurid descriptions of his criminal activities, had built up his reputation.

Top hats and mob caps all jostled together, as their ill-mannered wearers tried to obtain the best vantage point. Retailers near to the site were earning a shilling or two by renting out their upper floor windows as viewing points. Dignity, decorum, and in some instances, décolletage, went out of the window as excited spectators taunted those who were about to die.

One or two pickpockets were working the crowd, taking full advantage of this golden opportunity; but even they were compelled to stop their activities as the condemned men came through the door in single file and mounted the steps to the perilous platform, built to execute a maximum of six persons at a time.

Seemingly deaf to the cacophony of noise emanating from all quarters, the hangman, John Langley, set about his grim task. One part of his mind was calculating how much money he would make from selling snippets of Fagin's beard.

Hiram Lesky took a last look to the east, where the risen winter sun was painting the sky with pink hues beyond the great dome of St. Paul's Cathedral. As young Richard Moore's lips moved in quiet prayer, Fagin suddenly appeared to accept the inevitable and gained some self-control. Baring his teeth, he glared defiantly at the baying mob; his fearsome visage causing some of the more sensitive among them to shudder.

The crowd fell silent as the nooses were placed carefully around the three necks. The ghoulish onlookers might not mind waiting fifteen minutes for a clumsily placed knot to kill a man, but Langley had his professional standing to think of.

With all eyes fastened on the doomed men, the onlookers held their collective breath, waiting for the dreadful moment.

The trap sprang open and the ropes snapped taut under the weight of human flesh. The crowd gaped and gasped, sucking in the life-giving air that was being denied to men in their death throes. While some of the females present belatedly covered their children's eyes and released pent-up emotions by bursting into floods of tears, everyone else let out a great roar of approval.

A letter from Jack Dawkins (Esq)

Dear reader,

Believe it or not, what follows is the truth, the whole truth and nothing but the truth (now there's a phrase that makes my memory shiver; my oath it does!)

By happy happenstance I ran into Mr Charles Dickens on the old stern-wheeler, the Delta Queen, as she made her way up the Ohio River in January 1842. Mr Dickens was on a literary jaunt in America at the time. More for my own amusement than anything else, I took the opportunity to join him as he leant on a rail looking down at the swirling river. I didn't tell him who I am, of course; that would have just been asking for trouble, and it's hardly likely he'd have believed me anyway. The world's full of tricksters. Instead, I just drew him out about his book, 'Oliver Twist', which not surprisingly I carry about with me much of the time. Although he's painted me blacker than I am and written some stretchers in it, it's mostly true. He didn't mind admitting to me that the story is based on discoveries he made when he was a young law reporter in London, about twenty odd years ago. Apparently, I was still famous in the law courts at the time, oh, all right; infamous, then. So was Fagin.

Mr Dickens, lest you hadn't noticed, is something of a campaigner. He went on to tell me he wrote *Oliver Twist* because he was upset about the unjust changes that had been made to Britain's Poor Law Act. I'm not sure whether a book can make the world a better place. Good luck to him on that one.

Tongue in cheek, of course. I asked the great man if he knew what had become of the Artful Dodger, and of Oliver.

'I have no certain knowledge of this,' he answered, 'but I've been led to believe that the rascal Dawkins of whom you speak, died some time ago in captivity in Australia, having been transported there. As for Oliver Twist himself, he assumed the name of his adoptive father, Brownlow, now long dead, and opened a bookshop. Unfortunately he was killed a few years ago when a crate of bibles fell on his head.'

I managed to stop myself from saying, 'Poor old Ollie!' Instead, I asked Mr Dickens what he thought of America.

'Many of the younger women possess great beauty,' he said, 'but I remain largely unimpressed by the bleak landscapes, and even less impressed by the obnoxious habit so many Americans have of chewing wads of tobacco. In addition, I've never known a people to eat as much, drink as much or expectorate as much; and the further west one travels, the worse it becomes.'

I laughed at that, then went below; anxious to see my dear wife Lysette and the children, who were waiting for me in our first-class cabin. I made thirty thousand dollars last year, but they'll be happy to know that while I was in the saloon I shook hands on a deal with a railroad man that will make us a whole lot more. Lysette is adding to our wealth by having her books on nature published. People have fallen for her beautiful illustrations of insects in 'Antopolis', the *same as they did for her birds and other tree dwellers in 'The Forest Canopy'. President Tyler, himself, has bought copies of them.*

I meet a lot of people in the course of selling my lumber; those who've read Oliver Twist tend to ask me if I'm related to the Artful Dodger. It amuses me to tell them that, as Dickens' book is all made up, his picking on my name is just a coincidence. Now I shall tell you what really happened to me all those years ago.

Yours sincerely
  Jack Dawkins.
  St Louis, Missouri
  Christmas 1844

CHAPTER ONE
In which Oliver does me a favour

Let's begin at the start, shall we? It's nigh on the end of February 1815 and I'm sitting on a damp mattress in Newgate Prison, wondering where my next meal's coming from. I'm down to my last sixpence after forking out a bribe so I can live in this quiet corner with my leg-irons removed. They call it 'Easement of Irons' payment, but as I said, it's a bribe.

Thanks to that young shaver Oliver Twist, Fagin's gone to join Bill Sikes and poor, murdered Nancy in the next world. I hope they do well there. As for me; by the by, you can call me the Dodger, or Jack, or even Mr Dawkins, if you've a mind to. I can't be too fussy about the nomenclature (no, I haven't swallowed Dr Johnson's *Dictionary*) you ascribe to me while I'm one of Newgate's unwilling guests. But panic ye not about my situation, because between you, me and the bugs in this mattress, I don't intend to overstay my welcome. If I did that, I'd hardly be worthy of the 'sobriquet' the Artful Dodger, bestowed on me by Fagin, would I?

When it comes to ducking and diving, that well-remembered escape artist, Jack Sheppard, has got nothing on me. I won't have to climb up the inside of a sooty chimney like he did to escape from here. I intend to get clean away!

Oliver was rightly named Twist, because he twisted Fagin, Sikes and all of his other enemies into knots they couldn't get out of. As for me, nabbed as I was for lifting a silver snuff box off a mark I'd followed half way up the City Road, I was already tucked away in here when the roof finally caved in on them. Instead of keeping my mind on the job that day, I'd been thinking about how Nancy had died at the hand of Sikes. She was only two or three years older than I am, and had just been taken on by Fagin when he came across yours truly, so we'd sort of grown up together; grown close, too. I'm not the sort who blubs if my feelings get hurt, neither am I ashamed to admit that I found a corner to cry in after I discovered her blood-soaked body. Sikes helped himself to her as soon as she was old enough, you know. He used her, abused her and ended up killing her. There was nobody to stop him. It really made my own blood boil, but what could a lad do against the likes of him? He flattened me once, just because I told him not to hit her again.

There were plenty of other girls on the loose, but they were unfortunate creatures I could only feel sorry for; although, on occasion, I did send my hands on what you might call 'voyages of discovery' if there were no objections. Pity for their condition and situation stopped me from doing the famous 'it' with them. Hold on a minute, I know you're thinking, 'Ha-ha, he's only saying that because he doesn't know how to do it!' Well, you're dead wrong. You don't spend your life living in overcrowded warrens without noticing things you ought not. I've seen just about everything from life being made and born, to death having the last laugh, so you'd better think again about what I can and can't do.

Anyway, that's enough of that. I'm only human, so dwelling on 'it' doesn't do me any good while I'm locked up in Newgate, as I'm sure you'll appreciate.

Charged with the theft of that snuff-box, which the perfumed fop I lifted it from could well have done without, I was hauled in to court at the Sessions House after being kicked about a bit by a policeman. The judge had to have his little joke after one of his flunkeys introduced me to him, formal-like.

'He's about fourteen or fifteen years of age and goes by the name of Jack Dawkins, m'lud.'

'Jack Dawkins, eh?' His honour sneered. 'Well, considering how he can't resist stealing shiny objects, he's certainly kin to a jackdaw!'

'And I know what sort of bird you are,' I called out. 'From where I'm standing, your beak looks like it belongs to the parrot family.'

I can't stand his type. They'll send an out-of-work man to the gallows for pinching enough stuff to keep his wife and children alive, then go home to a mansion and a two-hour dinner.

After everybody sitting in the gallery had finished laughing like the half-wits they were, and witnesses had dished the dirt on me, the big wig settled my future:

'I hereby sentence you to transportation to a penal colony for a period of fourteen years. If you return to these shores before that time has elapsed, you will be hanged by the neck until you're dead. Take him down.'

Some of those sitting in the gallery had the blasted cheek to applaud his lordship's verdict, but nobody actually laughed at it, especially me, if truth be told. I'd heard that a lot of those sentenced to transportation to the other side of the world don't live through the voyage. Some never make the journey at all, ending their days on a prison hulk; either way dying of the hardship.

Hardship? Now that is a laugh! I was born to it; and before you start looking down your noses at me as a dip and a vagabond, let me tell you a thing or three. I've spent most of my life trying to stay alive on the streets of London town, summer and winter. You ought to try it sometime. It's an education. Mother? I've got memories of arriving in London with a woman when I was about four or five years old. She may have been my mother and we may have come from Bedford, because that place name means something to me.

Early last year, I did something that made the whole Twist business come about. I got it in my noggin that I ought to try and find my mother. It was an idea that had been growing in me for quite some time. Crazy, eh? I mean, where the devil would I start looking for her; Bedford, perhaps? Deciding to give it a go, I'd actually got as far as Barnet before I began calling myself all kinds of a fool. It was there that I ran into Oliver Twist. A runaway, he was on his last legs and needed help, bad. I wasn't about to leave him to peg out on the steps of the town hall, or hand him over to those who'd send him to the nearest spike, that's a workhouse to you. Get stuck in one of those places and you're likely to come out feet first and be buried in Potters Fields. No, the best I could do for him was to take him to Fagin's den at Saffron Hill. He'd get plenty of grub, a warm fire, blankets and a lumpy mattress; all paid back out of easy pickings, once we'd taught him the ropes. How was I to know he would blow everything to smithereens?

When I add it all up, it strikes me that his guardian angel, I don't have one myself, must have stopped twiddling his thumbs and decided to give Oliver a helping hand. He made sure I turned up in the nick of time to save him from starvation then planted Brownlow right where Ollie would run into him. Now Ollie's living in clover.

To begin with, Oliver didn't know where he came from. He does now; and that's set me to thinking even harder about my mother. I don't expect I'll have the same sort of luck he had, but I'm determined to have a real go at trying to find her as soon as I get out of here. I must have had a father, too. I wonder what sort of cove he is or was? I don't remember the gent, and how I know my name's Jack Dawkins, is a mystery to me. Perhaps mama taught it to me at her knee while papa was away fighting the French.

Now why did I have a thought like that? It came to me like it was some sort of foggy memory.

For all I know, I might have half a dozen brothers and sisters, some dead and some still alive. They might even be out there, playing the same game I did until I took up lodgings here in

Newgate. Putting all that to one side for a moment; as I was trying to say earlier; what would you do if, when you were only knee-high to a grasshopper, you found yourself left all alone in a world that didn't care tuppence if you lived or died? I'll wager most of you would have just given up and been dead in no time. Well, I'm not like that. I've got something inside me, see? I don't know what it is, but it keeps me hanging on.

Casting my mind back, I recall how, when I'd grown a bit, but still only came up to a Dutchman's kneecaps, I'd crept among the crowds lining the river to watch a fleet of ships following the barge carrying Nelson's coffin to its resting place in St Paul's, while I slid my baby hands in and out of bags and pockets, helping myself to whatever would stop me from starving or freezing to death. That was January 1806, as I recall.

I did that sort of thing for years; running, hiding, thieving – surviving. I got a job once, delivering trays of hot pies to taverns. I soon got the elbow, though; my employer said I was eating too many of 'em.

I learnt the way of the world by keeping my eyes and ears open in taverns, gin palaces and outside of coffee-houses where dandies made and lost their money. I liked to know what was going on around me, in case I could make use of it. That's why I'm able to tell you that I fell in with Fagin in the winter of 1810. Mad King George's son had just been made Prince Regent and we were fighting those Frenchies again. He's another one who got sent down in the end; Napoleon, I mean. They've stuck him on an island, somewhere, but I bet he's still got a lot more than sixpence in his pocket. Kill one man and you'll get hanged. Kill a hundred thousand and they'll put up a statue with your name on it.

Anyway, I was leaning on some railings in Drury Lane, minding my own business and in need of a warm coat, when a hand grabbed my shoulder and spun me round. I thought I'd been took until I saw that the man holding on to me wasn't an officer of the law; not with the straggling beard he had, or the rag-bag of clothes he was wearing. Everything about him was dark, reminding me of one of those ravens you see strutting about, scaring the pigeons. He had a nose you could make two of, darting eyes and hunched shoulders with a moth-eaten black cloak hanging from them. He introduced himself as,

'Jedidiah Fagin, saviour of the young and needy.'

It was the only time I heard his first name spoken, by him or anybody else. In fact I've just had to scratch my head to try and remember what it was. It woke the lice up but brought the name to mind.

Fagin always spoke in a whispery kind of way, as though he was sharing a secret. He did on the day we met.

'You're just what I've been looking for; a boychik at a loose end. How are you at climbing drain pipes, my dear?'

It didn't take much for him to persuade me to join his merry little band, who all thought they knew the secret of how to get rich before they grew old. I ate well and dressed warm after that.

'Artful' was one of Fagin's favourite words, so it wasn't long before he'd declared, in front of Nancy, Sikes and the young 'uns, that henceforth I was to be known as The Artful Dodger. I knew the miser inside out by then. He was just trying to flatter me so I'd put up with him keeping all but one of the thirty guineas I'd just handed over after I'd taken all the risk in lifting them. Still, as I stood head and shoulders above the other guttersnipes in his employ, I was happy to accept a fancy title. It was better than the cuff round the ear he liked to dish out to the rest of them every now and again. To give him his due, by that time, he'd started teaching me how to read and write-and had me studying a dictionary. With one of his bony arms round my neck and a long finger pointing at some scribble on a piece of paper, he'd said to me.

'If you can't read, how will you know the value of documents that might fall in to your clever little hands; and if you can't write, you won't be able to forge signatures, will you, my dear?'

As it turned out, I was a quick learner. Fagin said I had a good brain. All it needed was filling.

I know I'm down at the moment, but I'm not out; far from it. They can keep their transport ships and prison hulks. Crossing the Thames by wherry is about as far as I'm prepared to go on water. Any day now, prisoner escorts will be coming to take several of us to a ship that will deliver us to Southampton. Once it's got a full load, and that won't take long, the transport will set sail for New South Wales. I'd prefer it if it was going to old South Wales, myself. But they'll have to manage without me. One way or another, I'll lay my hands on a key that'll unlock the leg irons I'll be wearing. Then I'll be gone; out of sight before they can shout, 'Oi'.

I inherited this straw mattress from the man who died on it. When I say 'inherited' I mean I rolled his body off and laid claim to it before anybody else did. It's better than trying to sleep on a stone floor. I'm sorry if that sounds cold-hearted, but at least I had the decency to let him die before I took possession. He was so weak, I could have helped myself three days earlier if I'd wanted to. You've got to be tough if you want to go on living, but there are limits.

I keep tight hold of this shiv I made out of a beef-bone, even when I'm snoring. Good thing I do, too. I drew blood with it only yesterday when some ragamuffin tried to snatch my bread ration from me. He went away sucking his knuckles. You can't trust anybody in here.

Hello, that turnkey Ryan; the one who enjoys kicking a man when he's down, is sauntering towards me, keen to knock some-body's block off with that cudgel he's swinging about. The way he's scratching himself, he must have the same amount of fleas as the rest of us.

Standing over me, looking as though he'd like to bash my head in, he asks,

'You're Dawkins, ain't you?'

'No, I'm the King of Spain,' I tell him. 'What d'ya want? Can't you see I'm busy?'

'That's enough of your lip,' he snarls like the mangy cur he is, 'come with me; you've someone waiting to see you at the Lodge.'

That gets me to my feet, double-quick. 'Somebody to see me? Who might that be, then?'

Ryan jabs me with the thick end of his cudgel. 'It's a high-nob who don't want to get his nice, shiny boots dirty by crossing the prison yard, that's who. Move yourself, he ain't got all day.'

Just to keep my hand in, I search Ryan's pockets while we're on the way to the Lodge. All I get for my troubles is a filthy wipe and a twist of tobacco, so I give them back to him.

'Here cully, you look as though you need these more than I do.'

'You thieving young varmint!' He isn't happy about it and proves it by grabbing hold of me and shoving me through the entrance to the Turnkeys' Lodge.

I see straightaway that here's a chance for me to get my hands on one or two of those keys I was talking about. There are plenty of them hanging on a board behind that desk.

These keepers like their home comforts. They've got a kettle singing away on a coal fire in the grate, and I can smell fresh bread - and is that cheese? I like a nice bit of Cheddar myself.

Ryan still hasn't got over me lifting his goods. One of his feet connects with my rear end, sending me sprawling and giving me a close up view of a pair of leather boots. Ryan was right; they are nice and shiny.

'Is it necessary for you to treat your charges so roughly, sir?' a plummy voice enquires.

Ryan probably wants to say 'yes' to that, but keeps his mouth shut.

Looking up, I see a pair of britches and a green waistcoat buttoned over a stomach to be proud of. It's crossed by a tasty gold watch chain. The frock coat doesn't have a single speck of dust on it, as far as I can tell, and the gold stick pin in his silk cravat makes my fingers twitch.

The old gent wearing this rig is looking down at me through a pair of spectacles. I recognise him right off. It's John Brownlow. His being here can only mean one thing for me—trouble! I scramble to my feet as he looks me over and says:

'Ah, Mr Dawkins, our paths have already crossed, have they not?'

Not knowing what I'm in for, I answer that as carefully as I can. 'We sort of met when I was doing my best to take care of young Oliver Twist. Anyway, you can't touch me. I've already been given my punishment.'

Brownlow waves this away with a gloved hand. 'I intend you no harm, young man; far from it. Against my better judgment I have come here today in order to help you.'

I screw up my face and try my best to look tearful. 'You've left it a bit late. I'm due to be transported any day now.'

'Please don't despair, Dawkins,' Brownlow says, as though he cares about what happens to me. 'The child whom you knew as Oliver Twist has begged me to intervene with the authorities on your behalf. Although he is sensible enough to realise that your motives were far from altruistic, Oliver agrees that you helped him when he first came to London. You led him to shelter when he needed it most. By doing so you may have inadvertently saved his life. Oliver is also of the opinion that you were instrumental in re-uniting him with the remnants of his family and fortune.'

His lofty tone deepens and he starts spouting like a parson in a pulpit. 'It is shameful that, even in this great, wealthy capital city of ours, it is all too easy for orphaned children to starve to death, be murdered for a pair of shoes, or die of the cold. Disease is rampant, our water unsafe to drink - poverty and ignorance abound -.'

He stops talking, looks up as though he's expecting a halo to be handed down to him at any moment, then, getting back to the subject in hand, says, 'There is truth in what Oliver says. Because you found him, he found me. You will be pleased to know that, in memory of my friendship with his father, the boy will soon become my adopted son.'

Well, bully for you, Ollie! But I want to know what's in store for me. My wish is granted when Brownlow gets down to business.

'Oliver is good through and through, so I cannot stand in the way of his noble intention to help you. Fortunately for you, I have friends in high places who have agreed that under certain conditions you are to be given a second chance.'

For a moment I couldn't draw breath. 'You don't mean they're letting me off?'

'Yes I do, in a manner of speaking. I have posted a bond and signed legal documents my lawyer, Mr Frank Jaggers, drew up for me. Having been signed by Mr Justice Stareleigh in the Court of Chancery, they allow you to be released in to my charge. I have also arranged for you to be removed from the temptations of London. You will be sent to the country and given every opportunity to become an honest, hardworking citizen.'

CHAPTER TWO
Mutton chops for breakfast, courtesy of Mr Brownlow

I could have turned somersaults. No transportation. No prison hulk!

'I'm ready when you are, Mr Brownlow, sir.'

Brownlow turns a bit snappy. 'Not so fast, sir; you shall not be leaving here today. A police officer shall collect you tomorrow morning. He shall escort you to Gravesend where you will be met by a very good friend of mine. His name is Mr Gilbert Godden. He shall conduct you to Shippenden Farm, a place he now owns on Romney Marsh. You will be out of harm's way down there. I must warn you that should you attempt to abscond or commit any sort of offence whilst you are bonded to me, the consequences for you will be severe; which reminds me that, under the terms of agreement, you are obliged to report yourself to the local magistrate upon arrival, and once every three months, thereafter. Do you understand and agree to these conditions?'

'Yes, I understand, all right, but how will I live, guv'nor? What'll I do with myself all day?'

'You shall work for a living, sir. That is what people do.'

That sets me back on my heels. 'What, me - work?'

'Yes, indeed.'

'What at?'

'Farming, Dawkins, farming! Plenty of exercise and fresh, country air will do you the world of good. In the meantime you may wish to spend the next twenty-four hours contemplating your good fortune and giving thanks to the Almighty for His mercy. We shall not meet again until I visit Shippenden to see how you are faring. That is all I have to say to you at the moment, sir. I bid you good day.'

The thought of becoming a work slave has got my full attention, so Brownlow's departure takes me by surprise.

'Mr Brownlow, sir, Mr Brownlow ---.'

He ignores me. Twitching his top hat, held in both hands behind his frock-coated back, he's gone.

Ryan gives me an almighty smack round the head before taking me back to my mattress, or where I'd left it. Somebody has helped himself to it. As I said, you can't trust anybody. Still, I'd picked Ryan's pocket again, so at least I had a twist of tobacco. I tamped half of it in to the bowl of a clay pipe I had stowed away. In exchange for the other half, I got a light from a skinflint crouched over a small fire he'd made out of I don't know what. You get nothing for nothing in Newgate.

Then I sit with my back against a wall, smoke my pipe and try to get used to the idea that I'll soon be free, after a fashion. Whatever happens to me from tomorrow on, will be better than travelling to a land I've been told is full of cannibals and monstrous beasts.

It was a long night. I slept for a while, though, and had a dream. My mother was laughing and holding her arms out:

'Come to me, Jack. You can do it, darling child; just a few more steps.'

I was a babe, learning to walk, and she was very pretty.

It depends on my mood, but mostly, I don't believe in other worlds, and stuff like that, but that dream has left me feeling as though my mother's still calling out to me from - somewhere. I expect my empty stomach's making me a bit light headed.

I was wide awake long before daylight crept in through those barred windows set high on the walls. I watch the bread stealers, bawdy-house keepers, footpads and fraudsters as they lie like corpses all over the floor. The only way you can tell they ain't dead is by the noises they are making. Coughing, snorting, gurgling, and calling out in their sleep. It's Newgate's dawn chorus and I can't wait to get out of here.

'There's a Runner come for you.' It's Ryan, my favourite gaoler.

With my heart thumping away in my chest, I jump a foot in the air and click my heels together. It would have been two feet, but I'm in a weakened condition.

'That's me out o' here!'

Ryan's most put out at the thought of losing me. 'You've had a stroke of luck,' he jeers, 'but I'll be seeing you again, and next time you'll be here for the drop.' He draws a dirty finger across his dirty throat then makes me grab hold of my spare rags.

After that, I swagger along behind Ryan, acting like I'm the cock of the walk. That's the Dodger in me. Another part of my brain is wondering what my life will be like without having the dark cloak of London covering me.

The Bow Street Runner waiting for me in the turnkeys' office is a tall streak, about thirty years old. His jaw is shaved clean and, judging from the trim of his black hair, he's just paid a visit to a barber's shop. He's dressed in one of those new blue uniforms, but I can see he's hung on to the red waistcoat left over from the days when the Runners were known as 'Redbreasts'. Us young 'uns would catcall and shout 'Redtits' at them from a safe distance, then run off, busting our sides with laughter. This one's sheathed cutlass and the stave he's leaning on, helps me keep my mouth shut. He's twirling a top hat on his free hand and doesn't bother introducing himself before telling me,

'There's a parcel of *Ede and Ravenscroft's* finest apparel waiting for you there on the desk, me lad. Clean that carapace of prison filth off your vile body and get changed in to it, tout suite.'

I take offence at that. 'Hey! Who are you to call me vile?'

27

'My name, sir, is Martin Hawke, and I can tell at a glance that there's enough dirt between your toes to grow a row of turnips.'

He turns to Ryan. 'Can you oblige with soap and water, Mr Ryan?'

'There's soap, basin and a jug of water right there.' Ryan nods in the direction of a table standing hard by the back wall, right next to where those keys I don't need any more are hanging. 'He can pour it himself. I'm not here to wait on the likes of him.'

Ryan's a laugh a minute.

All I have to wash with is cold water and hard, lye soap, so I don't go to a lot of trouble.

My hair's like a rat's nest, I can see that when I look at myself in a piece of mirror glass. I'm not a great admirer of my own phizog. My nose is crooked and my ears stick out - but I've seen worse. I give myself a wink, saying hello to a face I haven't laid eyes on for weeks.

When I undo the parcel, I find a complete set of clothes; a linen shirt, new-fangled trousers that prove to be a bit too long for me, and a double breasted coat that almost reaches my knees. The boots fit, but there's a dent in the conical hat Brownlow's provided. After straightening it out, I make a show of placing it on my head at a fine, jaunty angle then strike a pose.

'Stap me vitals!' the Bow Street Runner says. 'It's Beau Brummel's younger brother!'

'Pick that stuff up,' Ryan orders, casting a beady eye on my old rags. 'You're not leaving that lot here.'

After wrapping them in the paper my new outfit arrived in, I bow low and offer them to Ryan.

'Here's a little gift, sir, for your chee-ild!'

'Best not do that Dawkins,' Hawke says, 'Mr Ryan's offspring will only get to playing dice for such a prize.'

Before I have time to think, the Runner grabs my arm, locks a handcuff over my left wrist, then snaps the other over his right one. It's very smartly done.

So much for my freedom! I decide to put in a complaint.

'What's all this, then?'

Cool as a cucumber, Hawke says, 'I should hate to lose you after so brief an acquaintance. Those whom God has joined together, let no man put asunder! Now, I'm to buy you breakfast from funds provided. I'm sure you can manage to eat a morsel or two after your sojourn here.'

Next minute, he's pulling me through the door. 'Good day, Ryan,' he says. 'I'm much obliged to you.'

'Me too,' I tell him.

Ryan, sounding as though he's lost a shilling and found sixpence, answers, 'The outer door's unlocked. I'll be along directly to secure it.'

Hawke's parting shot is, 'The Lord looseth men out of prison, eh, Mr Ryan?'

'Not if I had my way He wouldn't,' comes the reply.

A second door opens straight on to Newgate Street. The noise and bustle hit me right away. I'm deafened, and half blinded by nothing more than grey daylight. People are hurrying this way and that as if they haven't got a minute to live. Horses, hand-carts and wagons. Wagons, handcarts and horses. It's funny how I never noticed all this traffic when I was dipping and dodging on these very streets. I feel as though I've been born again.

There's hardly room for us to walk, but Hawke forces his way through the pedestrians, dragging me with him.

Well, would you believe it! There goes a geezer carrying a tray of hot pies on his head!

On Ludgate Hill, a fat porker of a man, dressed as though he's going to a funeral, waves a broadsheet under our noses.

'War in America! A tanner for the latest news, sir?' Hawke ignores him, and with me in tow, changes direction. Ducking his head, he pulls me through the entrance to an eating-house. Glory be!

The place is as full as my belly's empty.

Hawke has problems with his height, his stave, his top hat and his cutlass. He's trying to squeeze his long frame between a bench and a solid oak table. The fact that one of his wrists is joined by iron to one of mine isn't helping him. He gives me a filthy look when I start cackling at the sight of him trying to get his knees under the table.

I'm seated on the bench at last, hard against Hawke's thigh. If I reach across with my free hand I'll be able to take hold of the keys hanging from his belt.

An urge to escape takes my brain over, but Hawke is looking at me as though he's reading my mind. Now he's changing the lay of his cutlass and placing his free hand over those keys, rot him.

Not a bit put out, he asks:

'What's your fancy then, young Dawkins? I'm under orders to allow you the freedom to choose your own victuals.'

It was stupid of me to think about escaping before I'd had breakfast on Brownlow. 'I've been dreaming lately of mutton chops and porter,' I tell him.

'That's a good choice for a body that's only got one free hand to eat with. You can use your fingers; they were invented before forks, anyway.'

He signals a waiter by raising his stave.

I decide that a show of good manners might go down well. 'Aren't you joining me, Mr Hawke, sir?'

'No, thank you. I was having my breakfast while you were still in the hands of Morpheus.'

I tackle those chops like a wolfhound. The bread's very good and the beer even better.

Feelings seem to be running a bit high among the three wharf rats sitting at the next table. One of them shouts:

'Call me a liar again and I'll cut your gizzards out!'

Hawke's body stiffens. He's about to do his duty as a policeman when one of the scruffs says, 'Sit down, Tom, you couldn't cut butter with a hot knife.'

Hawke turns to me. 'Finish up. It's time for us to depart this Utopia for trenchermen. We have a boat to catch.'

I gulp the last of the porter and quickly pick a chop clean. I'm about to wipe my greasy fingers on my new coat when I think better of it and suck them instead.

'I'm ready when you are.'

As we begin to leave, I notice two, long apron-ed, lank haired waiters staring at the handcuffs. I have a word or two with them.

'What are you ugly whippersnappers looking at; ain't you got any work to do?'

One of them looks me up and down, and says, 'I don't know what you are, 'aircut. Your name plate must have fell off.'

The second one laughs like a drain. 'Keep your eye on him, officer,' he advises Hawke. 'He looks like a desperate character to me!'

I leave my parcel of rags on the bench, hoping one of them will notice it and think they've found something valuable.

Now that we're back on the street, I suddenly realise what Hawke had last said.

'Boat, what boat?' I ask him.

He explains. 'One of those modern marvels, a paddle wheeler, is leaving Old Stairs for Gravesend this morning, and we're travelling on it. Come along, the *Belle Sauvage* is nearby. One can always find Hackney carriages waiting for customers there. We'll need one to get us to Wapping. *Tempus fugit.*'

I think he means, 'We've got to get a move on.'

I could have told Hawke about the carriages. I've ridden on the backs of them enough times; staying ready to duck the driver's whip if he spots me. I tell Hawke so after we climb in to one, and get the second smile of the morning.

The streets are crowded with traffic as our carriage heads east. Still pinching myself at this sudden change in my life, I lean back against the upholstery and look up at Hawke. That's how it is with us two; he looks down at me and I look up at him.

'Going on a boat, am I? So I'm being transported, after all.' It's my idea of a joke.

Hawke manages yet another smile. 'That remark contains a nice touch of whimsy, Dawkins. You are not quite the common or garden delinquent I've been chasing and catching for nigh on six years. You're the first one I've ever suited, booted, breakfasted and seen off to live in Arcadian bliss. I'd release you from these cuffs, but there's something about you feral boys that compels you to live the way you do. Why, you'd be gone in a blink of an eye if I relaxed my vigilance, would you not?'

The man seems to be able to look right inside my head. 'I can't help what I was born to, can I?' I tell him.

'You think not? As the Immortal Bard wrote, we make guilty of our own disasters, the sun, moon and stars; as if we were villains by necessity.'

I work that out, then reply, 'Villainy often starts out of necessity, Mr Hawke, then becomes a way of life because nobody will take a chance on you; unless you want to spend your life keeping the streets clear of horse manure, or something.'

Hawke may have to look down at me, but he doesn't talk down. 'I agree,' he says, 'it is close to impossible for a person to get on in this fair land of ours if he is born to the lower orders. It takes exceptional strength of character and intelligence to do so; which prompts me to ask you if you have ever read a book? Oh, what a silly question that is!'

'I have, as it happens,' I tell him.

'Have you, indeed?'

'Yes. *Aesop's Fables* was the name of one of them. Fagin said it was first writ hundreds of years ago in some foreign tongue. It's all about animals and such. I liked *Robinson Crusoe* better. He knew how to look after himself.'

Hawke dips his free hand inside his coat and pulls out a leather bound book; the sort that are worth a bob or two. 'I shall put you to the test, my friend. Tell me the title of this tome, if you will?'

I study the words on the cover. 'It's called, *The Ad-ventures of Rod-er-ick Ran-dom* by Tob-ias Smoll-ett.'

My learned escort tucks his book away. 'I'm deeply impressed. As I said, you are a rather uncommon criminal. Only one in a hundred of your kind can read; and as for script, most can do little more than make their mark with a cross.'

At Wapping, the dome of St.Paul's, which I've sometimes stood under, rears up beyond the bare masts and spars of ships at anchor. I draw Hawke's attention to it.

'It's queer how that big church always seems to be looking over my shoulder wherever I am in London.'

'That is your guilty mind at work, Mr Dawkins; the pricking of your conscience over your un-Godly life.'

'Call me un-Godly, if you like, Mr Hawke, but I've got feelings. I'm not what you might call holy, but I've been known to say a prayer or two-and not for myself, either. They'd be wasted on me. Not so long ago, you could have seen me saying one over the dead body of a girl I liked; no, more than liked, as it happens. The last one I said was for my mother, wherever she is.'

'My apologies,' Hawke says, hanging his head. 'Do you have a name for her - your mother, I mean?'

'Only Dawkins,' I tell him, 'and I'm not even certain sure about that. It would have been impossible yesterday, but now I'm out, I'm going to do everything I can to find her.'

Hawke clears his throat and studies the upholstery on the opposite seats. 'A noble intention, sir, but I fear it will be an impossible task for a young man with no resources. I will make some enquiries and see what I can do to help you, but please don't raise your hopes. As you are well aware, London is nothing but a seething mass of humanity; its common people live and die in their thousands, unknown to all but the few who are close to them.'

I nod my head in agreement and thank him. It's a small hope, but I can feel it inside me, like a warm drink.

CHAPTER THREE
No pies at the inn

On the quay, we join a group of passengers waiting for watermen to take them out to the steam boat. My stomach, already complaining about the sudden arrival of all that meat and drink I had for breakfast, takes a turn for the worse at the thought of riding on it. Like as not, it'll blow up and send me to kingdom come. I mean the steamer, not my stomach.

Still linked to Hawke, I manage to keep everything down as we step aboard a small boat; too small, if you ask me! I've never liked being on the water very much.

Hawke airs his knowledge. Poking a finger at the back of the old rum gagger sculling us out to the paddle-wheeler, he says:

'These watermen are kings of the river. They refuse to allow passenger vessels to tie up at piers or jetties for fear of losing their livelihood.'

We pass close to a paddle wheel and bump against a platform with steps running up from it.

The steam boat is trembling from one end to the other. Perhaps it don't want to leave London, either. To take my mind off things, I look up at the tall chimney sticking up from the middle of the boat. It's shooting gobs of black smoke in to the air. I get the fancy that they're escaping from whatever devil-demon it is that's making all the noise down below.

Hawke, stepping lightly on to the platform, stretches out an arm and pulls me on after him. Somehow or other we climb the steps and stand together on the quivering deck.

'Let's not go below,' Hawke says. 'It's not so cold today and staying on deck will give us both the opportunity to get some much needed fresh air in to our lungs. I'm convinced I have an inch of soot in the bottom of mine. Truly the light is sweet and a pleasant thing it is to behold the sun, as it says in Ecclesiastes, and I say it certainly is in the month of February when the icicles are normally hanging. By the way, can you swim?'

'Like a stone,' is my answer to that one.

'I thought as much.' Hawke produces a key and unlocks the handcuffs.

The first thing I do is shake hands with myself. 'How-de-do! Well, thanks for giving it back to me, Mr Hawke. I've missed having it, you know. It's the one I use to scratch myself with.'

Sitting beside me, the friendly officer extends his long legs. 'Being locked together with someone is just as onerous for me, you know.'

'Not quite,' I tell him. 'You're the one with the key.'

Somebody starts shouting orders and blowing a whistle. The boat's moving; edging its way to the middle of the river. The paddle wheels are nearly as big as the one I saw at a flour mill on the Lea, when I was up that way. They start to churn the water; throwing it about as though they're trying to dig furrows in it. That noisy thing, somewhere under our feet, is stonking away louder than ever.

The boat is slipping easily along now; the smoke being blown to nothing by the wind. Tell me to shut up about her if you like, but I get the funny feeling that every minute of the journey I'm taking is bringing me closer to my mother.

There's plenty of traffic on the Thames today. Brown-sailed barges, rowboats of all sizes, and here's a man o' war! Whatever my faults, I love the way we English are always beating those Frenchies when we get to grips with them. Old Fagin fought them once. He told me the history of it all, one dark night when we were waiting for the lamps to go out in a certain house. The warship's gun ports are closed, which is a shame, because I'd like nothing better than seeing cannon sticking out of them. With only a few topsails showing, she's heading in the same direction as us; only we're moving a bit faster. I wonder where she's bound for - who knows? It's a mighty big world and I haven't seen any of it.

Those paddle wheels keep driving us forward. I close my eyes. Here I am, out of Newgate, stuffed in a suit that don't suit me, if you catch my meaning, and riding on a boat noisy enough to frighten the horses. I've been fed and watered, too!

I know I'm not dreaming it all when Hawke pokes me in the ribs.

'That's Greenwich,' he tells me, pointing at some grand palaces that reach down to the river's edge. 'The royals lived there upon occasion.'

A lot of passengers line the rail to admire the place.

'Well, good luck to the royals!' I say. 'It looks big enough to house half of those who live on London's streets. But they'd never think of using it to give the likes of them a roof over their heads, would they?'

Hawke gives me smile number three, or is it four? 'Only if they were made to, as they were in France. Twenty years ago the masses finally, if somewhat brutally, brought an end to their Ancien Regime.'

'Their ancient what?' I ask.

Hawke sighs. 'No, not ancient, although it is French for ancient, or more accurately perhaps, 'former', but when one says, 'Ancien Regime' one really means, the old order.'

'Well, why don't one say what one means, instead of one talking in riddles?'

As I sit back and start drifting off to sleep, it occurs to me that I'd better read a lot more books, because I don't know much about anything at the moment.

In what seems to be no time at all, Hawke wakes me with another poke in the ribs. Opening my eyes, I see that we're angling in towards the shore.

There's a town straggling up a hillside. It doesn't look like much. A church spire shows itself above a collection of low buildings. They're mostly made of wood.

All around the deck, people are gathering up their brats and baggage, in a hurry to get off the boat.

Hawke stands up.

'This, my light-fingered friend, is Gravesend. A sepulchral place-name with a hint of hope attached. It's where your deluded benefactor's associate, Gilbert Godden, should be waiting for us. He'd better not be late, I need to be back on board when this marvel returns to London this afternoon. As a matter of interest, do you know that Gravesend is the last resting place of the Indian maid, Pocahontas?'

'Poker who?' I ask.

Hawke, who I somehow can't help liking, gives me the benefit of his know-it-all brainbox. 'She came to England from the Americas as the wife of one, John Rolfe, in 1616, but after being presented at court, the poor girl quickly succumbed to our climate and diseases.'

Placing his top hat firmly on his head, he produces the handcuffs. 'I'm obliged to do this because I still don't trust you.'

There's no point in arguing, so I offer up my wrist. 'Here we go again.'

Boats are bobbing about, waiting their turn to get near the boarding platform. I hang on to Hawke's sleeve, and down the steps we go.

I swear there's four inches of Thames water swilling about in the bottom of our little ferry.

'No modern jetty here, either,' Hawke complains to no-one in particular. 'It must be due to these Luddite watermen again.'

As he pulls at the oars, ours manages to gasp out, 'That's right; do me out of a living!'

He brings us to a set of steps on what might be called 'dry land' but all I can see is mud.

38

'You nearly took the skin off my wrist,' I tell Mr Hawke, as he pulls me on to the bottom step.

I have to go along with him when he says, 'Better that than a ducking, don't you think? Now then, where's Godden? He's supposed to be meeting us here. Let's see if he's waiting at that inn over there, shall we?'

I like the way he offers me choices when I haven't got any.

'Yeah, let's,' I say, 'a nice mug of ale wouldn't go amiss.'

The Thames is very wide here, with plenty of boats running up and down it. There's no shortage of gulls either, wheeling about and swooping down to grab a piece of whatever takes their fancy on the ground.

The *Three Daws* tavern stands at the bottom of a narrow street. Being no better than those you'll find in Seven Dials, it makes me feel at home for the first time today.

Three sailors, drunk enough to make them easy pickings for me, if I was still in that line of work, stagger out of the saloon door, just as we are about to open it. When one of them falls down, laughing helplessly, the other two grab hold of his arms and haul him to his feet.

'Whoops-a-daisy, Denny.'

As they bar our way, Hawke grips his stave and tries being polite.

'Excuse me, gentlemen. Allow us to pass, if you please.'

The seamen put their arms around each other's shoulders, focusing their attention on him as best they can. The shortest of them examining Hawke's tall frame from toecaps to top hat.

'Stripe me! Is it a main mast or a mizzen we've got here, mates?'

'It's neither, Shorty,' Denny says, 'it's one of them there totem poles we saw when we was up the St Lawrence last year.'

I hear Hawke give another one of his sighs. 'Let's have none of your foolishness, men. We would like ingress to this tavern, if you please.'

One of them notices the handcuffs. 'Look at that, boys! I thought long, tall papa was a-holding hands with little Willy, but the lad's cuffed to him. He must be a runaway. You know how short-handed the old *Hunter* is; p'raps if we unlock the young rascal, we can press him in to service and take him with us when we slips anchor tonight. On top of that, I want the copper stick the lofty one's carrying.'

'You can have it!' Denny cries. What I want is the fancy topper he's wearing! Let's have a bit of fun, lads, afore we fall under the bosun's lash again.'

Next minute they're on us. Hawke swings the stave, cracking one of them hard across his nose. Blood gushes from it as he squawks and falls to the ground. Hampered by the handcuffs, Hawke tries to draw his cutlass from its scabbard, but the other two drunks tackle him round the knees. He falls and takes me with him.

I'm in a tangle of arms and legs with only one hand free.

'Shorty' shouts, 'Hold the lank down, for Gawd's sake. I can't reach the hat on his top deck!'

A face appears, close to mine, then a hand clutching Hawke's keys. 'Take 'em,' the drunk tells me. 'Unlock yourself.'

I'm not going to be dragged off to sea, if I can help it. I've seen enough water for one day. I stiff finger him in both eyes.

'Aaah! You young –.'

I heave at him and he falls backwards, still rubbing his eyes. Hawke pulls his hand free from the seaman's grasp and chops at the man's neck with it. He lets out a horrible choking noise, sticks his backside in the air and twists his head, trying to draw breath.

Put together, the three drunks are a sorry sight as they give up, stand up and head for the Thames shoreline. One of them is dripping blood from his nose, one is half-choked and the third, half blind.

Hawke gets to his feet, taking me with him.

'Well, that was a short, sharp encounter,' he declares, as he dusts himself down and straightens his coat. 'Thank you for your help.'

'Are you hurt, Mr Hawke, sir?' I ask him, as I bend to pick up our hats.

'No, I'm perfectly well, thank you, Jack. What about yourself? You keep remarkably cool under fire, don't you?'

Well, what do you know? He used my first name.

'I've been in a few scrapes in my time, Mr Hawke.'

'Now, where is Mr Godden?' Hawke asks himself. 'Sitting in this tavern enjoying a tankard of ale while we fight the navy, I suppose. Let's join him if he is; and if he's not, why, we'll buy our own ale. What say you?'

I couldn't agree with him more.

The parlour is full of Thames watermen and seafarers smoking pipes, supping ales and talking loudly. A thick cloud of tobacco smoke hovers just below the ceiling.

Hawke finds an empty table. It's awash with spilled beer. Speaking loudly, in order to be heard above the noise, he asks the customers,

'Is there a Mr Godden in the house?'

'I am he, sir,' comes the immediate answer.

A slim gentleman, carrying his hat and cane, pushes his way forward, smiling at us in friendly fashion. With his dark suit of clothes and white cravat, I have him pegged as a school master type. He's the image of those I've seen coming and going at Latymers. It's a conceit to say it, I suppose, but I only have to glance at somebody to know what their line is and what side of the law they're on.

41

Hawke stands up and I follow suit. He extends a hand and so do I.

'I am very pleased to meet you,' Godden shakes Hawke's hand, then mine. 'So you are Jack Dawkins, the young gentleman I'm going to take under my wing?'

'That's right, sir,' I answer, 'but I don't know about being under your wing, as you put it. I'm used to taking care of myself.'

Godden clears his throat as though he's about to make an announcement. 'We'll see, we'll see. I would have been waiting for you at the landing place, gentlemen, but your boat arrived fifteen minutes early. I'm afraid I'm a stickler for punctuality.'

I want to tell him that next time we'd get the thing to go a bit slower for him, but decide to keep my powder dry.

'No matter,' Hawke tells him. 'All's well that ends well.'

'As you say,' Godden replies, 'I caught a glimpse of your altercation with those sailors. You settled it before I could come to give you what aid I could; fisticuffs not being my line.' He stops speaking, examines me closely, then says, 'Well now, Dawkins, when my friend, John Brownlow, asked me to take you on, I had doubts, sir; serious doubts. Still have, as it happens. Can you allay them for me?'

It's my turn to clear my throat. I'm now living in the civilised world, so although I haven't had much practice at it, I try to act civilised. 'I would like you to know, right off, sir, that I'm not wasting the good fortune that's come my way. I haven't been properly educated like you or Mr Hawke, here, but I'm not stupid and I'm a quick learner. Someone who noticed that said I must have good blood in me, whatever that means.'

Hark at me talking! I've put the Dodger back in his box for the time being. Best keep him handy, though.

'That's exactly what I wanted to hear from you!' Godden says. 'I can see we are going to get on famously.'

The pot boy finally arrives to give the table a wipe and take our order for Kentish ales.

'Got any pies?' I ask him.

'Sold out,' he says.

Just my luck!

When he returns with the drinks, the boy slams the tankards down, spilling beer, scoops up the coins Godden throws on the table, and goes off to do someone else's bidding. He obviously enjoys his work. Work? That's a word I wish I hadn't thought of. Have you ever noticed that it's mostly people who don't have to labour, day and night, who say it's good for you?

The Bow Street Runner finishes his drink.

'They serve very good ale here, but I must return to that latest product of our inventive age - the steam boat. I would never venture on to a great ocean in one of them, and I doubt very much if others will, but I trust it to return me safely to the city of lost dreams and dashed hopes.'

Hawke has been very decent, considering he's a policeman, so I let him know I appreciate it.

'Although I haven't understood some of what you've said, Mr Hawke, sir, you've treated me well. Not many of your sort have done that, so I want to thank you for it. I don't know what's ahead of me,' I give Godden a quick glance, 'but I won't forget your kindness.'

'Ah,' says Hawke, 'the happiest conversation is the quiet exchange of sentiments. There is always hope, Jack Dawkins, remember that during the dark days that may indeed lie ahead of you. I promise that you will hear from me in the not too distant future, because I intend to make some enquiries regarding your parents. Goodbye, my youthful Orion, may your hunt be successful, and goodbye to you, Mr Godden, sir. It was a pleasure meeting you both.'

Godden shakes the Bow Street Runner's hand. 'Goodbye, sir. Keep an eye open for drunken sailors.'

'I shall, Mr Godden, I shall!'

We watch him duck through the low doorway then catch sight of him through a smeared window as he heads for the waterfront. For some reason best known to him, he's placed his top hat over the end of his stave and is holding it aloft as though he's carrying it forward into battle. A good man, that.

CHAPTER FOUR
Angels don't have to have wings, do they?

'Now then, do you have your possessions with you?' Godden asks me.

'I've only got what I stand up in,' I tell him.

He frowns, says, 'How very sad,' then gives me fair warning when we go outside and begin to climb a narrow street that rises up from the water's edge.

'You will not think of decamping, will you, Jack? Believe me, you don't want to risk freezing to death under a Kent hedgerow, and what's more, when you are inevitably re-captured, it'll be straight back to prison for Jack Dawkins Esquire.'

With one of his hands gripping my arm, I tell him, 'Don't you worry on that score, Mr Godden, sir. I've no intentions of going anywhere, except where you take me. There's just one thing. I plan to find my mother, if I can, and as soon as I can. I'm chomping at the bit, but it'll have to wait until I have your permission and the means to do it.'

'Oh, so that's what Mr Hawke was referring to when he told you he would look for your parents?' Godden says. 'I can't help noticing that you only refer to your mother; not your father.'

'I think that's because I don't have any memories of him at all, but I do have a picture of my mother in my mind. It's not a word I use much, Mr Godden, but she shows up looking beautiful.'

Godden's grip on my arm loosens as he gives it a couple of friendly pats. 'Let us hope that the Bow Street Runner is able to throw some light on the matter.'

He pulls out a pocket watch and snaps it open. 'In half an hour or so, the Dover coach is due to leave from the inn that lies beyond the top of the hill. My daughter is waiting for us there. I was unwilling to have her accompany me to a riverside tavern.'

As we walk together I raise a question with Godden. 'May I ask why you didn't come to meet me in London, sir?'

'Ask away, Jack,' he says. 'John, I mean, Mr Brownlow wanted me to do that, but meeting you off the boat, gave me the opportunity to visit my sister first. She lives near Rochester. My daughter and I stayed with her last night. We could all have done so again tonight, but she's gone away; acting as travelling companion to a wealthy, young lady; Miss Cassandra Havisham, by name. There's a wedding in the offing for her, so they've gone to Tunbridge Wells to visit the shops there. The girl's father owns a brewery, among other things. There's a lot of money in beer, or so I'm led to believe. I prefer wine, myself.'

Just for the sake of keeping everything on a friendly footing, I boast, 'I've always done my best to help keep the brewers going.'

When Godden gives me a disapproving look, I realise I should have kept my street urchin trap shut.

After a bit of a walk we arrive at a hostelry in time to catch the coach. It's waiting in the yard, with fresh horses standing between its shafts.

The coach driver appears, pulling on a pair of gauntlets. He's chatting to a bow-legged man carrying a wide muzzled blunderbuss and a post horn.

Two army officers, marching like they're on parade, beat us to the door of the coach. Then a rather stout, moon-faced man, dressed even more soberly than Godden is, dashes from the inn, obviously afraid he might miss the coach. And then, oh, my eye! An angel wrapped in a travelling cloak appears through a door marked 'Ladies Only'. Dark curls show beneath the bonnet she's wearing. I can see that her blue dress scarcely reaches her ankles-and-and, I'm in heaven because she's smiling at me; all red lips and gleaming white teeth.

Light as a feather, she comes up to Godden and kisses him on the cheek.

'Hello, Papa. I see that you found the boy.' She turns her wide-open eyes on me and I fall in to them and keep falling for about a thousand years.

Godden is saying my name.

'Jack... Jack.'

'Yes, sir?'

'Jack, this is my daughter, Lysette. Take her hand like a gentleman.'

She's still smiling as we touch fingers for a second.

Feeling like an ugly, dirty, sticky-out eared, long-haired idiot, I say, 'Very pleased to meet you, Miss Lysette.'

'And I am very happy that you are coming to the farm, Jack,' she says. 'It's lonely for me because there are no other young people nearby.' Her voice is like soft music.

Godden says, 'Come along, we mustn't keep the mail waiting. Six is a tight squeeze in these conveyances. Would you mind riding on top, Jack?'

'Not at all, sir,' I tell him, knowing all the time that I'd rather be squeezed up against his daughter than sitting out in the cold. What boy wouldn't?

While they get in to the warm and cosy coach, along with the officers and the man who looks like a preacher, I climb to its roof, feeling glad the coat Brownlow provided me with is a good one.

A young hostler hands the reins to the driver who murmurs a couple of words to the horses, moving them slowly forward.

Just for a lark, I lean over the side of the coach and knock an already battered hat off the hostler's head as we pass by. It's the first good laugh I've had for many a long day.

As he swings the coach out of the yard and on to the road, the driver calls out to the weasel with the horn, standing in the boot,

'It sounds like we've got a happy customer, Peter!'

'First one this year,' Peter calls back.

'You're wrong there,' the driver tells him; 'you're forgetting them twin boys we had with us when we took on that run to St Albans, last month. They were what you might call Cheeryble by name and cheeryble by nature!'

Peter cackles, 'That's nicely put, Tony. I was forgetting them two. Same cheeky faces, same clothes, same fat bellies; just looking at them made me want to laugh. The only difference between them was their Christian names. Call me Ned, says one. I'm Charles, says the other. They not only kept our spirits up by singing carols while we did battle with all that snow, they gave us both a guinea at journey's end. Your boy, Sam, was given a florin or two, as well, wasn't he? How's the lad doing, by the way?'

'Sam's a chip off the old Weller block,' Tony says. 'He's as smart as fresh paint, and growing fast.'

Seeing the beautiful Lysette, has set me to day-dreaming about girls as the coach rattles past the last houses in Gravesend. They meant nothing much to me until, for some reason or other, I started to think of Nancy as being a bit more than someone to feel sorry for. We were sort of drawn to each other in our secret misery, I suppose. As I think I've told you, I was always there for her after Sikes, who must have been nigh on twice her age, had bashed her about a bit; same as I was for some of the eight year old youngsters Fagin used to help line his pockets; cheering them up with my daft games and stories.

As we both grew older, stopping Nancy's tears sometimes led to me kissing them away. I would feel strange stirrings as she clung to me and kissed me in return. I knew how to go about

48

doing you know what, but held back because I thought she'd had enough of that sort of thing from Sikes. Strange stirrings? I could only speak to my pal, Charlie Bates, about those. He was a bit more open about what he did to relieve them than I was.

'Well, it's only doing what comes natural, innit,' he said.

I bluffed it out with him, telling lies about my experiences with girls, but then I've always acted cocky. That's all it was, though; an act. I kept it up, partly to hold my position in Fagin's gang and partly because it had always been me against the world. The trouble with that is, if you do it long enough, you're not acting any more.

When I find my mother, I don't want her to be ashamed of me, so I hope she'll understand.

I'm hungry; so using that as an excuse to have another look at the dark-haired angel, I lean over the side of the coach and poke my head through a window, encountering one belonging to an officer. It's blocking my view a bit, but there she is, sitting on the far side of the coach. She turns towards me, making me feel as weak as a kitten, as I ask my question within six inches of the officer's moustache.

'Excuse me, Mr Godden, sir; how long will it be before we get where we're going?'

'Well, really!' The officer, I'm so close to him, I can feel his breath, speaks to me in the superior manner many of that sort use. 'Isn't it time you were taught how to behave in public? Please be so kind as to get your hair out of my face.'

Mr Godden intervenes. 'My dear sir, this young man may not possess the fine social graces of an officer of engineers, but he is, nevertheless, a perfectly decent fellow, so please allow him some latitude.'

Well said, Mr Godden! But I didn't get an answer to my question!

In the boot of the coach, Peter is trying to sing:

'Oh, brave Benbow was his name.
How he fought all on the main,
You shall hear, you shall hear!'

Luckily enough, given his lack of talent, we don't hear, because he stops singing and, raising the post horn to his lips, produces three loud blasts from it. It's only then I notice that just ahead of us there's a gate across the road. Mail coaches pass straight through these places without stopping to pay toll money. The gate lifts and we speed past a cottage shaped like one of those threepenny bits. It does look odd.

As we pass through, Peter calls out to the gate keeper.

'G'day, Joe. See you at the *Bull* tomorrow.'

'If you're buying,' Joe shouts back.

With the coach wheels grating on a paved road, we go down to a valley. I can see a big river running through it. Just for something to say, I ask the driver:

'What river's that?'

'Why, that's the Medway,' he answers. 'You ain't no Man o' Kent, then?'

'No, nor is he a Kentish Man, either!' Peter calls out above the noise of groaning brake shoes as the coach makes its way down a short, sharp hill.

The road is good. We pass several farms and cross a bridge that provides views of a castle and a big church standing opposite each other. After travelling a short distance up a cobbled street, I'm obliged to bend my head as the coach passes through an arch and comes to a halt in a yard.

'Here we are; the *Bull Inn*, and right on time, too,' the driver calls out. 'Those going on to Canterbury and Dover have got fifteen minutes to do what they have to do.'

The two army officers leave the coach and don't waste any time. Off they go, high booted, straight-backed, marching in step with their hands on their sword hilts.

Mr Godden alights, as does the priestly-looking man. I'm right about him being some sort of bible-basher, because Godden says:

'Goodbye, Mr Crisparkle. As you are already the curate here, I'm sure you will achieve your ambition and become an ordained minister in the not too distant future. Your point about the juxtaposition of Rochester's castle and cathedral representing war and peace, was well put, sir. It set me to thinking that, throughout history, the church has frequently caused an urgent need to construct castles.'

As the curate strolls through the arch, Godden looks up at me and says, cheerfully, 'Here's a florin, Jack. You also have fifteen minutes to do what you have to do,'

Thinking of my stomach, I scramble down the side of the coach and make straight for the entrance to the inn.

I'm pleased to tell you they've got plenty of beef and mutton pies. They're selling oysters, as well; harvested from the nearby river, if you want them. I don't.

There's room for me inside the coach when we continue on our way. I find it easy to drift off to sleep, despite the lovely Lysette being only two feet away from me. Thoughts of her should lead to pleasant dreams, but they don't. A great, black horse is rearing up in a busy street. I'm small. The hooves come down. There's a scream; not mine. I'm running between someone's legs. A hand tries to grab hold of me.

'Mummy!'

I wake up. Mr Godden and worst of all, Lysette, are staring at me. Damn and blast it! Now she'll think I'm a big baby because I called out for my mother.

'Are you all right, boy?' Godden asks me.

What else can I say but, 'Yes, sir. Sorry if I called out. It's just that, after years of not giving them a thought, I can't get my ma and pa out of my head; especially my ma. Now I've started dreaming about her.'

I lift my chin and look straight at Lysette, sitting opposite to me. She lowers her eyes and concentrates on her knitting.

'What do you know of them?' Godden asks me.

'Nothing at all, sir; but I intend to find out whether they are alive or dead.'

'Dreams can be very significant, you know, Jack,' Godden says. 'Mr Brownlow told me, that, according to what the child he intends to adopt has told him, you were with your mother until you were about five or six years old. If that is true, you would surely have a few memories of her. If you haven't, then something must have driven them from your young mind. Perhaps the parting of the ways, itself, was the cause.'

I ask what I suppose is a stupid question. 'Are dreams and memories the same, Mr Godden?'

'I think not,' he says, 'but dreams can certainly be caused by memories, fears and experiences.'

'I saw a big, black horse in my last one,' I tell him. 'I was only little and it was rearing up.'

Lysette is looking at me again. 'I've got a beautiful, black horse, Jack. Papa gave it to me for my fifteenth birthday.'

What's that got to do with anything? I don't even know when my birthday is.

I've got to tell you this; here goes... Lysette's adorable face reminds me of one of those hearts people cut out of coloured paper to give to their sweethearts on Valentine's Day. I gave one to Nancy, once.

I smile at her without showing my teeth. It's the first time I've thought what they might look like to somebody else. The only horses I've sat on are those big ones that pull brewers' drays.

'In the famed play *Hamlet*,' Godden says, 'a character makes the comment that a dream itself is but a shadow. In that instance it is a reference to a person's ambition. Perhaps, now that you have decided to look in to your past, your own, long repressed memories are returning to you through dreams, Jack.'

The coach lurches, throwing us about a bit and causing Lysette's knitting to slide from her lap. She bends to pick it up and so do I. My scruffy head comes into contact with her sweet smelling hair. Her knees touch mine.

That's it. I'm done for. Angels don't have to have wings, do they?

CHAPTER FIVE
A wolf in shepherd's clothing!

There's a church tower standing up out of watery marshland criss-crossed by big ditches. Mr Godden has told me they're known as 'sewers' in this neck of the woods, except there aren't any woods, just marshes, water and sheep.

Our light carriage rolls along a rough and ready road, raised above miles of waving grass and the water-filled ditches, oh all right, sewers, then. We've got sewers in London, but they don't run as sweet and clean as they do down here. I expect it's because there's hardly anybody to go to the lavvy.

Arriving late in Dover, yesterday, we spent the night at a coaching inn where Mr Godden had stabled a pair of horses and left his carriage.

At breakfast, I asked him who was paying for my room and the food I was eating. He told me how things were and how they were going to be.

'Mr Brownlow has provided me with sufficient funds to cover these costs, Jack. Never forget that he was obliged to pledge a two hundred pounds bond before the authorities would agree to release you in to his care. Once you begin working at Shippenden, you ought to at least repay some of these travelling expenses. You will have the money to do so. In return for your hard work, you will receive twelve pounds per annum, your work clothes and free board and lodging. In addition, I will ask my man, Webster, to teach you all he knows about sheep and other aspects of farming.'

There's something else I want to know. 'If you don't mind me asking, Mr Godden, sir, how did you end up having to take the likes of me on?'

'Don't put yourself down, Jack. It came about because Mr Brownlow and I have a mutual friend in Dr Strong, a fine gentleman who has recently opened a school in Canterbury. As he jokingly put it the last time the three of us met; being birds of a feather, philanthropists tend to flock together!'

Curiosity forces me to admit to him. 'I'm showing my ignorance again, sir, but can you tell me what one of those philanthrops is? I studied any amount of words while I was with Fagin, but missed that one.'

He laughs, of course, but not exactly at me. 'Your modesty and eagerness to learn does you credit, Jack. Put simply, a philanthropist is a person who supports good causes.'

Oh, one of those. Something else occurs to me. 'Will I have to stay put after I find my mother, Mr Godden?'

His answer comes as a disappointment to me. 'I can see this objective of yours is fast becoming an obsession,' he says. 'After giving the matter some thought, my advice, and I mean this most kindly, is that you try put it out of your mind. How can you possibly find a person who disappeared from your life ten years ago?'

Godden doesn't know me yet. I'm not giving up on his say-so.

Feeling that I'm not going to enjoy life down on the farm if it gets in the way of looking for my mother, I tell him I'll find her if it takes me another ten years.

I believed Mr Godden when he told me, just now, that Romney Marsh covers an area of one hundred square miles, and those living on it like to believe they govern themselves.

I've never seen so much sky or so much flat land, either - and no people, at least, not since we passed two characters walking the rutted road, a mile after we left a place called Ham Street. With a name like that, they must keep a lot of pigs there.

It's a cold morning. Every now and again, rain showers sweep across us, so I'm glad Godden's carriage is a covered one. Its roof extends over the driver's seat, so Mr Godden is keeping dry, along with me and Lysette.

I say something obvious to no one in particular. 'It's a long way from London.'

'How right you are, Jack,' Godden says, turning his head towards me a little. 'It's fortunate you are a reformed character, isn't it?'

'What do you mean?'

'Well, there are hardly any pockets for you to pick. Romney Marsh people mostly wear smocks!'

All three of us enjoy that. As Lysette laughs, she shows the tip of her pretty, pink tongue. Straight away, I'm in love with that bit of her, as well!

I don't think Mr Godden understands the business of survival, otherwise he wouldn't have mentioned I'm reformed. I had to become thick-skinned while I lived as I did. It was like wearing a suit of armour, but I wore it so long it won't come off all at once. It started being peeled off me yesterday and some of it is coming off today. I'll tell you something else. I'm surprised at the kind of thoughts I'm having. It's as though my brain's started working in a different way than it had to before; restoring the original, not quite dead, Dawkins, to life and burying the Dodger.

'It's a good job you and me are never going to meet, isn't it? I'd never let on about these things if there was any chance of that happening!'

As another burst of rain hits the carriage roof, Lysette airs her knowledge about Romney Marsh, and I don't mind at all, because she's actually talking to me.

'People say there is more sky to be seen here than anywhere else in England, and the lanes twist and turn more, as well. We live two miles from Ivychurch, Jack, but have to travel four to get there!'

I keep trying to gaze in to her eyes as she talks, but she won't have it. I notice she's looking flushed; is that because she's put something on her downy cheeks to give them colour, or is it because of me? Keep talking. I'm listening as well as looking, Lysette!

She does.

'Once, a long time ago, most of Romney Marsh was covered by the sea. One can still pick up seashells in the meadows. The sea tries to take it all back, sometimes, doesn't it, Papa?'

Godden looks at me from beneath the brim of his hat and says, 'Lysette is quite right, Jack. Not counting the miasmas that cause so much sickness; floods and Owlers are the two main anxieties for the decent folk living on this desolate land, and the reason why so many have gone to live elsewhere.'

I'm a bit puzzled. 'Forgive my ignorance again, Mr Godden, but what are Owlers?'

'Smugglers, Jack,' Lysette bursts out before her father can answer me from where he's driving the carriage. 'They smuggle wool to France and smuggle tea, tobacco, brandy and even silks from far away China, to England; but my father refuses to buy any of it for me - silk, I mean.'

Godden lets it be known he's not best pleased with her for saying that. 'It's nothing to joke about, Lysette. Their criminal activities deprive the exchequer of large amounts of revenue. They are dangerous men, too. People have been killed for trying to put a stop to their activities. Best leave the Owlers to the militia and the excise officers.'

Godden, who strikes me as being a quiet, reserved man, suddenly bursts in to surprising song, startling the sheep grazing nearest the road, as well as me:

'And when the lad became a man,
The good old farmer died
And left the lad the farm he had
And a daughter for his bride!'
And now the lad a farmer is,
How he smiles and thinks with joy,

Of the lucky, lucky summer's day
He became a farmer's boy!'

His voice rings out across the meadows, scaring even the more distant sheep in to movement.

'My singing always frightens the animals.' He laughs, Lysette claps her hands and there we are again, all three of us in the best of moods, and I for one am glad that Owlers are people. I thought for a minute they might be some sort of dangerous wild animal roaming Romney Marsh, 'owling their 'eads off!

A rising track heads off to the left and we take it. I can see smoke coming out of a chimney beyond a small group of trees.

'Shippenden Farm,' Godden announces. 'We made very good time.'

Mr Godden steers the carriage up the lane, past a low cottage and in to a farm yard lined with a barn, a cart shed and stables.

I try to take it all in as two black and white dogs bark loud enough to let the world know we've arrived.

A man carrying a shovel comes out of the barn. Lysette squeezes past me with a rustling of skirts, steps down from the coach and waves at him.

'Hello, Charles!'

He looks about thirty, so I'm not put out. I don't want any competition as far as Lysette's concerned, see.

'Afternoon, Miss Lysette,' he calls out, before telling the dogs to shut up.

After sitting in the carriage for the best part of four hours, it's good to feel the ground under my feet again.

Leaning on his shovel, Charles stands right in front of the three of us as though he's on guard, or something.

'You made good time, Mr Godden, sir. I didn't expect you back until tonight.'

Something's up. He said that as though it's inconvenienced him.

I take a close look at him and see something that I recognise right off. The man's capable of almost anything. It's got nothing to do with the leather coat and moleskin trousers he's wearing or even the knife in his belt. What he is, shows in his face and in those eyes. He's tough; dangerous too; a man who would stoop to anything. Can't this philanthrop - whatever he is, see that? Honestly! Some people wouldn't recognise the devil if he sat down to tea with them.

'Yes, Charles,' Godden is saying, 'the roads are still good, but have you smelled the weather? I think we're in for it. I have the feeling we're going to be blown in to March.'

'More likely float into it, if you ask me,' Charles says. 'There's a lot of rain in the air, too.'

Mr Godden is talking about me now. 'Allow me to introduce you to Jack Dawkins, Charles. I intend to help him lead a better life than he has experienced so far; and you can help by letting him work with you.'

'Let him work with me, sir? That's all right, he'll come in handy, I'm sure.'

I stick out my hand and say, as polite as can be, 'How do you do, sir. I'm very pleased to meet you.'

There's no eye contact when he replies, 'And I'm pleased to meet you, Jack. My name's Webster, but you can call me Charlie. I'm Mr Godden's looker.'

'Looker?'

I hear Lysette giggle at my puzzlement. She's not half as grown up as Nancy had been at her age; but she'd had to get there fast, hadn't she.

'Oh, I forgot you're a townie,' Charlie says. 'A looker is the Romney Marsh name for a shepherd.'

'Right enough,' Godden agrees. 'Let's go and get Jack settled in now, shall we?'

Charlie continues to blocks the way. 'Excuse me, Mr God-den, sir, but I must explain something to you before you go to your house.'

Right there and then, a man looking as though he's been rolled in mud and dirt, and sprouting half a haystack, comes out the barn, stares at us for a second or two then makes a dash for it. It's no use shouting 'stop'; that's the last thing a runner does when he hears it.

Webster grunts and smashes a fist into his other hand.

With the man making a bee-line for the marsh, Mr Godden exclaims:

'What's happened, Charles? Who's that man?' '

Charlie talks fast, as liars often do.

'I was just about to tell you, Mr Webster, I caught him hang-ing around, sir. He put up a fight when I asked him what he was doing, so I used this here shovel on him. He got over it quicker than I thought he would.'

'Did you know the man?' Godden asks.

'No, sir, he was a stranger to me.'

'All right, Charles. We'd better report this to the authorities. In the meantime, please be so kind as to take care of my carriage and the horses. Come and see me afterwards, will you?'

'Aye, aye, sir. I mean, yes, sir,' Charles replies.

The daft dogs have ignored everything. They're too busy look-ing up at Charlie with their tongues hanging out. I could look at Lysette like that, I suppose.

As we begin to walk towards the house, I'm pleased as Punch when she slips her cool hand into my hot one.

Watching Webster turn the carriage round, Godden murmurs,

'I've noticed that whenever Charles is discomforted, he re-sorts to naval expressions.'

I think to myself, you ought to have noticed a bit more than that about him, guv'nor.

CHAPTER SIX
Permission to kiss, granted

I've found out several things since I arrived here yesterday afternoon. Mr Godden has told me that I would 'understandably suffer a period of adjustment before I settled in to my new life'. Webster lives in that cottage near the top of the lane, the countryside is creepy quiet at night, and Lysette sleeps in a room immediately below mine. After we 'retired for the night' which is the fancy term Godden uses for 'going to bed', I couldn't hear her moving about, or anything, so I stomped round my room just to let her know I exist. Childish of me, but I'm still adjusting, ain't I.

When I woke up this morning I wasn't sure if the end of a dream I'd been having was still stuck in my head, or I was actually remembering something to do with my mother.

In the dream or memory, whatever it was, I'm small again, and my mother is handing me over to a woman I don't know. Mother turns to board a coach that's ready to leave. She rushes back to me, lifts me off the ground and kisses me. Then she's gone and the other woman is holding my hand very tight. I'm the smallest thing there is because everything, people, buildings, carriages, even a black dog, is towering over me. There's noise and confusion. Where's mummy!?

That's it; there's no more; and I'm still a bit cut up about it when I go down to breakfast.

There's a lot to be said for civilised living. I'm no longer in Fagin's den, so there's no mad morning scramble for the last sausage. Here, the table is laid up for breakfast; white linen napkins, and all, and I don't know which smell I like best, hot coffee, fresh bread or fried bacon.

'Good morning, Jack,' says Mr Godden, seated at the head of the table. He's wearing a pair of those modern trousers that need a belt round the top to keep them up, carpet slippers on his feet and a fancy, brocaded jacket. He's not dressed for outdoor work, that's for sure.

'Good morning, sir,' I answer, feeling stupid in the farmer's boy smock they gave me to wear last night.

'The one thing I miss down here, are the London newspapers,' Godden tells me as he pours coffee for both of us.

'You came down from London to live here, sir?' I ask.

'Yes. Thanks to my success at Lloyds and as a business lawyer, I was able to do so; not to farm, I leave that to those who know how to do it, but in order to pursue my other interests.'

Before I can ask him what they are, Lysette enters the room. She's dressed in a high-waisted, dark green gown and carrying a riding jacket. When she curtsies to her father, I know at once she's putting on a show for my benefit.

'Good morning, father, dear. Did you sleep well?'

Godden puts his coffee cup down. 'Very well, indeed, my daughter. Now come and give your father a kiss.'

While she's stepping to the table and bending towards him, my brain is shouting, NO! Come and give me a kiss, instead!

After planting her lips briefly on her father's cheek, Lysette looks at me and smiles that smile of hers; the one that makes me feel a bit dizzy, and says: 'Good morning, Jack. Will you be ready to go riding after breakfast? The sun is shining.'

'Riding?' I splutter, 'but I told you I can't ride a horse, miss.'

Godden laughs. 'Lysette is teasing you, Jack. What she means is, are you ready for your first lesson? I am not setting you to work immediately, so I recommend you make the most of the next few days. By the way, I must remember to introduce you to the New Romney magistrate as soon as possible. Seeing him on a regular basis is one of the terms under which you were released in to Mr Brownlow's care. We'll both be in trouble if you don't attend!'

In the stable, I finally manage to get a saddle and bridle on a horse that looks at me as though he's never seen anything like it in his life.

It proves to be as reluctant to go with me as I am with it, but I drag the daft thing to the paddock. Lysette walks beside me as sedate as can be, with her hand holding the bridle of her own nuzzling pony. She's decided to call it Roland. According to her, Roland was a brave knight who saved France from being invaded by foreign hordes. He had a great horn which only he could blow and a sword that split a mountain in half, making a short-cut for his army to get through and slaughter the enemy. It's a good story, but that's all it is.

I get a lot of advice from Lysette on how to sit in the saddle, hold the reins, use my heels, steer the horse, and I don't know what else.

Here we go; I stand on the mounting block, swing my leg over the horse's back and plant myself on the saddle. Seconds later, here I am, lying flat on my back in the grass, looking up at Lysette's laughing face and the inquisitive muzzles of two horses who, judging by the amount of teeth they're showing, are also laughing their silly heads off.

It's worth being thrown off the horse, though, because Lysette puts a soft hand in mine and helps me to my feet. Give a dog a bone.

Then I see that Charlie Webster is leaning on the paddock fence. He's not laughing.

'That nag's got a soft mouth, Miss Godden,' he tells Lysette. 'You let Jack put the wrong sort of bit in it.'

While Lysette returns to the stable to find the right piece of harness, I give Webster a hard stare in return. A few seconds of that and he walks away, knowing that I know he's a wrong 'un.

My five feet four inches tall dream girl returns with a bit protected by woven cotton. Her riding boots make her seem the same height as I am, and I'm five seven - well, nearly five six, anyway.

'I hope you don't think I let that happen to you on purpose, Jack,' Lysette trills.

'Course not,' I tell her. 'Let's give it another go, shall we?'

Lysette keeps me practising for half the morning. I don't fall off again; pleasing my rear end, no end. On that very point, as we return the horses to the stable, she says:

'You already have a very good seat, Jack.'

I feel quite proud of myself for resisting the temptation of saying something similar about hers, in return.

Back in the - I think the word I'm looking for is 'intimacy'- of the quiet stable, with its mixture of pleasant smells; leather, fresh hay and horses, Lysette shows me how to curry comb mine. It's my chance to talk properly to her.

'Do you like living down here, Miss Lysette?' That's my feeble, opening question.

She looks at me across the back of Roland. 'I like the country, Jack, but I miss my friends in Chelsea. I miss my mother, as well, even though we don't get on, and quarrel about my future.'

'S'funny you should say that,' I tell her, 'because I miss mine, these days, and I scarcely remember her. I suppose that's the way it is with mothers.'

'How romantic,' she murmurs as she strokes Roland's shining, black mane, 'a lost boy, looking for his lost mother.'

'I might be lost, but I'm not a boy,' I tell her. 'I'm man enough for anything.'

'That's boastful,' Lysette replies. 'Do you know what I see when I look at you, Jack?'

'No, but I expect you're going to tell me, whether I want to hear it, or not.'

Taking careful aim, I toss the curry comb in to the wooden tub where I'd found it.

Lysette rests both her arms on Roland's back. 'You are not handsome, but you are not ugly, either.'

She shushes me when I say, 'Oh, thanks a lot.'

She goes on: 'although you have been a thief, you are basically kind and honest, after a fashion.'

'Anything else?'

'Yes, there is.' She flashes her green eyes at me as she leans across Roland's back in order to get closer. 'You want to kiss me, but I'm not going to let you do it, yet!'

Well, of all the...!

The girl's full of herself as she pats her horse and comes to stand close to me. 'Shall we go and have lunch with papa, then decide what to do with ourselves this afternoon. He says I'm to study the Arthurian legend and read Scott's *The Lady of the Lake* today, but that can wait if we think of something interesting to do together.'

Something interesting to do together!? Ah me, oh my!

Now here I am, taking an afternoon walk on the marsh with Lysette by my side. I feel quite noble and protective, and the child in me wishes I was wearing a sword like that knight, Roland. In between her attempts to spot water voles and stoats along the banks of a sewer, I manage to get out of her the fact that her father is writing a book about Sir Isaac Newton, the gravity man, and the mother she misses, is French. Her name is Yvonne, and she frequently visits Paris to help manage her family's millinery business.

The grass is too damp for us to sit down on, so we stroll along a footpath that's just about wide enough to allow us to walk side by side. My arm seems to insist on touching hers until, to my surprise; I find we're holding hands.

Lysette stops walking:

'Just a moment, Jack. This is interesting. There's a three hundred and sixty degree view from here, and if you look carefully, you'll see two church steeples and one tower in the distance. Draw a line to connect them and you'll have a neat triangle.'

I keep hold of Lysette's hand now I've got it, and begin to take notice of sounds and scenes. A whispery breeze is stirring the long, salty grass that surrounds us, I know it's salty because I've touched it and tasted it. Bird calls are almost lost in the huge space between watery marsh and cloudy sky; and there are Lysette's church steeples and the tower - steeples but no peoples - sorry, it's the mood I'm in! But there's not a soul in sight; only the grey-white blobs of sheep scattered everywhere, and fluttering, small birds; circling high and flying low.

We walk on until we see one of those brick-built looker's huts with a chimney sticking out the top of it, like a stubby finger.

'They usually have a bench to sit on, Jack,' Lysette says, gripping my hand a little tighter, 'shall we sit down for a few minutes?'

She's right about the hut having a bench seat. There's also a small window, a couple of shelves, what passes for a table, and an empty fireplace.

According to what Mr Godden has told me, shepherds live in these huts during the lambing season, which is just about to start, apparently. They also come in handy as a shelter if the weather turns rough.

The second we sit down, Lysette turns to me and whispers:

'All right, you can kiss me now if you still want to.'

A stolen kiss isn't worth much, but the real thing certainly is! I expect everybody closes their eyes when they do it, don't they? It helps shut the world out and takes you to a magic place while it's happening. Me and Lysette close ours when our lips come together. How soft and warm hers are! Oh, she smells of perfumed bath soap and one of her hands is resting on the back of my head. Her fingers are in my hair (thank heaven I washed it) and mine are in hers. It's the most glorious thing when, after a few seconds, she removes her lips from mine, kisses my cheek several times, then brushes her own against it before moving away, not suddenly, but kind of reluctantly.

We both open our eyes and here we are, sitting on a bench in a looker's hut on Romney Marsh. Although her face is flushed, I don't exactly know how Lysette is feeling. As for me, well, I'll be able to float straight out of that door and all the way back to the farm without touching the ground.

Lysette's right hand caresses my face.

'You are such a gentle boy, Jack.' Then she stands up, straightens her blue bonnet and suggests we return to Shippenden, 'before Papa begins to worry.'

As we make our way home, Lysette helps me keep my feet on the ground, so to speak, by showing me the difference between evening primroses and red valerian; grebes, peewhits and wagtails. I try to listen, but it's not easy when you're walking with a beautiful girl who's just told you that you're a gentle boy. I've been called a lot of things in my time, but never 'gentle'.

At teatime, when Godden asks me if I'd enjoyed my walk on the marsh, I tell him that Lysette has taught me a few things about birds and plants and such, but knowing the differences between them won't be of much help to me.

He disagrees. 'All knowledge is useful to us, Jack, even if one only airs it in conversation at the dinner table.'

He smiles at Lysette. 'Did you enjoy your walk, my daughter?'

'Yes, Papa. It was very bracing,' she replies.

Now why did she have to use a word like that to describe our time together? It looks as though I'm not the only artful one around here! And I wish she'd take that knowing, half-smile off her face. Although he's gullible enough to let someone straight out of Newgate be alone with his daughter, her father's not a complete fool.

When Mr Godden reminds Lysette that she has two studies to complete this evening, she pulls a face but goes off to do his bidding, leaving me alone with him.

There are one or two questions I want to ask, so I start off with:

'How did your daughter get to be so clever, Mr Godden, sir?'

Godden give a nod 'My wife and I educated her from a very early age. Lysette is fluent in French and, like you, has a quick mind that not only absorbs information, it retains it. She has already expressed some very firm ideas about what a woman's place should be in the modern world, and I must say I agree with her. Women ought to be playing a role in everything from politics to poetry.'

I told you I had him down as a schoolmaster type, didn't I?

I nod my head, trying to look wise myself. 'May I ask you something else?'

'Certainly; ask all the questions you want,' Godden says.

I take the plunge, trying to make myself clear. 'It's hard to put into words, Mr Godden, but although I've heard a lot about what people like to call freedom, hardly anybody seems to have it. In one way or another, they are chained down, unless they're rich. Take me for example. I was about as free as you can get when I was on the wrong side of the law and fending for myself on the streets of London. Now that's all over and done with, I'm leading an honest life, but I'm not free at all. It's like I'm stuck in a big, open-air Newgate. The worst thing is, I can't go off and start searching for my mother without having the law after me and letting you and Mr Brownlow down. Is there anything you can do about it? If you can't allow me to go off by myself for a while, perhaps you could help me search, although I admit I don't know where to begin.'

Mr Godden looks thoughtful. 'I understand what you say, Jack. For your own well-being, I have decided that it must be put to rest, one way or another; so I will do this much. If you don't hear from Mr Hawke in the next few days, I will contact him myself and encourage him to diligently pursue his enquiries on your behalf. I will pay him to do so, if necessary. If he uncovers any clues to your mother's whereabouts, you and I will follow them up together, no matter where they take us.'

That's pretty fair on his part and it helps me sleep better.

I didn't realise that today is Sunday, until I came down for breakfast.

Mr Godden looks at my smock and suggests I go back upstairs and change in to the smart clothes Brownlow bought for me. We're off to church!

Lysette is there, looking fine in a bonnet whose colour matches her eyes, and a cream-coloured gown with touches of green on its sleeves and at the throat.

I seem to fall for that girl every time I see her. That may sound daft to you, but I know most of you fellows reading this epic won't need to have it spelled out for you. Your girl turns up, you take one look at her and, whoops, you're gone again; and on that score, you girls reading this should have a bit of pity for us, because you always seem to hold the whip hand. You've got power in those fluttering eyelashes, and I expect you know it.

For all I know, it works both ways, so I'd like to ask Lysette if girls have the same feelings when it comes to boys. Has she ever known one who had that effect on her? Maybe I'll find out the next time we're alone.

Right now I'm seated next to her in her father's carriage as we take a winding lane to church.

'Your little holiday is nearly over,' Lysette tells me. 'I think Papa will put you with Mr Webster tomorrow. A lot of lambs shall be born in the next two or three weeks.'

'That's all right,' I say, 'I'm getting bored with everything around here, except you.'

There's the smile I've already gone on about. 'It's sweet of you to say that, Jack. I'm glad to have a friend at Shippenden.'

'Friend!?'

Having heard what's been said, Mr Godden turns and looks at me from the driving seat: 'You don't know it, Jack, but one might say that you passed a test with flying colours yesterday when you walked on the lonely marsh with my daughter. I wouldn't have allowed it if I'd had any doubts about you, and Lysette has confirmed that you behaved like a perfect gentleman.'

The vicar's sermon this morning is all about the prodigal son. He's a bone-idle young cove who goes off to the city, has the time of his life while his brother's at home doing all the work. After spending all his money and wearing himself out having a good time, the prodigal goes back home with his tail between his legs. When he gets there, his father welcomes him with open arms, tells his brother to give him a big hug, then throws a party for him. There's something wrong there, surely?

CHAPTER SEVEN
Hawke's letter

I've been on this farm for over two weeks now. It's rained a lot lately; turning everything in to a mud pond.

Farming is a disgusting business. Horse dung, pig dung and cow dung keep piling up in pens and all over the yard. It makes me grateful that the two hundred sheep Mr Godden told me he owns are doing it in the fields, otherwise we'd be up to our necks in the stuff in no time.

Webster has shown me how to gut rabbits, help a slippery, slimy lamb get born early, and how to wring a chicken's neck before pulling out its liver and lights. It's putting me off my food, I can tell you.

I've got used to wearing the smock and a flat hat with a wide brim to it, but I'm glad my old pals aren't here to see me in them, or the haircut Lysette gave me. She's made me look like one of those choir boys at the church we go to every Sunday.

'Oh, Jack,' she said, giggling away after she'd finished with me, 'It's made your ears stick out even more than before.'

She's been enjoying teasing me ever since I kissed her in that looker's hut. Twice now, she's come to my attic room after work. She's knocked on the door and when I've opened it, stood there, or leant against the door post, twirling one of her black curls round a finger and acting all girly as she tells me that dinner's ready, or asks me if my bed's warm enough, or do I want another blanket. The bed is warm, thank you very much, and so am I when I look at her.

Last night, she asked me:

'Have you really done a lot of bad things, Jack; I mean, really bad?'

'No,' I said, 'but I'll do something bad to you if you don't stop acting the fool.'

I could hardly believe it when she raised both her arms above her head, wriggled her body, tapped her feet in a little dance, then laughed and said, 'Will you really, Jack? You are a bad boy.'

Then she scuttled away, leaving me with my mouth open. If her ma had been around to hear that, she'd have spanked her, and no mistake; but she's still in France.

When it comes down to it, I can't make head or tail of Lysette. One minute she's flirting with me like that, and the next - well take yesterday morning for example. I was cleaning out a stable, when she appeared in the doorway, looking like an angel as usual. Daylight streamed in all round her, showing up her shape something wonderful. It made me reach out and try to touch her with my dirty fingers. I just couldn't help myself.

'Don't you dare do that!' she squealed, as she hitched up her dress and scampered away.

Later on I took a deep breath and asked Mr Godden, who doesn't look particularly happy himself, why Lysette is so moody. It turns out that the carrier had brought a letter from her mother, informing them both that she has been delayed in Paris for at least another month. It's the first I've heard of it, but it means they have to put off a foreign trip Lysette was looking forward to.

Webster is taking me to see the magistrate tomorrow. According to Webster, the farm needs some more cart grease, a new chaff-cutter and grain for the animals. He asked Godden if it would be all right with him if we come back quite late, because he has some personal business to take care of.

'Your time is your own after six,' Godden told him.

Lysette is still in a mood, so she refuses to come with us in the rain. It's a shame, because I was looking forward to sitting next to that girl, putting my arm through hers, perhaps, and listening to her chatter on about the pretty willow trees and how she loves listening to skylarks and such. Lysette knows a lot about nature.

The court house in New Romney isn't much to look at, but neither is the magistrate, Henry Fitch. After making sure we aren't going to drip rain all over his office floor, he lets Webster and me inside. Magistrates mostly all come from the same mould. This one sits there with a nose narrow enough to belong to one of the snipe I've seen hanging in poulterer's windows. He uses it to sniff at me as though I've gone off, or something. The first thing he wants to know is:

'What's the world coming to, Mr Webster?'

Then he goes on to slander me. 'Here we have an incorrigible rogue, given a new chance by a generous judiciary and sent to live among decent people. It's a scandal, sir!'

Webster looks solemn. 'I agree with you, your honour. It never ought to be allowed. Serve them right if this ne'er do well absconds, carrying everything he can lay his thieving hands on. It would put an end to such soft-headed ideas.'

I stand there and take it as Fitch nods in agreement. 'You're quite right, Mr Webster. I don't envy you your role in teaching a felon to be a shepherd. It goes against his very nature, and I fear he might do harm to the Godden family, living with them as he does.'

That's enough! I'm not having that. 'You just wait a minute, Mr Fitch, sir. That isn't me you're describing. I don't do violence, especially not to those who are giving me a helping hand.'

'Be quiet, sir!' Fitch orders, 'I'm addressing Mr Webster.'

'Don't worry, your honour,' Webster says. 'I live in the cottage out there, so I'll be able to keep my eye on him.'

As the magistrate pulls a face that does nothing to improve his looks, Webster adopts a 'concerned citizen' attitude. 'Have you heard anything further about the encounter the revenue men had with those smugglers a couple of weeks ago, Mr Fitch?'

The magistrate can't wait to tell us. 'I have, as it happens. After some unnecessary delay, another attempt to find out where they are hiding their ill-gotten gains is going to be made. The whole area will be swept, end to end, by a large number of soldiers from Brabourne Leas Barracks. No cottage, house or corner of the marsh will be left untouched this time. A ten pound reward is being offered for the one who finds their hiding place. That should ensure a thorough search.'

Fitch puffs up his cheeks then expels his breath as though he's trying to blow out a dozen candles. 'In the interests of security and with the co-operation of the postmaster, I have intercepted a letter addressed to you, Dawkins. One cannot be too careful when one is dealing with the criminal fraternity.'

I'm more than a bit astonished. 'You're holding a letter for me? I want it, then. It doesn't belong to you. Interfering with mail is a serious offence.'

The jumped-up, officious official produces my letter from his desk drawer. 'I can tell you its contents. It's been sent to you by a police officer named Hawke. Having carried out an investigation he confirms that your mother is dead; which is, no doubt, a blessing for her.'

'No she ain't! She's not dead. Give me that letter.' I take a step nearer the desk, lean forward and snatch it from his hand.

Fitch says, 'Well, really!' but I don't give a damn about the likes of him.

As he said, the letter is from Mr Hawke.

Dear Jack,

Thanks to my contacts among retired Bow Street Runners, it did not take me long to find one who remembers that, in the year 1805, in the month of June, your mother was killed by a horse being ridden recklessly by a disgraced cavalry officer named Captain Randall Swithin. I am so sorry to have to impart this terrible news to you. He subsequently disappeared from view. His whereabouts are still unknown and his estate in Derbyshire went in to receivership some time ago. You are remembered, Jack. In police records there are brief descriptions of the occurrence. A small boy became terrified when the incident happened, and ran off, never to be seen again.

Your mother proved her own identity. In response to being asked her name as she lay dying, her last words, noted by an officer, were, 'I'm Molly Dawkins. Please take care of little Jack for me.' It was assumed the unfortunate lady meant to say, until your father, or perhaps a family member claimed you. No-one came forward or made enquiries about you.

As far as could be ascertained, your mother did not live in the locality; and where she came from remains a mystery.

Described as being a well-dressed woman, she was carrying no identity, but had funds on her, more than sufficient to pay for her own funeral. Should you come to London, you will find me waiting for you at Bow Street, ready to conduct you to her grave in Camberwell Cemetery.

The letter went on, but I don't bother to read any more. I screw the thing up and stuff it in a pocket. Fate, or whatever you like to call it, got me out of Newgate. Now it's spitting in my eye.

I should have known better. Fitch is talking, but who cares?

'Well, Mr Webster, you may take Dawkins away and make what you can of him. If he should transgress, tell Mr Godden to inform me immediately. I'll make certain he is never troubled by him again.'

'Thank you for that, sir,' says Webster, still acting as though he's a gent, born and bred, which he ain't. 'I must bid you good day. Come along, Jack. We've got work to do.'

'That's the way!' cries Fitch. 'Work him hard, Mr Webster, sir; work him hard!'

Outside, on one of New Romney's narrow streets, Webster is suddenly in a hurry.

'Come on, Jack. I've got a job to do and like it or not, you're going to help me.'

I wipe some of the rain from my face. 'What's up?'

Webster is showing his true colours. They are dark; very dark.

'My men are either dead or scattered, and I've a buyer for some smuggled goods I've got hid. He's coming to take them off my hands tonight, which is just as well, seeing as how Fitch has told us there's going to be a search made for them. That's why I talked 'head in the clouds' Godden, into letting me come to New Romney with the wagon today. I fell on my feet when he bought Shippenden, and no mistake. The man's all brains and no common sense. He gives everybody the benefit of the doubt, lets his wife go off on her own whenever she wants to and fills his daughter's head with silly notions. It almost makes me feel sorry for him.'

I just listen and say nothing.

'Now then,' Webster goes on, 'tomorrow, after I'm better off, and you're still trying to get on the right side of that girl, you'll be keeping your trap shut if you know what's good for you. The man I caught up with after I found out he'd been asking questions about our last run, didn't live long. I'll tell you something else, just so you know what'll happen to you if you cross me. When you turned up early at Shippenden, I was getting ready to use a cross-cut saw on him, so I could feed one big squealer to a lot of little squealers in their pen; and if you can't work that out, I mean I was going to feed him to the pigs. I didn't hit him hard enough. The fool should have run towards you, when he came round, not into the marsh. That's where you'll find what's left of him if you search hard and dig deep.'

After reading Hawke's letter, even the ghastly thought of being cut up and fed to pigs doesn't stir me up that much. Feeling I might as well let life do what it wants with me, I give him my answer.

'You don't have to threaten me, Webster. I'll give you a hand if you pay me. I won't do it for nothing, and I don't scare easy. I've met worse than you on a dark night. I don't blab, either. That's the code I live by. You might as well know that I had you down as a wrong 'un the minute I laid eyes on you.'

Webster gives me a look that could knock a sparrow, stone dead, out of the sky. 'I know you did; ain't you the clever one? Don't worry; you'll get paid, all right. I'm all heart. Now, let's collect the wagon, get Godden's stuff and get out there before the marsh turns into a boating lake.'

Perched up here on the wagon seat, I ask myself, *Are you a happy, Jack? Your mother's dead and you're sitting next to a murderer who's taking you out to somewhere in the middle of a flooded marsh to pick up a load of smuggled goods, and it'll soon be night. Oh, and if you don't get caught in the act by the law and end up swinging on that gibbet you saw just outside New Romney, Webster might try to do you in, once he's got what he wants. You've got plenty to look forward to, haven't you? The rain's lovely, too, isn't it?*

Our wagon is on a narrow track that seems to lead straight to nowhere and I'm sitting up there next to Webster. He's wrapped the reins from both horses round his wrists in order to give himself firm control over them. The clouds are so low I feel I could reach up and touch them. How much water can those things hold? It just keeps on falling out of them.

Webster gives me a quick glance.

'That letter you had knocked the stuffing out of you, didn't it?'

'I'll get over it,' I tell him. 'I'm already making a start.'

'Game for anything, eh?' he says.

'Pretty much; except for murdering people.'

He shuts up and flicks the reins over the horses' backs while I take another look at all the water that's lying around, and rising.

'How much further is it?' I ask. 'There's nothing in sight yet, except the same old bushes and long grass, and they're starting to drown.'

Webster looks at me from beneath the dripping brim of his hat, his weather-beaten face reminds me too much of Sikes's. It has that same 'don't get on the wrong side of me' look. 'There's a sewer that cuts us off from where the goods are stashed,' he says, 'but I've got some planks of wood hidden up there, so we can cross it on foot. Then it's you and me, carrying what we can. The whole area will be under water if this rain goes on much longer. Like I told you before, we'll have a devil of a job getting my stuff away if things get any worse. Come on, you brutes!' He slaps the reins across the backs of the horses, increasing their speed somewhat.

'Why bother with it, then?' I ask him, 'the soldiers won't be able to search, either.'

'You don't know this country,' Webster says. 'The whole lot could drain away by tomorrow night, and I'm not trusting two thousand pounds to the weather.'

Two thousand pounds! You could live in comfort for ages on that. We are halfway across a field covered in six inches of water, when the track comes to nothing. I can see the line of the sewer and beyond that, the broken walls of a ruined church and a row of wrecked and abandoned cottages.

A church out here!? It must be quite a nice spot to bring a girl on a sunny day, but it looks grim under the grey skies. I wouldn't fancy spending the night out here. It's headless horse-men country.

Webster answers my question before I can ask it.

'Those in the know have told me that the people who lived here a long time ago, all died of the Black Death; men, women, children and all. Some other villages went the same way. This is as far as we can go with the wagon.'

He jumps down and I follow him. Getting my feet wet completes my all-over bath for today.

After Webster has dragged two thick planks of wood from among the reeds, I help him bridge the sewer with them. The water is flowing fast. Dirty brown in colour, it's quite close to the top, too.

Crossing the makeshift bridge is easy enough. Webster leads the way to what's left of the church tower and begins pulling slabs of stone away from its base. I lend a hand and before long, we've made a ragged entrance big enough to allow us to get at a fortune in kegs of rum and brandy, and bundles wrapped in sailcloth.

'Here, Jack, carry as much as you can,' Webster tells me, as he heaves one of the bundles on to his shoulder with one hand and rolls a keg of brandy beneath his armpit with the other, 'and step careful, those slabs over there hide what used to be a cellar.'

When this man wants a favour done, you'd think he wouldn't say boo to a goose.

'Silks, baccy, tea and brandy,' he says, 'they'll help me retire right soon, if I play my cards right.'

After making a dozen trips across our improvised bridge, I'm beginning to think I can't carry another bundle. The two, miserable horses are standing between the shafts with their heads down, and a sheet of water is creeping towards us like a live thing; filling the hollows as it comes. It's getting dark, too. I say as much to Webster, adding:

'Let's get away from here while we can!'

'You're right,' he says. 'The revenuers can have what's left, if they find anything.'

CHAPTER EIGHT
The devil drops in on Shippenden Farm

With flood water halfway up its wheels, the wagon has been trundling along for about twenty minutes. Although the rain's stopped, I'm still wet through from the last vicious downpour. Too tired to think straight, I'm trying to get my mind back on track, just as Webster is doing with the wagon. The bitter disappointment Hawke's letter brought to me has faded away and become nothing more than an ache in the pit of my stomach; and I've no intention of turning that in to a joke about my being hungry, which I am. The search for my mother is over before it got started; so what now. Ah, Lysette; you think you know me but you don't really, and I don't know you at all either, do I? There are things going on behind those green eyes of yours. As I start re-living the moment when I kissed her, Webster asks:

'What are you brooding about? Your dead ma, I suppose?'

'Her, and some other things,' I tell him, 'including what you intend to do with this wagon load of goods. You can't take it to the farm, can you? On top of that, Mr Godden will want to know where we've been half the night.'

'Don't you worry about Godden,' Webster says. 'He never knows what's going on around him. When we get back to Shippenden, he'll either be tucked up in bed, as will the girl, or have his head stuck in a book. The buyer will be waiting for me at my cottage, so the goods shall be gone by morning, and the wagon with the stuff I bought for Godden, in it, will be back in the cart shed before he wakes up. If he bothers to ask me, I'll tell him we had trouble getting back because of the floods; everything's taken care of, see? I spent seven years eating ship's biscuits and salt pork before I got enough prize money to set this business up. I'm closing it after tonight; going off to pastures new to put my feet up.'

He looks beyond the high-stepping horses to a line, darker than the night, crossing the horizon. 'That's the causeway up ahead.'

Now the flood is swirling about the horses' bellies. It's beginning to feel as though we're floating. I don't want to float!

One or two grey bundles bump against the side of the wagon and slide by. I'm trying to stay calm, but show I'm not, when I wail,

'Sheep! They're drowned sheep!'

Webster couldn't care less. 'Yeah. Those are Godden's sheep, I reckon. He's probably lost dozens of 'em.'

Then the wagon lurches in to what feels to be a deep rut, sending dirty water splashing over our legs as its front tilts to an angle I don't think it's been at before. Kegs and bundles crash and roll about in the wagon bed. I'm out of my depth in more ways than one on Romney Marsh.

'We're off the track!'

Webster claws at the reins. 'Whoa, there!'

The horses struggle to keep their footing as one of the rear wheels lifts clear of the ground.

'We're going over!' I shout; but the wheel falls back, sending up a fount of water.

'Damn and blast it.' Webster gives up wrestling with the reins. 'Come on, we'll have to manhandle the horses out of here, if we can. Take hold of their heads and lead them.'

The dark water comes up to my chest. All right, so I'm not very tall.

I plunge through it, and none too happy about trying to get one of these big shires to do as he's told, take hold of a bridle.

Two more dead sheep drift slowly by.

Between us, we manage to get the horses moving forward.

'Stop!' Webster bellows, as another of the wagon wheels rears up. 'We'll have to back up again, and try to get all four wheels on the track.'

The wagon, pushed back by, I don't know how many tons of horse flesh, moves easily enough, but the shafts start going in the wrong direction, taking the wagon with them. Now we've got two back wheels stuck in the marsh and the goods in the wagon are sliding about; shifting the weight and allowing water to creep under the tailgate.

Webster ploughs his way through the water and, reaching beneath the driver's seat, produces a whip. Striking first one horse, then the other on their rumps, he encourages them to move forward. I don't like to see that, even though we're in a fix.

How they strain their great muscles and stretch their necks! Finally, the wagon moves and we're off again. Cold, worn out, empty in more ways than one, and with water running off me, I sit next to Webster on the wagon-seat.

A lot of very scared sheep have found safety on the causeway. It's a weird scene. The wind has got up now; blowing enough of the clouds away to allow the moon to shine on the restless animals as they move about, sticking close together and looking as though their nerves are in shreds. I know sheep don't smell that good at the best of times; wet through, they smell even worse.

There's deep water stretching away on both sides of us, with only a few of the taller shrubs and willow trees sticking out of it.

If there are such things as ghosts and hobgoblins, this place must be swarming with them tonight!

As we move up the lane leading to Shippenden Farm, we see that lamps are alight in Mr Godden's house. Have you noticed how welcoming lamplight appears to be when you arrive somewhere on a dark night? I like to see it across water, too. It always makes me wonder what's going on 'over there'.

As we pull up by the cottage, the front door of the farm house opens and, talk about hobgoblins! I can see that the man standing in the doorway, holding a lantern, would easily pass for one.

Webster sees him and shouts,

'Madeley! What the hell are you doing in Godden's house? You're early, too.'

He jumps from the wagon and I follow him, bracing myself to face what past experience tells me looks like being something painful or bloody - or both.

'You were supposed to come in the dead of night and meet me at my place, with my money,' Webster rants.

Madeley is a twisted, deformed little man with a powerful torso and a head on his shoulders such as I have never seen. It's too big for his body and shaped more like a nightmare monkey than those you see sitting on an organ-grinder's shoulder. Deformity doesn't always make a person evil, but it obviously has in this instance.

He's pointing a pistol at us as we walk up to him. Webster doesn't seem to be worried by it. Indeed, I've got the feeling that if he didn't have money on his mind he would knock Madeley flat on his broad back and shove his own pistol up the dwarf's pimpled nose.

'You were supposed to meet me at my place after Godden settled down,' he snaps. 'Where is he?'

Madeley bares his broken teeth. 'I've done for him, just as I intended to after I saw that fine girl of his, the last time I called on you. I had an idea he wouldn't hand her over to me, quiet like. Enjoyable work, it was, listening to him plead for his pretty, young daughter just before I sent him to meet his maker. He was an odd sort; didn't seem to care a whit for himself.'

I knew it! It's the return of blood and horror and I'm caught in the middle of it again. Lysette!

Before I realise what I'm doing, I'm knocking the monster's pistol aside and shoving him in to the hallway. I'm taller than him. 'What have you done with the girl, you piece of filth?'

'Oi, oi', he says, as Webster gets hold of me. 'Is this the young villain you told me about, Charlie boy?'

'He's the one. Jack Dawkins, by name,' Webster tells him. 'He's sweet on the girl. Now I'll ask you the same question he did. What have you done to her?'

'Why, nothing at all, Charlie,' Madeley wipes the back of his hand across his mouth and makes a disgusting, slobbering sound. 'I wanted to, but damaged goods fetch less than a virgin. She's in Godden's little library, dosed up with opium and something extra a Chinee sold me to help keep her quiet.'

I've suddenly grown very cold. What have I fallen in to? I've got to play a waiting game here. At least Lysette is still alive.

Webster says, '1 need a drink, after the day I've had.'

'Let's all have one!' cries Madeley. 'Follow me, gentlemen. There's no charge.'

In the drawing room, I gulp down the biggest measure of brandy I've ever had.

'Everything's in place,' Madeley is telling Webster. 'The boat is waiting for us beyond New Romney. The crew will take us, the girl and the goods, round to a creek near Faversham, to begin with; then on to Limehouse Reach.'

'What's all this "us" business?' Webster wants to know. 'I'm not going with you any further than the boat and I'll do for you right now if you ain't brought me my blasted money.'

'Everybody loves it, don't they?' Madeley sneers. 'I know I do. I plan to be a money lender myself, one fine day. Worry not, Charlie, boy. I have yours with me, but with Godden's dead body lying on the kitchen floor, you'd better get out of here fast. Come with me to Limehouse. When I set up my business, I'll need a man like you to persuade those who haven't paid, that they really should.'

Webster has other ideas. 'That's not for me. I've already thought it out. Young Dawkins killed Godden, not me. He disposed of the girl, too; somewhere out there on the marsh. The local magistrate already thinks he's no good and, this is a bit of luck, he was on the receiving end of some bad news about his ma today. Bad enough to send him off his head and do a thing like this.'

I'm not cold now; I'm thinking fast and trying to interrupt.

'Why do that to me after I've proved I'm on your side? Didn't I work my guts out helping you get your stuff through the flood? I'm famous where I come from, you know. I'm not just anybody. I used to be a gang master's right hand man. I can copy anybody's script, lift anything you like to name, and follow a mark up a ladder without being spotted, if need be.'

Webster looks at Madeley.

'He's useful, all right, but I'm still going to lay Godden's murder at his door. It's a shame I've got to do it, because he ain't short of brass nerve, either. Do you want him, Madeley? He could come in handy in your line of work, and he'll stand a better chance of not getting his neck stretched if you take him with you.'

As worked up as I am, I can't help thinking, *never mind my neck, Webster; at least I've got one*. Madeley's head seems to sprout straight out of his shoulders. It makes me wonder where the hangman will put the noose on him when Madeley's time comes.

It's strange what goes through your mind when you're up against it.

'He can help with loading the boat to start with,' Madeley nods and slurps. 'After that, I'll take him on and see he gets fed and watered while I put him to the test. If he don't come up to scratch, I'll split any reward money with you.'

I don't like being talked about as though I'm not there, and I'm making my own plans for my future, thank you very much.

'Can I have the girl, then?' I ask Webster.

Madeley gives what passes for a laugh. 'Got a thousand pounds to spare, have you?'

Webster answers that question. 'No, he ain't, but you've got two thousand for me, haven't you?'

Madeley's hand is touching the butt of the pistol he's placed on the table. 'Market values have dropped, Charlie. I can let you have fifteen hundred. Five hundred now and the rest after the boat's loaded. I've left the thousand on board, just in case you intended burying me on the marsh, as well.'

As Madeley starts counting out paper money, Webster says, 'I told you I wanted gold coin. These notes had better be genuine. If they're not, I'll hunt you down wherever you choose to hide.'

I ask, as polite as can be, to help me get my own way. 'Can I just take a look at the girl, then, Mr Madeley?'

He clasps his hands together and puts them beneath his chin. 'Oh, so it's Mr Madeley now, is it? Well, seeing as you've asked me so nicely, dear boy, you can most certainly look at the lovely creature. Look, but don't touch.' Waggling his fingers at me, he lets go with another one of his skin-crawling laughs.

'Don't do a runner,' Webster warns me.

Madeley says to him, 'If things don't work out for you, Charlie, my offer's still open. You'll find me up Limehouse way. I'll be using my ma's given name, which was Quilp. So I'll be Daniel Quilp, Banker and Pawnbroker. It'll look fine on my office door.'

I'm weak in body and mind, but I drag myself from the room and make straight for the kitchen.

When I get there, I find a lamp burning. It's smoking a little because its wick needs trimming. Mr Godden is there as well.

He's lying lifeless on the floor, almost surrounded by a pool of blood.

It's not the first dead body I've seen, but I feel sick, remembering how decent he'd been to me.

I haven't had a bite since breakfast, so I know I've got to eat something to help me keep a clear head. Fagin always used to make sure we had a good dinner before going on a jaunt. He maintained that having a full stomach helped us keep our minds on the job, instead of dreaming about sausages and hot pies.

Thoughts of vengeance fill my mind. I picture myself rushing up to Madeley and shooting him dead. Perhaps Mr Godden kept a brace of pistols somewhere?

Not surprisingly, I can't find one, let alone two barkers in the silent kitchen, so I swallow about a pint of milk, then cut myself a thick slice of ham and put it between two chunks of buttered bread; eating it as I head for Mr Godden's library.

Oh, Lord. Wearing a green and white gown, decorated with little flowers and buttoned up to the neck, Lysette is lying on a chaise longue with her head thrown back and her hair all a-tumble. That animal-swine must have looked at her legs, because she is showing a lot more than her ankles. I pull her dress down as delicately as I can. I'm all choked up now. She looks very pale, especially around the lips, so I breathe deep and touch her face. She's warm enough and her bosom is rising and falling. My God, I want to shoot Madeley more than ever now. Perhaps those pistols are in Mr Godden's desk. I begin opening drawers.

'I'll take her,' a voice says.

It's Webster. 'Let's get her to the wagon. Madeley's ready to go, and I'm ready to see the back of him.'

He notices the look of despair on my face.

'Believe it, or not, Jack, I'm sorry about the girl. I didn't want anybody hurt. All I wanted was the money. My goods should have come and gone in the night without anybody being the wiser. I always take care of number one; but seeing as how I like the cut of your jib, here's twenty pounds to help you get away, if you can.'

Webster hands me the brand-new notes, then says: 'As for this girl; well, the ugly brute still owes me money and even after he's paid me, the day might come when I need him, so I'm afraid she'll have to take her chances with him. As I said, with me it's number one, first and last.'

He lifts Lysette and without any help from me, carries her from the room.

I'm helpless in the face of the pistols held by these dangerous men; for the moment, that is; because, come what may, I'm determined to save Lysette.

Madeley is stuffing a bottle of brandy in to the pocket of an overcoat that reaches the ground.

'I'll have to give that girl another dose of my special mixture soon. We don't want her waking up and screaming her pretty head off, do we?'

It's black as pitch outside. Madeley uses a lantern to light our way to the wagon.

I follow Webster and watch him place Lysette among its cargo. He's quite gentle with her. Now he's saying to me:

'I'll wait 'til late morning before I report the deaths, Jack. It'll give you half a chance if you make a break for it.'

Keeping my voice down, I tell him, 'You do what you like, Webster. Whatever happens, I'm going to survive this. I'm not leaving Lysette in the hands of that... that thing. Do you hear what I'm saying?'

He hears but doesn't answer me; just climbs to the wagon seat that I for one have seen and felt enough of for one day.

There's no argument from him or Madeley when I crawl in to the back and sit down among Godden's sacks of grain and the smuggled goods.

I do what I can with Lysette's hair, then straighten her limbs and rub her hands to try to wake her as the wagon starts moving. We are on our way to the sea, a waiting boat and who knows where, after that?

The deep silence of the night is broken by the sound of our iron-bound wheels grating on the roughly paved road as we pass through the centre of a small village. Being well past midnight, every cottage is in darkness.

As I lay back with my arm around Lysette's shoulders, I imagine the reaction of someone who can't sleep, looking out of their bedroom window and seeing the scarcely human figure of Madeley sitting up there in the ghostly moonlight, next to grim-faced Webster. It would be 'bedclothes over the head' time, for them, and a tall story to tell in the morning.

I can hear it, I can smell it and I can even taste it, but before I get the chance to take my first ever look at the sea, Lysette begins to stir. I hold her close:

'Don't scream, don't scream, darling. It's me, Jack. I'll look after you.'

She opens her eyes and makes a moaning noise; quiet, but enough to scare me in to worrying that either Webster or Madeley will hear her. She struggles for a moment, then with her head on my shoulder, whispers one word:

'Jack?'

'I'm here,' I murmur. 'Listen to me. Are you strong enough to stand and run? I want to get you off this wagon before it's too late. We can hide somewhere out there on the marsh.'

'Papa!' she's able to shriek the word, because I hold back from clamping my hand over her mouth. It don't seem right to do that to her.

Madeley turns his fantastical head and, showing teeth that look like they belong to a wild beast, leers at me and says:

'My little treasure's awake, is she? Well, let her scream if she's a mind to. There's nobody to hear her now, except for us and Peachey. He's waiting by his boat, not far from here.'

Lysette has taken hold of me. 'Oh, Jack, my dear papa is dead. That monster killed him. What will happen to me now?'

'I know what won't happen to you,' I tell her, not caring whether Madeley hears me or not, 'I ain't going to let your pa's murderer take you with him. And if Webster doesn't change his mind and help me stop him, he's no sort of man. I wouldn't spit on him if he was on fire.'

It's Webster's turn to look at me. 'Watch your mouth, boy. I told you how the land lies.'

My first sight of the sea should have amazed me, but I have far too much on my mind to allow me to take it all in. Waves are breaking on shingle and a man is standing beside a small boat drawn up on it; that's all I notice at first.

The man crunches his way towards us as we climb from the wagon, leaving Lysette sobbing her heart out.

A horrible feeling of helplessness has swept over me again. I know I can get away from here in a flash, but how can I leave Lysette? The short answer is, I can't, so I'll wait it out.

There's no hand shaking when the three meet up. The fisherman, Peachey, is another Romney Marsh man; a strong body, formed by hard labour, and a weather beaten face, half hidden by a grey beard. He looks old but acts like he's as fit as a fiddle.

'What's that girl doing here?' is the first thing he wants to know.

'She's mine,' Madeley hisses. 'I'll dose her up again when we get her to the boat. Let her snivel for now. It does me heart good to watch beauty suffer.'

'Goods first, though,' Webster tells him. 'The sooner you give me the rest of what's owed, the sooner I can get out of here.'

CHAPTER NINE
A cannon ball kills the sparrow

I haven't slept a wink since yesterday and here I am, doing the same thing I'd done hours ago, because there's no sense in getting myself killed by not doing it. In other words, I'm carrying contraband again; crossing a pebble beach to a boat, this time. Oh, goody. It ain't raining.

Madeley takes great pleasure in tying Lysette's hands and feet, so she can't run off while he's busy, and I don't know how to save her.

Peachey's fishing boat, the *Sparrow*, is anchored about a hundred yards off-shore. Getting everything out to it is proving to be a long job. While Webster and Peachey take turns in rowing boat loads out to the larger vessel, where a man is waiting to haul the cargo aboard, I plod to and fro, piling stuff up on the beach.

The sky is lightening over Romney Marsh when Webster starts demanding the rest of his money, again. Peachey and his one-man crew are on the *Sparrow*.

Madeley puts his hand into his overcoat pocket. 'I've got it here. Put the girl in the row boat for me, and I'll count it out.'

'What about me?' I ask him. 'What do I get?'

'Your life, and that's generous of me,' Madeley says, waving his pistol under my nose. I'd like to smash his face in, but can't risk it. Lysette is causing me agony because, with her face smudged with dirt, she's pleading with Webster as he places her in the boat.

'Please let me go, Mr Webster, I beg you, please.'

'Sorry girl. It's out of my hands,' he tells her.

All I can do is call out to her. 'I'm coming with you, Lysette. Don't be afraid!'

Madeley pays Webster the rest of the money then clambers awkwardly into the boat. With his face twisted in to a display of wicked self-satisfaction, he threatens me with the pistol:

'You ain't coming with us, after all,' he tells me. 'I've got no use for the likes of you. I'll let you live, so I'll have the pleasure of knowing you'll be grizzling over this girl you're soft on when the hangman puts the noose round your neck for something you didn't do.'

Knowing I'm a match for him any day of the week, I want to tackle Madeley, but I won't be able to help Lysette if I'm shot dead, so I'll stay alive and swear to God I'll get her back, somehow.

Keeping the pistol close, Madeley unships the oars and starts pulling towards the fishing boat, cresting small waves as I follow it out, wading through the surf until I'm in danger of being swept off my feet.

'I'll find you, Madeley and when I do, you'd better watch out!' I'm yelling at him like a hurt schoolboy.

When I turn round, trying to stay upright in deep water, I see that Webster is crossing the shingle, heading for the wagon.

I stumble ashore, reaching it as a warning comes from the man helping to crew the *Sparrow*. He shouts one word from its deck.

'Soldiers!'

Everything happens at once.

Madeley begins rowing faster but not very well. I swivel my head and see six or eight uniformed men carrying muskets, pounding towards me. Webster leaps on to the wagon. Musket balls strike him at the same moment as the noise of their firing reaches my ears. He falls forward between the two horses as they panic and set off at a pounding gallop, dragging him and the rocking, bouncing wagon along with them.

I throw up my arms.

'Don't shoot at the rowing boat - there's a girl...' I'm shouting as loud as I can.

Half a dozen well-built, red-coated soldiers, panting like over-grown puppy dogs, form a half-circle round me. Two others are chasing after the wagon.

The clock seems to stop when things like this are happening, because I can see Lysette is already being hauled aboard the fishing boat.

I haven't got time to feel afraid of these lump-head soldiers.

'That girl's being kidnapped. Can't you do something to help her?'

Their sergeant pays me some attention. 'There's not much we can do to stop them getting away, but those gunners manning the cannon on that Martello Tower can... and will. Trouble is, if, as you say, there's an innocent girl out there, I don't give much for her chances. That fishing boat will be turned into wet fire-wood if it's struck by one of our thirty-two pounders. We're here because my officer, Lieutenant Harman, saw what you lot were up to through his spyglass. He sent us running after you before we even had time to have our breakfast. By the way, you're took, lad.'

I lower my arms so that he can use his lanyard to tie them behind my back. It's the end of the road, and the hangman's rope's in sight.

I express how I feel, out loud. 'Things just keep getting better for me, don't they?'

'Yeah,' the sergeant replies, 'and it's early yet.'

Now the wagon's on its way back to us, following the line of the beach. One of the two soldiers is running ahead of it. He's getting plenty of exercise this morning. As he veers towards us, it's his turn to do some shouting:

'He's still alive, sarge! Shot twice and still alive!'

Another of the soldiers raises his voice, 'Hey, sarge, there's a ship beating its way up the channel. A frigate, I think.'

I hadn't noticed the odd-looking round tower standing close to the sea, a few hundred yards away, but before the sergeant can answer either of his men, its cannon booms.

The *Sparrow* is dipping and rising, heading out to sea as the cannon ball raises a splash far beyond it.

'Can't you signal that tower and tell them there's an innocent girl on that boat?' I ask the sergeant.

'Just a minute,' he turns on the soldier who'd shouted that Webster was alive. 'Now then, Private Gibbs, I've told you before, ain't I? You don't shout at me from a distance. You come up to me, stand smartly to attention and make your report, geddit?'

Private Gibbs doesn't quite hang his head. 'Sorry, sergeant, but that man we shot is still just about alive. He needs a doctor; though there ain't much he'll be able to do for him, I reckon.'

The big gun on top of the tower booms out again and we all duck our heads; which doesn't make any sense at all, because we're on land and it's aiming at the fishing boat. I actually catch a brief glimpse of the cannon ball as it hurtles over the *Sparrow* and sends up another spout of water, no more than a few yards from it. That frigate is bearing down, as well.

'Will you signal those men on the tower!?' I scream at the sergeant.

'The man's still alive, is he?' he says to Private Gibbs. 'Well, get him to the Martello as quick as you can, he's got questions to answer.'

Why am I always so helpless? Too young for a man to pay attention to, am I? We'll see about that. With my hands tied, I can't punch the sergeant, so I kick him in the shins as hard as I can.

'Listen, you cretin, make them stop firing, or I'll-'

The butt of a musket hits me hard in the back, and I'm on my knees in the shingle, gasping as the cannon roars for the third time.

The soldiers start cheering:

'Bullseye!'

'Third time lucky!'

'Who'd a thought it!?'

The *Sparrow*, now a long way out, has sort of folded up and has all manner of floating objects swirling round it. I carry on watching as what's left of the fishing boat slides beneath the waves and more of its contraband cargo starts popping to the surface like a magic trick.

The sergeant is looking down at me.

'I'm sorry, lad, but I couldn't have stopped them from firing, you know. For a start, nobody on that Martello would have been looking in our direction. They'd have been too busy loading, firing and watching for the fall of shot. Perhaps the girl will be picked up by that frigate. They're just now putting a boat in the water. Your sister, was she, I mean, is she?'

I'm dead inside as I leave the beach, with three soldiers encouraging me to walk faster. The wagon is far ahead of us and already nearing the tower.

There's nothing left for me to aim for now. No mother to find, no idea where my father might be, if he's still in the land of the living, that is, and no girl to win over. Why was it all put in front of me and then snatched away? Damn everything. From now on I'm going to do what Webster said he did. If I escape being hanged, which don't seem likely, I'm going to take care of number one. For some reason, the thought makes me feel sadder than ever.

I look up at the Martello Tower as I stand outside it with two soldiers guarding me. Without even a slit in its walls for windows, it bulges out round the bottom and gets narrower at the top. One of my guards, seeing me look at it, says:

'Them walls is eight feet thick, them walls is. Makes a body feel safe when he's inside it.'

He snaps to attention when a young officer emerges from a doorway in the tower.

'Put the prisoner in the wagon, along with the wounded man, Private Lister. Escort them to New Romney, hand them over to the civilian authorities, then return here, post haste. There's to be no hanging about in the taverns, understand? With Bonaparte back in France, we are in the middle of an emergency.'

Lister salutes. 'We'll be back 'ere before you know it, sir.'

Webster, now laid out in the back of the wagon, has been shot twice through his shoulders. It looks as though he was knocked about a bit by those horses, too.

Between them, Lister and his companion have done their best to stop him bleeding to death; ripping his shirt to pieces and using it as wadding and bandages.

When I sit down beside him, I notice that his blood has already turned the white dressings very red. He's had it.

Lister has placed himself as far away as possible from me, although what he thinks I can do to tackle him while my hands are tied behind my back, is a mystery to me. I ask him if he knows the fate of the people who were on board the fishing boat.

'No, I don't. Nobody tells me nothing,' he says. 'You picked the wrong day to go a-sailing, didn't you? You'd have got away with it yesterdee, 'cos we didn't man the Martello 'til last night. We were rushed here from Dover when word came through that Boney has landed in France. As for your mates surviving that wreck, they do say a longboat put out from the frigate to look for survivors.'

My brain starts working again. Here I am, sitting next to a dying man with at least a thousand pounds in his pocket. It goes against the grain to rob someone in his situation, but if I'm given the chance to get my hands on it, I can put the money to good use; maybe bribe my way to freedom. Something he'll never be able to do.

Filching from a man's pocket is normally over in a flash, and you're out of sight in another, but this job has to be done little by little. Luckily for me, Lister starts gossiping with the driver. He's a talker, is Lister. According to him, if Bonaparte tries to invade England, his fleet will be blown out of the water. He's looking forward to playing his part in doing it. Why didn't they hang Boney last time? It's typical of the 'gold braids' who don't have to do any fighting, to send an enemy 'gold braid' off to live in luxury on an island, even after he's killed millions.

Keep going, Lister, while I try to stuff all this money down the back of my trousers. With my hands tied behind me, I can't reach anywhere else.

Webster is offloaded at a doctor's house at the beginning of New Romney's narrow, winding high street. Everything looks normal, but I feel it shouldn't, not after everything that's happened. Even the blasted sun is shining a bit. There's a hint of green in the trees growing here and there and some birds are flying about. Life goes on, as they say.

The gaol looks more like a cottage with barred windows, but it's a gaol all right.

To stop the money I've lifted from falling down my trouser legs, I have to walk from the wagon as though I've done something in them.

Lister notices and says,

'Scared to death, are you? Well, you'll have to clean yourself up, somehow. If you're like that now, I don't want to be too close to the gibbet when they hang you. I suppose I'd better untie you. Sergeant Hays will want his lanyard back'

Averting his head, he releases my hands.

'The wagon and horses belong to the Godden family at Shippenden Farm,' I tell him. 'You'd better let somebody know that Mr Godden's been murdered by the same man who kidnapped his daughter. His body's lying in the house out there.'

'I'll tell our lieutenant,' Lister replies and departs, leaving me with the turnkey. He's a skinny, bent over sort of fellow who seems to think he's running a guest house.

'You ain't had nothing since breakfast, I'll be bound. Give me the wherewithal and I'll get you a dinner the likes of which you've never had before.'

The way things are, I can't eat, and tell him so. 'All I want to do is get some sleep, so lock the door on me and leave me alone.'

'Right-o,' he says, 'my name's George, George Theobold. I'll look in on you later.'

I fall onto a low, wooden-slatted bed, covered by a thin mattress and a couple of blankets, and try to block everything out.

No dreams, but I wake up in a panic. It's dark, but someone's standing over me holding a lantern. It's George:

'Mr Fitch is here to see you.'

'Let him in, then,' I tell him, 'he can hang me as soon as he likes.'

'Don't talk daft,' George answers. 'He ain't here for anything like that.'

Feeling like death, I sit up and swing my feet to the floor.

'Come ahead, your honour,' George calls out.

He does, and he's full of the little-bitty power he holds over people.

He looks down at me; I mean, what else would he do?

Thinking he's being clever, he says:

98

'Well now, Dawkins. Here's a pretty kettle of fish, and you are sitting right in the middle of it. Somehow, though, you seem to be climbing out without any stink attached to you.'

'What?'

'Don't "what" me, young man. Along with the Reverend Hood, I have just come from Dr Mercer's house. We were both there at the request of Charles Webster. Before, and indeed, during, the last rites he confessed that you were forced at pistol point to help him and a man named Madeley, bring contraband goods from off the marsh to the waiting fishing boat that now lies at the bottom of the channel.'

I interrupt him with, 'Do you know if there were any survivors, your honour? Mr Godden's daughter...'

Fitch holds up a hand. 'Allow me to finish, if you please. I was going to add that one must accept the word of a dying man. Webster also told us how Madeley killed the unfortunate Mr Godden and took his lovely, young daughter aboard the boat. What a fiend that man must have been.'

Now I know. 'You mean, nobody survived, sir?'

The magistrate shakes his head. 'I fear there's little hope; although Lieutenant Harman did observe the frigate *Wyvern* lowering a boat to search for survivors. We shan't know whether they had any success until we get word from her. She was obliged to continue to the Downs on the king's business.

I lose control of myself and burst out, 'Girls like Lysette Godden just can't be allowed to die like that! What's God up to?'

'No matter who they are,' Fitch says, 'people frequently get carried off through accidents, disease, or die at the hands of villains such as Madeley. It is a cruel world, Dawkins. A person like yourself should know it and get used to it.'

'What's going to happen to me now that Mr Godden's dead, Mr Fitch?' I ask, but I don't care.

'You will remain a bondsman, of course.' He tells me from on high. 'I will send a message to Mr Brownlow, informing him of the situation. He will, no doubt, make other arrangements for you. Indeed, he has to, if you are not to be returned to Newgate and transportation. In the meantime, I think it will be in everybody's best interests if you remain in this cell. Have you any money to feed yourself with?'

I answer 'yes' to that; but don't tell him just how much I've got. Not having had the chance to count it, I don't exactly know myself.

Fitch goes on, 'I have arranged for Mr Godden's body to be brought in from Shippenden Farm. Whilst you were with him, did you happen to learn the whereabouts of his wife or any of his family members?'

I tell him what little I know. 'Mrs Godden is somewhere in France; Paris, I think. I don't know where, exactly. He has a sister living near Chatham. I don't know if she's married, or anything else about her.'

'I'll see what can be done to find them,' Fitch says. 'Goodnight, Dawkins. I hope you realise that Webster's confession has almost certainly saved you from being hanged. I will call and see you again.'

'Good night, sir,' I say it absentmindedly because I'm back to thinking about Lysette - and Webster. I honestly don't know what to make of him, now. There was a man who killed and buried some loosed-mouth local out on the marsh, allowed Madeley to make off with a young girl after murdering her father, then saved me from being hanged as he lay dying. I thought I'd already met every kind of villain there is, but I was wrong. I'll have to revise my opinion about how clever I am at judging people, won't I?

CHAPTER TEN
Hope on two fronts

George and I have been getting on famously for three days now. I haven't spent a lot of money, but I've bought a change of clothes and the necessaries to get myself cleaned up, although not in the way Lister thought I needed to! I'm the only guest George has at the moment, and because I can pay for it, he brings me my dinner, fresh and hot from the *New Inn*, just like any waiter.

'We're all smugglers in New Romney, now, Jack,' he obviously enjoyed telling me this morning. 'When word went round that goods were being washed ashore from the wreck, everybody rushed like long dogs to the beach. We got most of it away before those dozy soldiers got wind of what was happening. Between you and me, I've more than enough tea hid up to last me 'til Christmas, and enough brandy stowed for me and my family to have a good one!'

If I'm sounding a bit more cheerful, it's because he also brought me news yesterday; news that gave me a little hope. Word has it that the frigate longboat only collected two bodies. They were apparently men who looked so much like each other, they must have been related. They can only be those of Peachey and a relative he had on board to help him. No girl or malformed man had been found. Other voices declared that a row boat with the name *Sparrow* painted on it, had been found abandoned on the beach, a mile or two from the Martello Tower.

I've been torn about by different feelings since George told me that. Is it just gossip and rumour, or is Lysette alive, after all? Did the vile Madeley manage to get them both clear? If he did, it means she's his prisoner and will be sold to the highest bidder. I know that sort of thing happens. I used to hear it spoken about. I've got to get out of here! Perhaps George will turn his back for a hundred pounds?

Limehouse! That's where I'll go. I'll have to be careful, though; If I ask too many questions round there, I'll find myself floating down the Thames with my head bashed in.

There's something else. While I was sorting out the incredible sum of one thousand pounds that I lifted off Webster, I came across Hawke's letter and finished reading it. The last part says that he was still forging ahead with his enquiries and I would hear from him again.

'More visitors!' George calls out in his usual cheerful manner as he enters the gaol. Lo and behold, Oliver Twist or Oliver Brownlow, whatever he calls himself these days, is peeping at me through the tiny, barred window set in my cell door. George unlocks it, and I see that Mr Brownlow is standing there, as well.

Like the dutiful boy he is, Oliver greets me with:

'Hello, Jack,' then steps aside for the man I must now think of as being his father.

Mr Brownlow stands in front of me, looking very much the gentleman as he clings onto his travelling cloak. 'Well, well, Dawkins, trouble seems to follow you around, doesn't it?'

I can only agree with him on that score. 'Yes, sir; I felt I was doing quite well, too.'

'That is a significant remark. I have seen Mr Fitch and given him the address of Gilbert's, I mean, Mr Godden's sister, Rachel, but I have been unable to provide him with one for Mrs Godden. She's French, as you will know, and spends a good deal of her time in Paris; which for a married woman, is very strange. Perhaps a search among Mr Godden's papers will reveal where she is living at the moment. As for the daughter; I can't help wondering why God turned his face away and allowed her to die in such a fashion.'

'She's not dead, Mr Brownlow!'

Saying it helps me believe it.

I'm obliged to sit down on the bed when Oliver joins us in my tiny cell and says, excitedly:

'Your mother may still be alive, as well, Jack. Show him Mr Hawke's letter, father!'

'One thing at a time, Oliver,' Brownlow tells him, then asks me, 'what makes you think Lysette Godden may still be alive, sir?'

I provide him with the facts as I know them. 'Only two dead bodies, both men, have turned up so far, and a small boat is said to have been found not far from where the *Sparrow* was sunk. They say it had that same name painted on it. I think Madeley got away, taking Lysette with him. She's worth an awful lot of money to him. I know where to look for her, Mr Brownlow, but I must do it soon before Lysette is... oh, what might happen to her is unthinkable!'

'It's also rumour and conjecture,' Brownlow observes, 'as is part of this letter Mr Hawke requested I bring to you. He disclosed its contents to me. Here you are; make of it what you will.'

Perhaps it's one of those premonitions or the result of everything I've been through that's making my fingers tremble as I break the seal, unfold the pages and begin to read.

My dear Dawkins,

I hope my previous letter did not cause you too much distress. Having now made further enquiries, I am happy to be able to inform you that your mother might still be alive in the world; your father, also. I stress the word 'might' because the information I have is several years old. Copies exist of notices that were put up in various parts of central London, two years after the woman who was presumed to be your mother, Mrs Molly Dawkins, died. They provide a description of a missing child and the clothing he was wearing. It offers a reward of fifty pounds for the safe return of Jack Dawkins to the adjutant at Hounslow Cavalry Barracks. I understand that some false claims were made and rejected.

I speculate that the following is what may have happened:

In the year 1805 a mass of British and allied troop movements took place due to the continuing ambitions of Napoleon Bonaparte. Your mother followed her husband, your father, to war, as many other brave wives felt it was their duty to do. Having spoken to its colonel, I can confirm that your father, James Dawkins, was at the time, a captain in the 7ʰ Hussars, stationed at Hounslow, but in 1805 he was sent on special detachment to join our forces in Sicily. Your mother's name was/is Mary. No doubt she left you behind in the care of your father's sister, Molly Dawkins. The unfortunate woman was killed by a horse ridden by one of your father's fellow officers', the reckless and unprincipled, Captain Randall Swithin. Ironically, he disappeared just as you did. In his case, he deserted his regiment.

What became of your parents? The answer to that, my dear Jack, seems to be a regimental secret. Solve one mystery and up crops another. I will dig deeper. Good luck in all your endeavours!

Martin Hawke
Bow Street, London

It's hard for me to take it all in. My father was or is an officer in the cavalry! It couldn't be true, could it? I've never had any time for officer types. And what about a mother who left me behind and went off to war? I don't know what to think about that, either. Hold it. Take one thing at a time, Jack. Concentrate on Lysette, if she's alive, you know where to look for her.

'Mr Brownlow, sir. I have to go to London. Will you take me with you?'

'Return you to your old haunts, Mr Dawkins? Even if I was willing to do so, which I'm not, I cannot leave New Romney until I have made arrangements for someone to take care of Mr

Godden's farm and, in particular, his livestock. That is my first priority. Next, I intend asking my friend, Dr Strong, who has a school in Canterbury, whether he will consider taking you on. I'm sure he'll be able to provide you with board and lodging, and employ you in some menial capacity. In the meantime, you look very comfortable here. It's a long way from Newgate, is it not?'

Oliver finally manages to get a word in edgeways:

'Dear me, Jack, I'm sorry the report you've received about your parents is not more definite. Perhaps, like me, you will come across some other relatives. You don't really wish to return to London and your old way of life, do you?'

'No, I don't,' I tell him. 'It's got nothing to do with that. Deep down, I know Lysette Godden is alive, and I know where she's been taken, so it's up to me to go and get her. I won't rest until she's safe.'

Brownlow shakes his head. 'Her body not being washed ashore can only mean it's trapped under water. I understand an attempt will be made to dive on the wreck. The shelf falls sharply away at the point where the vessel sank, but not to the extent that it can't be reached. Excise officers are interested in finding out how much of the boat's cargo remained with her when she went down. The bodies of Madeley and Miss Godden will also be discovered. In the off-chance that she is still alive, it is up to the police to make the necessary enquiries, not you.'

I dismiss that. 'They won't find her. Half the police are on the take in Limehouse, Mr Brownlow; and that's where she is. The other half barge about, not knowing who's doing what to who, and not caring very much, either. If by some miracle, they did come close to finding Lysette, Madeley would get warning of it, because they're all brother and Bob where he hangs out. He'd cut her throat and his losses, dump her body in the Thames and disappear, or pay a dozen witnesses to swear he was somewhere else at the time.'

'Brownlow's all "rules and regulations".'

'I'm sorry, Dawkins,' Brownlow returns, 'but I can't possibly help you with such a romantic undertaking. I'll speak to the police about the matter after I have seen you safely lodged with Dr Strong and returned to London. Come along, Oliver. I want to have another word with Mr Fitch.'

Oliver, looking dapper in his made to measure suit, shakes my hand. 'I'm sorry, Jack. I'll see you later, shall I?'

He gives me an odd sort of look as he follows his father out of my cell. Coming from anybody else, it would be letting me know some sort of mischief is afoot; but mischief and Oliver just don't go together, do they?

CHAPTER ELEVEN
Oliver does me another favour

It's turned out to be more than mischief, Oliver had in mind.

Half an hour's gone by and he's back, looking at me through that window in my cell door again; his eyes wide with excitement.

'Jack,' he whispers, 'I helped myself to a spare key when I left here. The warder is very idle.'

I hear the key grate in the lock, the door opens and Oliver is standing there, quivering like a puppy waiting for his master to throw a stick.

Life's full of surprises.

'What do you think you're doing, Ollie?' I ask him. 'You're going to get yourself in to a lot of trouble, coming in here like this.'

With his button eyes blinking away, he says, 'Please give me your solemn word that you will return here, or to my father's house in London, after you have rescued the girl.'

I think he's read too many of those books about knights in shining armour; which brings to mind Lysette's 'Roland'. Doesn't the young shaver realise that Limehouse isn't exactly a grand, old castle whose walls I've got to scale after swimming the moat.

'I know you can do it,' he says. 'I believe in you, Jack.'

At least I'm a hero in somebody's eyes; it sort of makes me want to be one. 'Well, of course I give you my word. You'd better tell your pa I swore on my mother's life that I'll come back. What about you? Helping a prisoner escape can land you in gaol yourself.'

Oliver's growing more excited by the minute. 'I've thought about that. There are no charges against you, are there; and now you've sworn on oath that you'll return, it's just like a captured officer giving his parole. It's a matter of honour. Come on, you must hurry. The turnkey is telling stories in the high street tavern, and there's an omnibus that will take you as far as Ashford, standing outside of it, this very minute.'

I gather up the bits and pieces George bought for me and stuff them in a bag. Then I'm out of that cell door like one of those long dogs he mentioned to me.

'Have you got any money?' Oliver asks, as we turn on to the high street.

'I'm all right at the moment, thank you,' I tell him.

Oh, yes. I'm one thousand and fifteen pounds, seventeen shillings and sixpence, all right! The thousand isn't warming my backside. This time it's wrapped in a dirty shirt, nestling against my chest, underneath a clean one. The other five hundred Madeley paid Webster must have been in a pocket I couldn't get at. I expect somebody's managed to by now.

'Father will beat me for this, Jack, but I don't care,' Oliver says, just before I climb in to the omnibus and join the other passengers.

I give him a pat on the shoulder. 'I hope it don't hurt too much. I'm in your debt again, Oliver. Thank you. I won't let you down. Tell your new-found father that, will you?'

'I feel as though I've paid back a little of what I owe you, Jack,' Oliver calls out, as our driver clucks his tongue at the horse and the long coach jerks in to motion.

I could have walked it faster! We finally arrived at Ashford after covering twenty miles at the pace of a particularly decrepit snail; stopping at small villages and hanging about in a place called Tenterden. Never mind, the ride only cost me that odd sixpence

I told you about. People here at The George have told me that it's sixty miles to London. It means a twelve-hour journey by post chaise. My impatience knows no bounds. I'd buy myself a horse if I could ride a bit better.

While I'm trying and failing to decide what to do, my mind wanders. An idea that's completely useless to me and the rest of the world pops in to my head.

This is my idea:

Everybody would get around a lot faster if someone built lots of little steam boats with wheels for use on the land and roofs on them to keep the rain out, put a tiller to steer them with and seats to sit on. I'm surprised nobody's done it. Forget horses; people could buy them and run them on roads as their own private coaches. I reckon they'd cover ten miles in an hour, or so. Imagine that! Merchants could make money by having stacks of coal at stops on the side of the road to sell to the steamer drivers as they went by. They'd have to tow a little cart behind them to carry it in, of course and if they made them so water didn't get in, you could take them on rivers, as well.

That's diverted me, but not for long. This delay means more terror for Lysette. I can't bear thinking about her situation, but can't stop doing it, either.

After picking at a roast dinner, I book myself a cheap room at The George and wait for morning to come.

I doze and dream muddled dreams. Death, blood, and cries in the night; the last being mine. It wakes me up, so I sit on the bed and wonder what leading a normal life is like. Working, nothing too hard mind; coming home to a family that's living in a nice, little house; going out with friends. Ah, forget it! There's no point in worrying about something I'll never have.

I'm happy to be aboard the coach and on the road again, this morning. The old boy with a bush of a beard, sitting next to me, has told me that Napoleon and his army which, according to him, is growing bigger every day, is marching on Paris. So he may be, but I'm too busy marching on Limehouse to care what Boney's getting up to.

Time passes, no matter what you do. Sometimes you curse it for going too quick, and sometimes because it's going too slow; like today.

Here we are, though, crossing Blackheath and plunging down Shooters Hill on the other side.

Not too long after that, we arrive at another George Inn. This one's in Borough High Street. I'm familiar with it.

I didn't make any friends out of the five passengers I travelled with. There they go, off to wherever their own small worlds are, never to be seen by me again.

I could cross London Bridge, turn right and be in Limehouse twenty minutes later, if I wanted to, but I can't face Madeley, bare handed.

I force a passage through the crowds on the bridge; rich pickings here in the old days, then turn left on the other side of it.

While passing St Paul's, I think of Martin Hawke and wonder if what I'm set on doing next could be called God's work.

I turn my head away from Newgate Prison when I pass near it. No thanks.

It's growing dark by the time I knock on Dick Jenner's shop door, tucked away in an alley near St Giles. He sells all sorts of junk, but his main source of income is providing wallopers, barkers, powder and ball, and such-like, and not to the kind of people you'd want to know, either.

This gloomy and miserable alleyway is making me feel hemmed in after being on Romney Marsh. There's no big sky or distant horizon here. The roofs of the buildings on either side of the alley, lean towards each other, forming an archway. It's what you might call, Tumbledown Town, all round here.

Jenner's filthy shop window, set in a wall that used to stand straight, but now leans all over the place, has nothing in it that I'd want to buy. Dick keeps that sort of stuff locked up.

I knock on the door again.

'All right, I'm coming. Give me a little time, won'tcha?'

After a rattle of locks and bolts, the door opens.

'Good evening, Mr Jenner, sir!' I say, as he holds a lantern on high.

'Dawkins, the Dodger!' he cries, taking a step backwards. 'I thought you were on your way to Van Diemen's Land, or some such distant part of the world. You'd best come in quick, if they're after you.'

'They're not, Dick,' I reassure him. 'I'm sort of out on a long bit of rope.'

Dick's quite fat, so his rear end wobbles like jelly beneath his silk robe as I follow it along a narrow passage. I know him of old. He loves eating bread plastered with beef dripping and pepper; washing it down with a good deal of porter. Given the price of it, he probably spends more money on pepper than he does on food.

The shop's a shambles, so walking in to the room he almost lives in, always comes as a pleasant surprise, with its fine carpet, best quality furniture and a piano standing across one corner. It's just the same as it was when I came here a year ago, and Dick's clothing is just as fine. He could pass for the Prince Regent.

'Have a pew, Jack,' he says. 'You've surprised the life out of me. Are you here on business, or pleasure?'

'A bit of both, as it happens, Dick,' I tell him, as I park myself in an armchair. 'The business part is, I want you to sell me a pistol and two bottle bombs, like the ones you made for those ann arkists, or whatever you called them.'

Jenner's as shocked as I thought he might be. ''pon my oath, Jack, when did war break out!?'

'It's only a small, private war, Dick. One I've got to win.'

The supplier of every, under the counter, item you can think of, ambles his way to a sideboard. 'Want a drink, Jack?'

'Thanks, Dick. I'll need a clear head tomorrow, so a beer will do.'

'Now then,' Dick says, after he sits himself down and we've both tasted our drinks, 'what's going on, Jack, me boy?'

Hoping for the best, I ask, 'Have you ever come across an ugly mug, and I mean ugly, who goes by the name of Madeley? He's as bad as you can get and lives up Limehouse way.'

Dick shakes his head. 'Limehouse? You know me better than that. It's outside my territory, Jack. You should stay out of there, too.'

'I can't,' I tell him. 'Madeley might be holding a girl I know, against her will, and I intend to get her away from him.'

'Might be?' he asks.

'It's a long story, but I know in my guts he's got her.'

'While I've been growing out, you've been growing up, Jack,' Dick says. 'Have you got money?'

'Enough for my needs,' I tell him. 'There's one other thing. Have you got a spare bed for the night? I can pay for that, as well, but I'll want a bit more than bread and dripping for breakfast!'

Dick laughs out loud. 'Why's that? It sets you up for the day. Now then, a barker with powder and ball, more black powder, two bottles, fuses and seals, bed and breakfast- that'll cost you five guineas, Jack.'

'Five guineas!' I go off like a bomb, myself. 'That's robbery without violence!'

Dick sighs. 'It's inflation, Jack, that's what it is. By the way, how are you going to light these fuses when the time comes? Flints can be unreliable, especially if you're in a pinch and you're trying to get a spark. I've got a magic something you can have for old time's sake.'

He hauls himself to his feet and goes back to the sideboard, returning with a flask that can scarcely hold two good swallows, and a small box.

'These came my way just a few weeks ago. As I said, it's a bit of magic. Watch this.'

I have to wait as Dick drinks most of his beer, then he opens the box and takes out one of the several little sticks it holds. One end has been dipped in what looks like black treacle.

'Now then,' Dick says. 'This can be a mite dangerous, so stand back a bit.'

He shoves the black end of the stick in to the flask and quickly pulls it out again. To my amazement it bursts in to flame!

'How's that, then!?' Dick throws the burning stick in to what's left of his porter. 'They're the invention of a Frenchman named Jean Chancel. Don't ask me where I got them, but I have a small supply of the special matchsticks and the foul smelling liquid.'

'Five guineas ain't so bad, after all,' I tell him. 'I'll have a couple of those.'

I only realise I'm bolting down the breakfast Dick's crone of a maidservant cooked for me, when he draws my attention to it.

'You're like a racehorse at the start line,' he said. 'Slow down a bit for your stomach's sake.'

'You worry about your own stomach,' I tell him. 'If I find Madeley today, then I'll get Lysette away today. I'm set on doing it.'

'You certainly are,' Dick replies. 'I might be able to get you some help, for a price.'

'No thank you, Dick. Madeley might kill Lysette if we go in heavy. Don't worry. I'll best him.'

Not feeling as confident as I sound, I place two black bottles filled with gun powder and with five minute fuses attached to them, in to a leather case Dick sold me for three and six. Inflation again!

'Have you ever fired a gun of any description, Jack?' Dick asks, as he hands me a smart, holster pistol, small enough to hide under my coat.

I admit that I haven't, 'but I watched Sikes at play with them, many a time.'

Dick hands me the magic sticks and the flask. 'Well, good luck, then. Try not to turn up dead, won't you.'

'Goodbye, Dick. Nice doing business with you.'

All right, so I've got my heart in my mouth after I pick up a cab in Wych Street and tell the driver to take me to Aldgate.

During the journey, I find I'm knuckling my forehead. I've started thinking too much. First of all, I'm telling myself there's nothing to be scared of because I probably won't find Madeley, let alone Lysette. Then it's about turn. 'Brace up, you coward. You'll find her and take care of Madeley, all right. You can do it!'

I unbuckle the case and take a crafty look at Dick's home-made bombs.

'Don't be around when these go off, Jack,' He'd told me. 'If you are, they'll need a dustpan and brush to pick up what's left of you.'

I'm not familiar with Limehouse, only its reputation as a noto-rious den of thieves, so I head for the most obvious places to get information; the taverns.

There's a curious mix of people going about their business in the passageways and on the streets, and a lot of sailors off cargo ships. There's no point in asking them anything, so I concen-trate my questions on inn keepers. Inn- and out of them I go!

'Look, you can't mistake him. He's almost a dwarf and he's all twisted up; nasty with it, too.'

'Don't know him, and wouldn't tell you if I did,' is what I get, or sometimes words to that effect, which I'd better not write here.

I'm down by the river, or at least, close to its stinking mud banks, walking along Narrow Street; you couldn't find a better name for it, I arrive at the Bunch of Grapes.

And what have we here? Why it's that rare bird, a friendly innkeeper.

'Madeley?' he says, 'yes, I know that wicked devil, all right. If you're going to sup tea with him, I advise you to use the longest spoon you can lay your hands on.'

My throat seems to have closed up, but I manage to say: 'I've just got a bit of business with him, that's all. Where does he live?'

He tells me.

The devil hangs out in a ramshackle, tottering hovel which some might call a house. Its upper floors extend over the river's muddy shore. If you've ever been down in the Thames mud, like I did in the dim, distant past, you'll know it's about two feet deep and stinks to high heaven.

Now's the moment, Jack! Knock on that wreck of a door.

My heart lurches when it opens.

A young urchin is standing there; ragged, dirty and so like I remember myself, I want to pick the wretch up and carry him off to somewhere safe; but I've got a job to do.

'Is Madeley here?' I ask him.

'Dan'l,' There's nothing wrong with his lungs. He screams at the top of his tiny voice. 'There's a cove 'ere who wants to see you!'

'Send him on up, then!' That's Madeley's voice.

The boy stands to one side. 'You heard 'im, mister.'

Every one of the thirteen steps creaks loud beneath my feet as I climb the stairs. There's no door at the top, just a kind of loft, with a hatch in its bare, wooden floor and two closed doors at the back of it. There's not much furniture in the room, and what there is looks as though it belongs on a bonfire. Madeley is sitting at a roll-top desk.

I'd almost forgotten what it feels like to look at him. If it was anyone else, I'd feel pity for them, but not for this creature from hell.

He bares his teeth; just one of his charming habits:

'It's Jack Dawkins, ain't it? I thought you'd be hanged by now.'

I put my case on the floor and open it. I'm not wasting time.

'I've come for Lysette Godden, Madeley. I don't expect you to give her to me. I aim to buy her from you.'

'Buy that pretty, little girl from the marsh? Why, she drowned, Jack. Nearly did meself, as it happens.'

I tell myself that I can do it. 'Drowned, did she? In that case you've just signed your death warrant.'

Quite casually, I take one of the fused bottles and the magic stuff out of the bag.

Madeley laughs and points a pistol at me. 'You'll be stone dead before you light that thing.'

I have my answer ready. 'Go ahead and shoot if you want to risk dying along with me. A pistol ball will work just as well as a fuse.' I hold the bottle in front of me. 'It's full of black powder. Now where's the girl?

I dip the matchstick into the flask, remove it- and there's the flame!

It sets Madeley back on his heels. He's as surprised as I'd been; as anyone would be, the first time they see it. While he's gasping, I touch flame to the fuse and snatch my own pistol from beneath my coat. Snapping its hammer back, I point it at the bottle.

'Take a chance and shoot me now, Madeley. Either you'll hit the bottle or this hammer will fall and we'll both be goners. You've got five minutes before you're blown to kingdom come. Now where's the girl!?'

'You're mad! Off your head!' Madeley shouts and spits; his eyes bulging out of that hideous, twisted-up face.

'About four minutes now,' I tell him. 'I'd sooner go now than be hanged later, but you want to live, don't you?'

'All right, all right, how much will you give me for her? She's sick, mind, which ain't my fault. She's gone down with something, otherwise you'd have been too late. She'd be doing the old business for somebody who's got more money than he knows what to do with.'

'I'll offer five hundred pounds,' I say.

His eyes narrow. 'Where'd a down and out nobody like you get five hundred pounds from?'

I'm not going to tell him I'm paying him off with some of his own money, am I; the money he'd given to Webster:

'Heard of a receiver called Fagin, have you? Well, I knew where he hid his gelt before he was took. Today's the first chance I've had to get at it. This bottle's getting warm, Madeley. What do you reckon; about three minutes?'

'Put it out. I'll get her.'

'I'm just about to light the other one I've got in this bag,' I tell him, reaching down for it.

He's sweating now. 'Give me the money, then, you crazy, young fool. You ought to be put in a mad house. '

I throw the purse at him. He dips his crooked fingers into it and pulls out a bundle of notes.

'A couple of minutes left, Madeley.'

Stuffing the money away, he turns and scuttles off, unlocks a door and disappears for a few seconds. He comes back fast, pulling Lysette along behind him as though she's nothing but a barefoot marionette; as pale as death itself, filthy dirty and wearing rags for clothing.

'Take her and get out!' Madeley says, then starts spouting some more words you wouldn't want to hear, or see writ down.

I light the fuse on the second bomb and lob the first one way over Madeley's head. Some days, everything goes right. My aim

117

is perfect. It lands on a pile of clothing. Stolen or pawned, no doubt.

Remembering what Dick had said, I tell him, 'You've got half a minute to put it out. If you don't make it, I'll come back with a dustpan and brush.'

'Damn you.' He's down among coats, dresses and I don't know what, trying to grab hold of the bottle as I help Lysette's tragic, silent figure down the stairs; hanging on to the second bomb at the same time.

With about two minutes of fuse left to burn on it, we emerge on to Narrow Street. I'd like to toss the thing straight through one of Madeley's windows, but can't bring myself to do it, so I tear out the fuse and stamp on it.

By some miracle, I've got what I wanted.

Scared off, the urchin who let me in to Madeley's place is standing by a handcart on the other side of the street, looking lost.

I call him over.

'Bring that cart here, whatever your name is. Give me a hand with this girl and I'll see what I can do for you.'

There's no argument. As small as he is, the boy manages to push the cart across the deserted street.

He looks up at me:

'Who are you, mister? I'm hungry.'

'I used to be what you still are,' I tell him. 'Come with me and I'll try and make sure you don't go hungry again.'

Between us, we manage to lay Lysette on the cart. Her eyes remain closed as I kiss her cheek and rub her hands. Then off we go, pushing our precious cargo up Narrow Street until I find a cab waiting for fares at a junction.

CHAPTER TWELVE
Doing the honourable thing

I can't remember Brownlow's exact address, but I give the cabbie a rough idea where it is, then ask him to take it easy because he's carrying a very sick girl, as well as me and a down and out boy.

The driver, worn thin as a rake, but decent enough; asks me:

'Why don't you take her to an orspital?'

'I want her to live. Ain't 'orspitals where most people end up dying?'

'Oh, ah, quite right, sir,' he replies.

It's mid-afternoon and the city streets are jammed with traffic, so we can only crawl along, anyway.

Lysette is lying full-length on the seat and I have her head in my lap. How pale and drawn she is! Her lips are trembling a little and there are dark rings beneath her eyes. When I bend my head and kiss her brow, I find that it's burning with fever.

'Is she dying, mister?' the urchin sitting opposite us, asks.

'No, she ain't,' I snap at him, although I'm fearful she might be. 'Anyway, what's your name, boy?'

'It's Desmond. What's yours?'

Lysette moans. I look down, see that her eyes are half open and begin to stroke her matted hair:

'It's all right, Lys. You're safe now. Jack's here.'

'Jack?' she murmurs my name then falls quiet.

'Hey, cabbie,' I shout, 'how much longer, do you reckon?'

'Ten minutes should do it, sir,' he answers.

Racked with fear for Lysette, I swallow hard and take another look at the urchin sitting stone-faced, opposite me; recognising everything that's in him:

'So you're Desmond, are you?' Well, my name's Jack- Jack Dawkins. Have you got a second name?'

'Yeah, it's Butler.'

'All right,' I say. 'I'm pleased to meet you, Desmond Butler. What's your story?'

I bend my head again and kiss Lysette's hot forehead. Oh, God. Don't let her die!

Desmond is saying, 'I'm nine. Pa went off to be a sailor. He didn't come back. Then Ma and me little brother, Philip, died. Typhus they called it. I've been on my own for six months. The ugly one said he'd take care of me. He did, in a way, but he did other things, too; nasty things. Are you going to take care of me, now, Mr Jack? I'm hungry.'

'I'll get you fed as soon as I can,' I tell him. 'What happened to your ma's stuff, Desmond? Didn't she leave anything?'

'They burnt what she hadn't already sold to feed me and Philip,' he replies.

Oh, yes. Typhus.

'Is this the place?' the cab driver asks.

I hadn't realised we'd stopped moving.

Looking out of the window, I see that Brownlow's town house hasn't changed at all. It still stands, white and proud, behind a wrought iron fence and gate.

My throat constricts again when I hear Lysette say the word 'Roland' ever so softly. The poor darling's worrying about her pony.

'Wait a bit,' I say to the cabbie, as I step down and open the gate.

Next minute, I'm banging away on Brownlow's front door. The brass knocker is shaped like a lion's head:

'Not so loud!' a woman's voice calls out before the door is opened.

She's a tubby little thing, about fifty and wearing a mob hat and pinafore.

'Can I help you, young man?' she asks.

I tell myself to be patient and say everything right:

'I hope so. My name's Jack Dawkins. Is Mr Brownlow at home? I have to see him right away.'

'I've heard your name spoken,' the motherly woman says. 'You're one of Mr Brownlow's good deeds, aren't you? He's away in Kent, so I'm afraid you can't see him at the moment. I'm expecting him back tomorrow.'

'Look, Mrs...'

'It's Bedwin... Mrs Bedwin. I'm Mr Brownlow's housekeeper.'

'I need a doctor, Mrs Bedwin. I've got Lysette Godden, the daughter of one of Mr Brownlow's best friends, in that cab. She's very sick. Mr Godden's been murdered and for all I know, Lysette may be dying. I've got enough money to pay for the best doctor you can get for her. Can you help me?'

I learn that Mrs Bedwin isn't easily shaken, when she says, 'Can I help? Of course I can. Lysette Godden has been in this house on more than one occasion. She's a rare beauty, if ever there was one. Bring the poor thing inside, if you can manage her on your own.'

'That's another thing, Mrs Bedwin,' I tell her, as she stands four-square in the doorway, like a sentry guarding a palace. 'There's a boy in the cab, as well. I rescued him from the same villain who was keeping Lysette prisoner.'

She takes that on the chin, as well. 'My, you have been busy. You'd better bring him in, as well, then, and mind how you go with that girl.'

She doesn't have to tell me that.

With Desmond helping me as best he can, we walk Lysette, her eyes open but unseeing, through the front door. After that, Mrs Bedwin takes charge.

'We can't expect the poor thing to climb the stairs, can we? I'll make up a bed for her down here. You can leave her to me. I'll tell the kitchen maid to go and fetch Dr Palfrey.'

Desmond says, 'I'm hungry.'

With both her plump arms holding Lysette upright, Mrs Bedwin manages to point a finger at a door at the far end of the hallway. 'Now listen to me, young fellow. Go down the stairs you'll find beyond that door. The kitchen is at the bottom of them. Tell young Vera to take herself smartly to Dr Palfrey's house and bring him here as quick as she can. Then you can stay in the kitchen and have yourself a feast. Tell cook I said it's all right. Have you got that?'

'Yes, lady,' Desmond says. 'Tell Vera to bring Dr Palfrey quick, and tell cook to feed me.'

With thoughts of being about to enjoy a good tuck-in, Desmond rushes down the hall and barges his way through the door.

'Right,' Mrs Bedwin says, firmly. 'Let's get this unfortunate girl to bed.'

Lysette coughs, opens her eyes and cries out, 'Daddy, oh daddy!'

Unable to stand seeing her brought so low, I say to Mrs Bedwin, 'Excuse me won't you, I must pay the cabbie.'

Desmond is getting on famously with the cook in the kitchen and I'm sitting on an upholstered chair in the hallway biting my fingernails and waiting for tall, slim, Dr Palfrey to come and give me his verdict on Lysette. With pure-white bed linen and a blanket tucked under her chin, she is lying on a divan in a side-room; comfortable at last.

You've never seen anyone stand up as fast as I do when Palfrey comes through that door.

'Is she all right?' I almost shout the words at him.

'Calm yourself, young man,' he says, combing his little goatee beard with three fingers of his left hand. 'The girl will make a complete recovery in just a few days. She has suffered a severe reaction to the opiates she has taken.'

I put him straight on that. 'She didn't take them, doctor. They were forced on her by someone you wouldn't like to meet, even in broad daylight.'

'My apologies,' Palfrey says, nodding his head. 'The girl is also dehydrated, so I have asked Mrs Bedwin to provide her with plenty of liquid nourishment, avoiding our so-called, fresh water, the quality of which continues to be a scandal.'

A feeling of relief sweeps over me. 'So Lysette will soon be all right, then?'

'Haven't I just said so?' Palfrey replies.

There are tears of relief in my eyes now. You might think I'm soft, but consider the day I've had before you start jeering at me. Could you have done what I did? Not a fair question, perhaps, because I didn't know I could do it myself-until I did!

I control my feelings and ask Dr Palfrey how much I owe him.

He looks a bit surprised, but says:

'Not on Brownlow's account, then? Very well, five shillings will suffice, young sir.'

Having money gets you a little respect, doesn't it?

I pay him what it takes a workman two days to earn, and off he goes, letting himself out of the front door.

I'm in her room and kneeling beside Lysette in about five seconds. With my fingers scarcely touching it, I stroke her messed-up, black curls and listen to her quiet breathing.

Mrs Bedwin is there as well, looking down at Lysette like she's her mother. Putting her fingers to her lips, she whispers:

'I managed to wash her face and put her in a nightgown. Everything else can wait. The poor thing's sleeping peaceful, now. I'll look in on her every now and again, so why don't you come back in the morning? You look as though you could do with some rest, yourself, if you don't mind me saying so; and you've got that vagabond boy to think of, haven't you. He reminds me of young Oliver when Mr Brownlow first brought him home. It's like history is repeating itself, in some ways.'

I want to grab a chair and sit by Lysette's makeshift bed until she wakes up, but Mrs Bedwin rules the roost, so that's not possible.

I stand up, go to shake her by the hand, change my mind and say:

'Thank you for your help, Mrs Bedwin. I'm very grateful. I'll come back first thing in the morning and wait for Mr Brownlow to arrive.'

'I'll be here,' she says, 'and don't you go worrying about Miss Lysette. I can tell you're fond of her.'

Mrs Bedwin knows how to get rid of people who've overstayed their welcome. Suddenly, without her even laying a finger on me, I'm back in the hallway and saying goodbye to her.

'Good afternoon,' she says, 'I'll see to it that the boy meets you at the servant's entrance, just outside.'

So it's back to Dick Jenner's place now. I'm sitting in yet another cab, feeling trapped and hemmed in; a prisoner of my own making. Desmond is with me. I suppose I could ditch the urchin; that would solve one problem. What am I thinking? I couldn't do that; not in a million years. I'm stuck with him. Could I break my word with Oliver and skip my bond, leaving Brownlow to face the music? I don't know why I even bother asking myself that question. Lysette is now part of my life, but I've got nothing to offer her. Dead ends, wherever I turn.

I might as well face it, unless I do something drastic, I'll never find my mother, or my father, for that matter. Which one of them are you going to let down, then, Jack?

I look at the complication to my life sitting opposite me:

'Have you got any family at all, Desmond; any aunts, uncles-grandmas?'

'I've got an Aunt Sophie and an Uncle Edward. He's only got one leg. He lost the other one in the war.'

'Do you know where they live?'

Desmond lets me know he's not a fool. 'Course I do. They're a long way off, though, in a place called Brede. My ma took me to see them when I was not much more than a baby. I would have gone to them after she died, but when Madeley got hold of me, he said he'd send people worse than him after me, if I ran off. He said they'd cut my hands and feet off when they caught me. It scared me something awful. I can tell you.'

I make another promise that'll stop me from doing what I want. 'You don't have to be scared any more, Desmond. I've never heard of Brede, but if you're sure your relatives will take you in, I'll get you there, somehow. I can't do anything until Lysette gets better, so I'll ask my friend, Dick Jenner, to put you up until then.'

'Is Lysette your girl?' the cheeky little devil asks.

I don't mind telling him that I want her to be.

Apart from being greedy for money, Dick Jenner's all right.

'I'll feed and water the brat for a florin a day,' he told me last night, when I presented him with Desmond. 'I'll find him a bed, too.'

'He needs some new clothes, Dick.'

'No trouble, Jack. A guinea should cover that.'

I handed it over to him, saying, 'You can rig him out for ten shilling, but you never miss the chance of making a profit, do you, Dick?'

'I need to, Jack. If they ever stop having wars in Europe, I intend to go and visit its great cities; Rome, Venice, Florence, Vienna-Paris, of course. Which reminds me, have you heard the news? Napoleon's back in Paris and all France is bowing down before him, again.'

'France will have to manage without my help,' I said. 'I've got my own problems.'

It's only eight o' clock in the morning and I'm already knocking on Brownlow's front door.

Here's Mrs Bedwin, standing there in all her glory.

'How's Lysette?' I ask, before she can open her mouth and tell me I'm too early.

'Good morning, Mr Dawkins,' she says. 'Lysette is much better after a long sleep and some decent food. You're very early, you know. Mr Brownlow won't be here until after lunch.'

I stop myself from pushing my way in to the house; instead, I ask, polite as I can. 'May I see Lysette, please?'

She stands to one side and gestures for me to enter. 'After what that girl has told me you did for her, I think you've earned the right, young man.'

If you'd put your hand on my brow as I open the door and saw Lysette lying on the divan, propped up by several pillows, you would have thought I was going down with something myself.

We sort of exchange names:

'Jack!' she says, although not so loud as I say,

'Lysette!'

I grab a chair and sit as close to her as it's possible to get. The dark rings beneath her eyes still show up strong on her pale face. Her hair has been washed, and brushed to the point where it shines. She smells wonderful, too. I want to kiss her, but make do with placing my cheek against hers:

'My Roland,' she murmurs.

Still thinking about her horse?

'Don't worry about your pony,' I say. 'Mr Brownlow's getting somebody to take care of him and all the other animals.'

'No,' she says, 'you are my knight, my Roland. You came and rescued me. How brave you are!'

I actually kiss her cheek this time. 'I'm not brave at all. To tell you the truth, I was scared stiff, 'specially when those bombs were fizzing.'

'Bombs?' she asks.

'Oh, you won't know about them, will you? That's how I got you away from Madeley. I had a couple of bombs made, and threatened to blow him and everything else to pieces if he didn't let you go.'

She turns her head slightly so that we can look at one another. 'Including yourself, Jack? You were ready to die for me?'

I manage to smile at her. 'Well, I knew it wouldn't come to that. Everybody wants to live. The trick is to make those you're trying to get the better of, believe you don't care one way or the other.'

I can feel Lysette's face getting warm as she asks, 'Is it wicked of me, Jack, to wish you had killed that beast who murdered my father?'

I move away a little to give her some breathing space. 'I'm going to ask Mr Brownlow to report him to the police. They might do something about him; then again, they might not. Madeley's a slippery devil, though, so I doubt they'll lay their hands on him. Now I think you'd better rest for a little while. The fever's coming back.'

'Oh, Jack,' she says. 'Nothing will ever be the same, will it? Although we don't get on, I can't help wishing that mummy was here.'

'Close your eyes,' I tell her. 'Perhaps your mother's not far off.'

Mrs Bedwin frowned on the idea of me having lunch at Lysette's bed-side, so I'm eating alone in Mr Brownlow's dining room when he arrives home with Oliver.

His housekeeper, who can talk the hind leg off a donkey, tells them everything before they can even get out of their own hallway.

Skinny and polite as ever, Oliver opens the dining room door and stands aside to allow Mr Brownlow to enter first. He's got good manners, that boy.

'Well, sir,' Mr Brownlow begins, as I stand up in order to show him I know a thing or two about good manners, as well. 'When Oliver told me he had freed you from New Romney Gaol, I ordered my manservant Garfield to give him six of the best. I can't remember when I'd last been as angry and disappointed as I was that day. Now I come home to discover that Oliver was right to trust your given word. Not only that, but you have carried out your intention of saving Lysette Godden from the hands of a monster. I congratulate you, sir. You have performed a brave and noble act, and honoured what Oliver likes to refer to as, your parole.'

Oliver is grinning all over his face as Brownlow shakes my hand.

CHAPTER THIRTEEN
Just one of life's little coincidences

Lysette was moved to an upstairs room this afternoon. It cuts me off from her; or seems to, because a lady's bedroom is private, isn't it; forbidden to the likes of me, anyway.

Mr Brownlow is busy dealing with domestic affairs, so while Oliver is showing me his room, which is big enough to house an entire family, I ask him if he knows where Brede is. He has no idea, but takes down a map from a shelf and unrolls it on the floor. We both kneel and use our fingers to trace Brede's position on it. Finding it becomes a light-hearted race that Oliver wins:

'Here it is, Jack! Why, it looks to be no more than twenty miles from Shippenden Farm!'

'That's handy, Oliver,' I say. 'When Lysette is well enough to travel, I'll be able to drop Desmond off on the way back to New Romney. I'd like to know what's happened to her mother. At the moment, we're both in the same boat as far as mother's go.'

I spend five whole days, impatiently huffing and puffing, because I'm dying to get going. Do something!

The cab driver who hangs about near St Giles, gets to know my daily routine, taking me from Jenner's to Brownlow's and back again, at the same times every day.

On day three, Lysette comes downstairs for lunch. My heart skips a beat when I see her, then speeds up mightily when she kisses me, right in front of Brownlow, Oliver and Mrs Bedwin.

I'm more than thankful for such small mercies.

On day four, the weather is fine and spring has sprung, so Lysette sits with me in the garden behind the house. The trees are coming in to leaf and flowers are sticking their heads above ground. I don't know the names of the birds that are twittering, but Lysette does.

When Mr Brownlow joins us, he brings news of a sort.

He places a fatherly arm round Lysette's shoulders.

'My dear girl,' he says, 'the reason for your mother's absence should have been obvious to us, or at least to me. I was obliged to ask a friend in government about it before the light dawned. She has been held up in Paris because Napoleon's bureaucrats have imposed severe restrictions on travel between France and England. There are strong rumours that the great despot will march on Brussels before very long.'

Lysette takes it well enough. 'I would like to return to Shippenden as soon as possible, Mr Brownlow. I must visit my father's grave and see my aunt at Rochester. I'm sure she will allow me to stay with her until mama is able to come home.'

I'm fit to burst, so before Brownlow can say anything in reply, I ask him:

'Do you trust me, sir?'

'You have proved yourself to be trustworthy, Jack, so, yes I do. Why do you ask?'

'Because, sir, I need to take Desmond Butler, the boy I rescued, to his uncle's house at a place called Brede. Oliver says it's only twenty miles from Shippenden Farm. If you were kind enough to allow it, Lysette could come with us, and I would make sure she got to Shippenden, after I've dropped Desmond off. I have enough money to take care of the expenses.'

'Honest money?' Brownlow asks.

'No, sir, it's dishonest money being put to honest use.'

Do you know something? Brownlow actually laughs out loud at that. 'Splendidly put!' he cries. 'Very well, Jack Dawkins, you have won me over.'

'Shall we go tomorrow, then?' Lysette asks, looking brighter than I've seen her since I tore her away from Madeley.

Journeys can be a bore, can't they? This one isn't. I'm not bored at all while I'm travelling in a coach with Lysette. Desmond chatters on and on about this and that as he sits by my side. Lysette is restored to her former loveliness but has an air of melancholy about her. It shows in her eyes. She is sitting opposite me, wearing a new, ankle-length, lilac-coloured gown and a Spencer Jacket. I bought them for her, along with the matching leather slippers on her feet. I treated myself to a new top hat, while I was at it. After all that spending, I'm still carrying a small fortune in a hidden pocket sewn in to my jacket by Mrs Bedwin. You can't be too careful; there are a lot of rogues about, you know.

Lysette, with thoughts of her father and mother on her mind, is keeping herself to herself, but manages to smile when I pretend to strangle Desmond to stop him going on about everything he sees as he looks out of the window.

The passenger sitting on my right, an elderly, moon-faced gent, says:

'I have never seen a boy made so excited by a journey. Your brother, is he?'

'Yes, he is in a way, sir.'

That puzzles him, but I'm not going to explain what I mean. Instead, I reach across and squeeze Lysette's hand. I do so want her to be happy.

'It's nigh on seventy mile, sir,' the coach driver had told me when I asked him how far off Rye was, 'but it's a good run. The turnpikes' will get us there in nine or ten hours.'

They did, with four changes of horses on the way.

Rye is perched on a hill, with its streets sliding in all directions. It's early evening and easy to see that Lysette is tired. Desmond has little to say, apart from:

'Cor, look at that big ship way out there, Mr Jack!' He's got good eyes, that boy.

There must be more coaching inns named The George than there are flies in a butcher's shop window, because here's another one.

Although something inside me is urging me to press on, I do the decent thing and book two rooms for the night. I'd like to stick Desmond in with Lysette, but it just isn't done, is it. I pay a chambermaid what she would earn in a week, to take special care of her. The plump-cheeked girl; she's about my age, curtsies low and says:

'Thankee, sir. My pleasure, sir.'

'Are you going to be all right?' I ask Lysette, as we stand outside her bedroom door. 'I'll get a chair and sit right here all night, if it will help you rest easier.'

'Don't be silly, Jack,' she says, taking hold of my hand and moving closer. 'I haven't recovered my strength yet, but I'll feel better in the morning. Kiss me goodnight, will you? It's very forward of me to ask, but I need the comfort it brings.'

Our lips touch; hers are as soft as thistledown. Eyes close: tingle, tingle on the back of my neck. Our lips separate. All over.

'Goodnight darling,' I whisper, embarrassing myself by using the word.

'Sleep well,' she says, and slips in to her room.

I turn to go to mine, and almost fall over the young chambermaid. She'd come up so quietly, I didn't know she was standing there. 'G'night,' I mutter, then go and find Desmond, hoping he doesn't talk in his sleep.

Two out of three of us are all smiles at breakfast, this morning. I'm the one who's moody. I woke up with Lysette on my mind; that's nothing new. She'd been there when I went to sleep, as well. I'm moody because I've made a decision about our future. I've got nothing to offer her until I find my parents. Yes, I'm still set on it, so after her mother turns up, I'll say goodbye to her until I find them. I can only hope she'll be true to me while I'm gone.

It's eight miles to Brede, so I go out on the streets of Rye and look for a carrier. Someone points me in the direction of Ben Chesney's yard. He's a whiskery countryman. I hire him for the day.

His cart is not so comfortable to ride in as a coach, but Lysette makes light of it.

'We'll all three sit in the back on these horse blankets and enjoy the ride. It will remind me of-,' she stops there, obviously not wanting to be reminded of whatever it was that had popped in to her mind.

'The year's slipping away fast, sir,' Ben Chesney says to me. 'Easter gone, and April's here already.'

Desmond is busy copying the noise a cockerel is making as our cart passes a farm; the road we're on is more like a track, by the way. 'Cock a doodle doo!' goes Desmond.

'I hope you remember where your aunt and uncle's place is,' I tell him.

He stops crowing and looks at me as though I'm a simpleton. 'Course I do. It's halfway up a lane next to the church.

'What's your uncle's name, boy?' the carrier asks him, 'I know most people in and around Brede, 'cept the new vicar. I ain't met him yet.'

'My uncle's name is Butler, and he's only got one leg,' Desmond answers.

'Ted Butler? I know him. He's a fine carpenter. He served with the colours, didn't he?'

'That's right, mister,' Desmond says. 'He was a brave soldier. Killed a lot of Frenchies, he did.'

The village of Brede is half-hidden by trees in full leaf, but here's the church. The carrier knows where he's going.

Lysette whispers to me:

'What shall we do if Desmond's relatives refuse to take him in, Jack?'

'Money talks, Lys,' I whisper back. 'I won't leave him with them if that's all they want him for, but I'll help them out if they seem all right.'

They do seem 'all right' when the cart stops outside of a five-barred gate leading to their cottage. A tail-wagging dog arrives first, sticking its heads between the bars, with its tongue hanging out. Two girls are the next to arrive; at a guess I would say they are aged between eight and ten.

'Hello, hello, Benjamin,' they greet the carrier.

'Hello, you two,' he answers. 'Have you been good girls?'

'Course we 'ave.'

I help Lysette down from the cart and Desmond climbs onto the gate as though he owns the place.

'Hello, Lucy; hello Barbara. Remember me? I'm Desmond.'

Another chorus; 'Course we remember you, Desmond. Come and help us feed the chickens.'

He jumps in to the garden and off the three of them go; hopping, skipping and running; passing a sturdy, barrel-chested man who has a wooden stump where his left leg should be.

He greets the carrier.

'Morning, Ben. I didn't expect to see you today, and I certainly didn't expect to see young Desmond. No Margaret or little Philip?'

'You'd better ask this young lady and gentleman about that, Edward,' Chesney says.

The heavily bearded, mottle-faced Butler, takes a long look at me and Lysette as we stand together, holding hands in that natural manner we now have.

'I don't have to, Ben. I haven't heard from Margaret for six months and one look at the faces of these two young 'uns is enough to tell me my sister and nephew ain't with us anymore.'

Relieved that he's guessed why we're here, I say to him, 'I'm afraid you're right, Mr Butler, sir. Desmond was in a bad way when I came across him, so I thought you might...'

Butler interrupts me. 'You'd best come in and tell me and my wife, Sophie, all about it. You can come in, too, if you're waiting for 'em, Ben.'

We follow Butler as he stomps his way along his garden path to the cottage door. Opening it, he shouts:

'Sophie! You'd best come here, gal.'

From what I can see, every stick of furniture in the cottage is home-made, but it's somehow fitting for the old place.

'Right,' Butler declares, after his care-worn wife has finished adjusting her dress and patting her hair. 'Introductions are in order, I think. You know who me and my missis are, but who are you two youngsters, and how did you latch on to Desmond? That'll do for a start.'

Here I go; ladies first. 'This is my friend, Miss Lysette Godden. She lives over New Romney way.'

Lysette charms us all with her curtsey. 'How do you do, sir and madam?'

'How do, miss,' Butler inclines his head.

'Sit yourself down, dear,' Mrs Butler says.

It's my turn. 'And my name is Jack Dawkins. I'm here because...'

Butler's eyebrows almost disappear in to his hair. He holds up a calloused hand. 'Stand fast, that man! Did you say Jack Dawkins?'

'That's right, Mr Butler. Jack Dawkins.'

Butler takes a close look at me. 'You're the right age and the right stamp, as well, and there can't be too many lads bearing that name. You're not by any chance the lost son of Captain- well he's a major now- James Dawkins of the 7th Hussars, are you?'

The details of Hawke's second letter are stuck firmly in my mind. 'According to a Bow Street Runner, I am, sir. I sort of got lost in London when I was younger than Desmond is now.'

'I know the story,' Butler says. 'Your father told it to me during a long night we spent together in the Galician Mountains. Near Christmas 1808, it was, and fearful cold. We talked the night away to stop ourselves from going to sleep and waking up dead. Your pa saved my life. With my legs froze and his horse done for, he got me all the way to Corunna, somehow, then on to a transport. My left leg was frost bit so bad the ship's surgeon had to saw it off.'

I don't believe in good deeds being rewarded, but there's no doubt about it; saving Desmond has brought me to someone who knew my father! What are the chances!? I'll have to think about this later. Right now, I ask Mr Butler:

'As I understand it, my mother went off to war with my pa. Was she with you when it happened?'

'No, son, Mrs Dawkins was with the baggage train, along with the other wives and children who made it that far. I do know she was desperate to get back to England when news came to her that her sister-in-law was dead and you'd gone missing, but it weren't possible for a long time. The captain told me how leaving you with his sister broke your mother's heart, but she was wise not to bring you with her, you know. He returned from Sicily to be with his regiment and serve under General Moore. You might not know it, but the expedition to Spain was a disastrous affair. A whole lot of soldiers and their families died during the retreat. I mean children like you'd have been, and their mothers along with 'em. Your ma and pa are all right though; at least they were two year ago when they went miles out of their way to call in and see me and my Sophie on their way back from London. He's a good man is Major Dawkins.'

With a mixture of hope, fear and excitement bubbling up in me, I ask, 'I don't suppose you know where they are now, do you?'

'Valenciennes,' Butler says, 'that's right, ain't it, Sophie? The major said he was living in Valenciennes.'

'That's right, dear.' Sophie confirms, 'except he's not exactly a major any more, he's a civilian, just like you are. Valenciennes is a funny name for a place, but that's where they said they were living, all right.'

My imagination takes over. It has me running hand in hand with Lysette, towards the heroic figure of my father and the beautiful vision I have of my mother. They are both standing in front of a grand house, waiting for us with outstretched arms.

Lysette, stirred up almost as much as I am, is sitting next to me in one of Mr Butler's home-made chairs. She claps her hands together and says:

'Your mother and father are in France, Jack. How extraordinary! Everything seems to point to France.'

The three children come noisily in to the room.

'Desmond says he's going to live with us, papa.'

I'm still in a muddled state of mind, but I think that's Lucy talking. 'He's not going to have my bed, is he, papa?'

'He's not having mine, either.' That's little Barbara.

'I don't want your rotten beds!' Desmond declares. 'I don't sleep in girls' beds with silly dolls and things.'

'Now then, you three,' Butler says to them. 'Nobody's going to be sleeping in anyone else's bed. Why, I can make Desmond his own before the day is out, can't I, Sophie?'

'Of course you can, dear,' Sophie looks kindly on her husband. 'The only thing is, I'm a bit short of blankets, and having another mouth to feed is going to put a strain on us, you know that, don't you?'

'Of course I do, my dear,' Butler agrees, 'and most of that strain will fall on you, but if Desmond's willing to do what I want him to do, and join the 50th as a drummer boy in a year or so, I think we can manage to get by 'til then.'

I'm looking at Mrs Butler when I ask, 'Would twenty five pounds help you get through?'

Her face lights up. 'Twenty five pounds! That's a year's earnings.'

Her husband's puzzled by my offer. 'Now, why on God's earth should you give us such a sum, Mr Dawkins?'

'Because I wish there'd been people like you on hand to take me in when I was living like Desmond, that's why.'

I can see the relief in Butler's face when he says, 'Well, if you've got it to spare, it'll come in right handy. Come here, Desmond.'

The boy gives up trying to impress the girls by standing on his head, and obeys his uncle. 'Now then, Desmond,' Butler gives him the once over, 'you need feeding up a bit, but other than that, you're a good, strong lad. How would you like to join your Uncle Edward's old regiment as a drummer boy in a year or two? I'll teach you all you need to know, by then.'

Desmond can't wait. 'What, be a brave soldier like you, uncle? Not arf!'

Butler grins at me. 'In case you don't know it, Mr Dawkins, drummer boys are a bit like regimental mascots, so they don't come to much harm, and woe-betide the soldier who lays a finger on any of them. They can progress, too; become a bandsman and get some rank.'

He turns his attention to his wife. 'Get our guests some of that cider, will you old girl - and some bread and cheese, while you're at it.'

I fiddle about, find my money and hand him twenty-five pounds.

CHAPTER FOURTEEN
There are dreams,
and then there's the real world

Lysette and me begin our return journey to Rye, or should that be Lysette and I? If it is, it's a bit late for me to start writing it that way now, but I seem to remember people like Mr Godden saying, Lysette and I, my wife and I, and so on. Whatever's right, Lys and I sit side-by-side in the cart, watching the Butler's family home fade from our sight.

It's a bright afternoon; peaceful, apart from the happy sound of children at play. The village church is nearby and the trees are turning green. Brede seems to be separate from the rest of the world. The sort of place where you can go to bed at night, leaving your door unlocked. I know there are better words to describe scenes like these, but I think it's what the Bow Street Runner, Martin Hawke referred to as 'Arcadian Bliss'.

Lysette puts her arm through mine, making me forget all about asking Ben to speak nicely to the horse and ask it to get a move on, because, at the rate he's going, I won't be able to start my journey to France before Christmas:

'You may have been forced to do bad things in the past, Jack,' Lysette purrs, 'but saving me and finding a good home for Desmond is enough to get you in to heaven. You are such a fine boy.'

What did she have to go and say a thing like that for!? Can't she see I'm trying to think straight?

I'm asking myself; how do I get to the place called Valenciennes? If people have been stopped from leaving France, no doubt the English have been stopped from going to it, unless they've got special permission and travel papers.

Next: I can't/won't/don't want to leave Lysette behind, after all. Between you and me, although I can't really lay claim to her, as yet, I'm scared of losing her.

Next: when I manage to find a way of getting to France, will Lysette agree to come with me? We could go to Paris, find her mother and ask her to come with us when we head for Valenciennes to look for my parents.

Yeah, it sounds like a schoolboy's idea of a plan to me, as well. On the other hand, it's so simple it might just work.

Hang on; if Valenciennes is a big city, how will we set about finding my parents when we get there? Lysette speaks French, so all the more reason why she ought to stay right by my side. Oh, blast! we've still got to get to Shippenden Farm, sort out whatever's got to be sorted out and visit Mr Godden's grave, before I can even think of asking, begging Lysette to come with me.

I must get myself a pocket watch; but if the church clock's right; it's three in the afternoon when we arrive back in Rye.

After paying the carrier, I'm about to ask him if there's any way of getting someone to take Lysette and me to Shippenden Farm that day, when he takes me by the arm and pulls me to one side:

'I kept my trap shut when you were talking to Ted Butler about your ma and pa being in France,' he says, speaking in a low voice that instantly has me on the alert. 'It's my guess, you'll want to see them, smartly, but you can't because Boney's on the rampage again. You've proved to be a sound lad, so I'll help you out. If you want to make the crossing, my advice is, ask Billy Hammond when you get to New Romney. You'll find him in the New Inn most evenings. Talk to him on the quiet and tell him I sent you.'

A problem solved? I don't know yet, do I? One day, everything goes as smooth as silk for me; the next, I find myself on the rocky road to death and destruction. It's not only me, of course. We all have to keep an eye on that tricky devil, called 'luck'.

After thanking Mr Chesney for his help, I ask him if it's possible to get to New Romney this afternoon.

'There's no-one here who'll take you that distance,' he tells me, but there's a place down the road that's got a couple of sway-backed nags for sale. They are going cheap, so if you knock 'em down a bit more, you'll make a profit when you sell them on.'

I'm not much of a rider, as you know, but Lysette's with me. She has a way with horses. It helps that my nag seems to be half asleep most of the time, so I don't have much trouble with it. Lysette insisted that she rode the livelier one I bought; and although she's not dressed for it, she does look lovely, sitting askew in the saddle and letting the pony know she's in charge.

The road is terrible, of course; rutted, muddy and overgrown with weeds, but by late afternoon, Lysette begins to recognise the area we are travelling through. She touches my arm. I don't mind:

'If we're going straight to Shippenden, Jack, it'll be quicker if we travel by way of Appledore.'

'Be my guide as well as my sweetheart,' I tell her.

Apart from the sheep and some circling birds, we are all alone out here on the marsh, so I don't really care how long our journey takes.

Although it's dark by the time we arrive at Shippenden, we didn't expect to see lamps alight in the farmhouse.

'Don't tell me the men Mr Brownlow employed are living in our house!' Lysette says, as she slides from her saddle.

'It's a blasted cheek, if they are,' I say, on her behalf.

Then a kind of shudder goes through me. The last time I approached this front door, the twisted up figure of murderous Madeley had appeared!

Not so this time. It does open before we reach it, but it's a woman who's standing there.

Lysette calls out, 'Mother!' and runs the last few yards.

I see right off that this lady is everything I imagine Lysette will be when she's about forty years old. Slim, elegant and still beautiful.

The hugging goes on until Lysette wipes her face with something lacy her mother gives to her, then pulls me in to the lamplight.

'I must introduce you to my dear friend, Jack, mama. After father was killed, he rescued me from a man, so terrible, he-.'

As I offer her my hand, Mrs Godden interrupts Lysette, saying, 'I know all about young Mr Dawkins, daughter of mine. Mr Fitch, the New Romney magistrate, has informed me that he is a young criminal, bonded to your father's friend, John Brownlow. In his opinion the ne'er do well is lucky not to have been hanged for his crimes by now. Escaped from the local gaol, he is certainly not the sort of person I want you involved with. Your father should never have agreed to have him work here; but he was always soft headed as well as soft hearted, wasn't he?'

While Lysette is struggling to find words, I'm trying to stop myself from saying something I might live to regret.

Finally, Lysette manages to say:

'Jack is a good person, mother, and a perfect gentleman. Father liked him a lot.'

It's hands on hips time for Mrs Godden. 'That tells me everything I need to know,' she says. 'I can excuse you, because you are young, but your fool of a father never really grew up, did he?'

I can see I'm not going to be receiving a knighthood or even a handshake from her, so I step back a little. This small retreat triggers her in to saying, 'Before you leave, Mr Dawkins, please be aware that, although I am grateful to you for restoring my daughter to me, I absolutely forbid you to see her again. I have plans for her future, and they do not include a young villain like you, sir. I bid you good night.'

I have to say something, don't I? Out it comes. 'I can see, madam, that while Lysette is all you on the outside, she is all her father on the inside, and he wasn't a fool by any means. He was one of the finest men I've ever met. I bid you good night.'

I don't think about it; it just happens. Suddenly, I'm holding Lysette in my arms.

'Go, Jack,' she whispers. 'Find some lodgings and a way of letting me know where you are. I'll see you again, I promise.'

'I'll be staying at the New Inn,' I tell her, as Mrs Godden pulls her away.

In a voice cold enough to freeze milk, she says, 'Touch her again and I'll lay charges against you. Goodnight, sir.'

How can such a nicely wrapped package hide something so nasty?

My imagination bites again. Snatch Lysette, run to the horses; they are still standing in the yard, and gallop away into the night.

The smarter part of me won't let that happen. If I did that, I'd like as not put myself on the wrong side of the law again, and end up back in gaol. Mrs Godden is the woman to do it. I know now why Lysette has hardly mentioned her since first we met. She's used her name once or twice when she's been in distress, but it's been mostly 'father' with her.

'Goodnight, Lysette,' I say, ignoring her mother. 'Be happy if you can. I won't be far off.'

Trying to show her that I'm not going away browbeaten, I march, straight-backed, to where the horses are waiting.

It's a long plod to New Romney for me and my born-tired nag. I couldn't make the thing go any faster, even if I wanted to. At least it gives me time to think.

I've hardly got started on my plan to go to France and things have already turned out different. Lysette and I won't be going to Paris, and I won't be saying to her mother, 'How do you do, ma'am. Would you like to join your daughter and me on a trip to Valenciennes?' No. I'm going to have to get what I want the hard way. I'll see Lysette on the sly, find out if the man Chesney told me about can get me to France, and find out where Valenciennes is. I grit my teeth and tell myself that I, Jack Dawkins, can do it.

Whatever you may think of all this braggadocio, a good word I picked up somewhere along the way; it's not in *Johnson's*. I don't brag out loud, do I? It's just the way I have of talking myself in to keeping going.

The lamps are lit in most houses lining New Romney's main street. Their bright windows are a welcome sight after the dark of the road. The New Inn is even more welcoming.

The first person I notice in the saloon is George, the New Romney Gaol turnkey. He chokes on his beer at the sight of me.

'Evening, George,' I say to him. 'Let me buy you another one. It's the least I can do.'

His drinking pal, a red-faced man with mutton-chop side-burns, asks him, 'Is this the youngster you let walk out the door without so much as a by your leave, George? Grab him quick. There might be a price on his head.'

George looks quite offended. 'There's no such thing, Billy. The lad was locked up for no good reason. There were never any charges laid against him.'

Billy? Billy? Not just like that, surely?

'Excuse me for asking, sir,' I say to the leg-puller, 'but would you happen to be Mr Billy Hammond?'

He puts down his tankard and wipes his whiskers. 'Who wants to know?'

I'm in a grim mood, so I come straight to the point. 'Me, Jack Dawkins, I want to know. Ben Chesney, the carrier working out of Rye, told me you can help me get to France.'

Hammond waves his hands about. 'Are you angling for the town crier's job? Keep it down, can't you? I don't want the whole blasted world to know my business.'

George says, 'You're a long way too late, Billy boy. Everybody in New Romney knows your game, and now Webster's gone to answer for his sins, most of them will be after doing business with you, won't they? The landlord of this here drinking den certainly will.'

'Webster's passing hasn't made much difference as far as I'm concerned,' Billy tells George. 'He mostly supplied the London market, which is where he made his mistake. He had to stock-pile his goods while mine are landed and sold before you can say knife.'

I take another look at Hammond and I'm glad to see he's not the sort who goes in for burying bodies on the marsh. 'Don't take any notice of mouth almighty,' he says, 'just sit yourself down and keep it down.'

Here goes, then. The three of us put our heads together in a manner which, to my mind, is enough to make the other customers think, 'Hello, that lot are up to no good.'

'The way things are for me,' I tell them, 'I can't just go and buy a ticket for France, and I've got to get myself there.'

Hammond asks, 'Have you got any money?'

There it is. Have you got any money? It's always the first question anybody asks when you want something done, isn't it?

'Yes I've got money,' I tell him. 'How much will it cost me?'

'Fifty pounds; that's twenty for me and thirty for those who take you across.'

I'm not having that, and let him know it. 'If you're going to rob me, why don't you hold a pistol to my head, so I know you mean business? Fifty pounds is too much. I'll give you ten for yourself and twenty for the others.'

'Fifteen for me and twenty five,' Hammond says.

I slap my hand on the table. 'Twelve pounds for you and twenty guineas for the workers.'

'Buy me and George a beer and we'll shake on it,' Billy agrees. 'And buy one for yourself why you're at it!'

'When do I go?' I ask.

'Ah, there's the thing,' Hammond says, rubbing his chin, 'it depends a lot on the weather. Word comes quick when a run's being made. You'll have to be on hand and ready to go at a minute's notice. Where are you bedded down?'

'I haven't got a place, yet. I was going to stay here.'

'Best not,' Billy says. 'Come and stay with me and the old girl. It'll only cost you five bob a day, all found.'

'Five shillings!' customers look up from whatever they're doing, when I let that out. 'Live in a palace, do you? I tell you what, Mr Hammond; I've got a broken down saddle-horse outside, it's worth a tenner. You can have that instead, after I've gone.'

'Fair enough,' he agrees. 'For a whippersnapper, you've got a hard head on your shoulders.'

That's the France bit settled. It happened pretty quick didn't it? I hope the rest of it will be as easy. My mind is buzzing now. The next thing is to get a message to Lysette. She'll be waiting to hear from me. After that, I'll send a letter to Brownlow. It's only right he should know that, although I'm going to France, I'll return to him as soon as I can. Mind you, when I do find my father and mother, them being officer types, they might be able to get me free from the bond. On top of that, Mrs Godden, being what she is, will look up to them and change her mind about me. Stripe me, Jack! You'll have to brush up on your table manners before she invites you to put your feet under hers!

If I get away to France in the next day or two, I could be back here in a week. A week? As a plan, I ought to write 'weak' but, seeing as how the first one died an instant death, this is the only one I've got left.

Hammond says to George, 'Time I was going; time you were, too. You're supposed to be on duty over at the gaol, ain't you?'

George looks at the clock on the wall. It's nearly ten.

He acts surprised. 'Lor, lummee, is that the time?'

Hammond falls about laughing. 'You say that every blooming night! Come on, Dawkins, you still owe me a beer, but let's get going. It's the best part of a mile to my place.'

Outside, I stop to free my horse. The daft animal has pulled its reins in to a knot:

'I'll catch you up, Mr Hammond,' I say to his back, as he carries on walking.

'Jack,' a soft voice whispers my name.

It's Lysette! She's hiding in a dark corner between the inn and the next building.

I'm with her in an instant. 'Lysette, what's happened? Are you all right?'

'I've had a big quarrel with my mother, Jack, so I decided to run away. Will you help me?'

'Help you? I love you. Where's your horse?'

'I haven't got it. I had to leave home without anything. Not even a change of clothing. I walked and ran all the way here.'

I put my arm round her. 'You came all that way, alone and in the dark? Ride my horse, then. It's got the wrong saddle for you again, but I'll lead it while you rest yourself. See that man up ahead? His name's Billy Hammond. He's going to get me to France, and I want you to come with me.'

Lysette doesn't answer for a minute or two as we plod along behind Billy's shadowy figure. Then she says, quite firmly:

'You have helped me make a big decision, Jack. I'm going to come with you.'

Well, what do you know? How about that for luck, then?

CHAPTER FIFTEEN
Down on the duck farm

'Runaways, are you?' Billy asks us when Lysette and I catch him up. 'That'll double the price we agreed.'

I don't argue with him, just reach up my free hand and take hold of the one Lysette offers me. It's cold.

'I keep ducks,' Billy tells us when we arrive at his small, isolated farmstead. 'I sell their eggs and feathers, then wring their necks for the butchers.'

Mrs Hammond is one of those large, bustling female types, with arms like legs of mutton. She's all over Lysette as soon as Billy tells her what's what.

'I've got a nice fire going in the kitchen, dearie,' she tells her. 'You come along o' me. I'll soon get you warm. I've got some soup on the go, too. That'll do the trick. Good for body and soul, my soup is.'

Billy wants paying 'up front' so I knock him down from sixty-six pounds to fifty-five. It gives me warning that the money I have is going to run out sooner or later. Nearly half of the five hundred I had left after paying Madeley has already gone. I can't see what lies ahead of me, so I tell myself to live, 'One day at a time, Jack. One day at a time'.

'That girl can't cross the channel in a fishing boat, dressed as she is,' Billy says. 'She'd better wear a pair of boots of some sort, a smock and a hat that'll hide those curls of hers. I'll get them for you—no charge.' He gives me a broad grin and licks his lips. 'I hope she leaves some of that soup for me.'

I'm a dreamer in more ways than one, aren't I? After coming up with plans and notions, I'm apt to have nightmares about them. Last night, my first under Billy's roof, I dreamt that Lysette and

I were in a small boat, adrift on a storm-tossed sea. There's no sound. The boat overturns and, while I cling on to it, Lysette is swept away until I can only see her fingers sticking out of the water. Then they too, are gone.

I'm sure Mr Godden would have told me I'd had the dream because I was afraid of losing Lysette. I'm not too ashamed to admit that I am. She's a weakness of mine.

Billy and his wife are outside, letting ducks out of sheds and collecting eggs, when Lysette, looking pale and sleepy, enters the kitchen.

I've just stuck a thick slice of bread on a toasting fork:

'It looks to me as though you didn't sleep much, either,' I say to her.

She comes straight to me and throws her arms around me. I forget all about toast:

'My conscience is bothering me, Jack. I've fallen out with mother and I still haven't stood by my father's graveside.'

Before I can give an answer, Billy Hammond and his wife enter the kitchen, looking very countrified in their rough outfits and dirty boots.

Billy says:

'A little bird walking up the lane outside, stopped to warn us there's a search going on for you two.'

He glances at Lysette. 'Your ma got the magistrate out of bed before the sun came up this morning, miss. She told him that Jack, here, spirited you away from your house last night. You haven't got too much to worry about, though, because when it comes to helping the law on Romney Marsh, everybody's mouth is shut tighter than a drum. Besides which, I've got a nice hidey-hole you can tuck yourselves away in if they turn up here to do a search.'

I haven't forgotten Webster's new receipt for pig feed. 'Not everybody keeps quiet around here, Billy. Somebody tried to give Webster up.'

'Him?' Billy asks. 'I happen to know he weren't no marsh man, and he wasn't after any reward money, either. He was sent down from London to try and sniff out the place Webster hid his goods.'

Madeley! It doesn't take much to work out that the grotesque was hoping to lift Webster's cache of contraband from right under his nose.

Impatient to get moving, I ask Mr Hammond, 'How long do you think it'll be before you can get us away to France?'

'Two or three days,' he says. 'I sent a message first thing this morning. A fishing boat will meet up, mid-channel, with one of Bonheur's, out of Boulogne. He's the man I deal with over there.'

His answer reminds me that I must write to Mr Brownlow. 'Do you have pen, ink and paper I could use?'

With Lysette looking over my shoulder and checking my spelling, I write, using a scratchy quill pen:

Dear Mr Brownlow, and Oliver,

This is to inform you that I am still honouring my parole and will report back to you when I have finished attending to some important family business. Miss Lysette Godden is safe and in good health. Rest assured, she is being well cared for.

I hope that you and Oliver are also in good health.

Signed etc, etc.

Not too bad, is it?

There's not much left for Lysette and I to do after we've picked our way round Hammond's muddy duck farm a couple of times.

Before he went to New Romney this morning, Hammond warned us that we would 'stick out like sore thumbs' if we made our way to Ivychurch to find Lysette's father's grave. That upset her so much I don't like to ask her why she told me yesterday that she was worried about making me unhappy. Things are a bit gloomy all round, but we do manage to have a laugh when, at about mid-day, I must get that pocket watch, Lysette comes downstairs, wearing a long smock and, judging from what I can see peeping below its hem, a pair of sailor's trousers. She has clunking great boots on her feet and a hat on her head that looks as though it's been trampled on by a mad bull.

'It's the very latest in ladies fashion,' she says, poking her tongue out at me. 'Anyway, I have my own ideas about what ladies should be permitted to wear; and I thoroughly dislike the word 'permitted'. Why should men decide these things? That's what I'd like to know. On the one hand, they set us up on pedestals and on the other, well, I won't shock you by saying what the other hand is.'

Mrs Hammond comes in to the room:

'Right, up the stairs you go. I've got to get you hid. Three uniformed gents are coming up the lane, searching for you. The silly fools are even looking up trees, to see if you're hiding in them. Come on; shoo-shoo! I'll show you where the hatch to the roof-space is in our bedroom.'

It's cunning that hatch is. You can't see it because it's hidden above a large, three-cornered cupboard, so tall the moulding round the top of it touches the ceiling. The hatch itself, masked by clothes hangers and coats on hooks, lets down inside the cupboard. Muscle power pulls you through it and in to the area beneath the thatched roof.

This is fun. I get myself in to the roof-space, lie flat and reach down for Lysette. Up she comes! a sheer delight in her smock and boots.

I close the hatch while Mrs Hammond makes sure it can't be seen. Warning us to be quiet, I hear her heavy tread as she goes back down the stairs.

Lysette and I are lying side by side in the dark, so it just happens. We don't think about it; we simply start kissing each other. Isn't it the finest thing?

Then the banging and crashing noises begin downstairs. With our warm breath mingling together, we pause to listen.

I can hear Mrs Hammond having a go at those who are searching for us:

'Don't you mess my larder up, not less you want a clout round the ear with this frying pan; and just because he likes to talk to ducks, don't make my old man a looney. Who's in charge here? I want to have words with him.'

We hear the sound of boots on the stairs, the bedroom door being flung open - and after that, the creaking of the cupboard door, directly below us.

A voice says:

'They ain't here. Where's the next house, Davey?'

'Just up the road,' Davey, whoever he is, replies.

After being noisy in every room in the house the searchers leave... noisily.

When I give Lysette a final kiss, she calls me a naughty boy. Judging by the look on her face, she's feeling as warm as I am. I open the hatch and lower myself in to the cupboard. Despite her protesting that she can manage all right on her own, I reach up hold Lysette by the waist and help her down.

Mrs Hammond opens the cupboard door and grins at us. She can see our flushed faces, all right:

'I've sent them off with a flea in their ear,' she says. 'Come downstairs and we'll have something to eat.' She gives me a sly look. 'It'll give you both a chance to cool off.'

'You'll be off tomorrow night,' Billy announces when he arrives home.

'At last!' was my reaction, but Lysette sits with her hands in her lap, looking sad.

'Excuse me,' she says, and leaves the room.

Mrs Hammond looks at me, and says, 'If the girl doesn't really want to go with you, Jack, you mustn't try and make her. Let me have a word with her. The poor dear's still missing her pa, and I expect she loves her mother, in spite of everything. She needs a woman to talk to.'

I stop worrying about myself and start remembering everything that's happened to Lysette. If she's changed her mind about going to France with me, I'll have to do the right thing and leave her behind. Billy can keep the extra money I've paid him, and use it to take care of her until I get back with my ma and pa in tow. Sounds easy enough, doesn't it?

'Women, eh,' Billy says. 'One minute they're up and the next they're down, but we can't live without them, can we? I'm lucky. I've got a good one in my Ruth.'

To take my mind off things, I say to him, 'I heard her telling the men who came here, that you talk to your ducks, Billy.'

Hammond grins. 'Oh, ah. We discuss the wonders of the universe together. It's either that or let 'em get down in the mouth!' He can hardly get the last word out for laughing, and here we are, both hooting away and banging our hands on the table.

'Nah', says Billy, wiping his eyes, 'the dafter you act in front of the law, the less likely they'll think you're capable of breaking it.'

His wife comes in to the kitchen, where we seem to spend most of our time.

'How's Lysette, Mrs Hammond?'

'You're a noisy pair, and no mistake,' she says. 'That girl's got things on her mind she don't want to talk about, but she'll be all right in the long run, Jack. I'm going to take her some hot milk. It'll help her get a good night's sleep.'

I should have drunk some of that hot milk myself, because I didn't sleep much again last night.

Just below my window there's a cockerel crowing its silly head off as I climb out of bed, knowing that today's the day. It's a fearful undertaking, but whatever happens, I'm off to France in a few hours to look for my parents, and all being well, Lysette's going to come with me. It's a big risk. For one thing, we'll have to steer clear of the law over there.

I know I probably shouldn't do it, but I'm impatient to know how the land lies with her, so I go and knock on her bedroom door.

'Who is it?' Her voice sounds normal enough.

'It's Jack. I've come to see how you are.'

'I'll be out in a minute.'

Damn these niceties! What's so shocking about going in to a girl's bedroom, anyway - 'specially when you don't mean her any harm.

Lysette opens the door and, you've guessed it; I fall in love with her all over again. When she's out of sight, I go drifting along, thinking about this and that, then she hoves in to view again and, abracadabra, every part of me comes alive.

'Good morning, Jack,' she says, kissing me on the cheek. 'Can you lend me some money? I need to buy a few things before we go to France. I'll pay you back when I can.'

Pay me back!? She's coming with me! Somersaults, fireworks and cheering crowds - in my head, anyway!

Talk about acting delicate with Lysette! I'm walking on eggs and treating her with kid gloves at the same time, trying not to give her a reason to change her mind about coming with me.

After breakfast I give her enough money to buy everything she needs. She says it's too much, but I risk a little joke by saying,

'Keep the change, miss.'

This encourages her to tell me, 'Mrs Hammond was very kind to me last night. Among other things, she said that I should let my mother know I'm safe.'

'Sounds fair enough to me,' I tell her. 'It's a funny thing, isn't it, Lys? I'm running towards my mother and you're running away from yours.'

That was a smart remark I shouldn't have made.

The day drags on. Mrs Hammond comes back from New Romney with most of the stuff Lysette asked her to buy.

Later on, Billy puts in an appearance and gives us boat cloaks to wear.

'It can be damned - sorry, miss - very cold on the sea at night.'

'Thank you, Mr Hammond, that's kind of you.'

Tick, blooming tock; I'm just beginning to think time has stopped altogether, when we're suddenly on our way. It's night, and Lysette and I, after a short walk, are standing on a pebble beach with Billy and a small group of men. The surf rolls in and drags noisily back again. My heart is thumping with excitement as I hold Lysette's hand to give her confidence.

Out at sea, lights have been flashing on and off, and Billy has been answering them by opening and closing the shutter on a dark lantern.

The lights have gone now, but something else is showing through the murk. It's a small boat, rearing up and over the waves then plunging in to troughs. Six oarsmen are struggling to bring it to shore.

Some of Billy's men wade through the tumbling water to meet it, their hands helping to bring it to the shore.

The oars are placed inboard and the rowers jump from the boat as it runs aground.

Now I see there's a rope trailing from the back of the boat. Some of the men haul on it until a thicker one, with kegs and canvas parcels dancing on it, appears.

Working quick and silent, two of the men slash the goods free with their knives, for others to take from them and stack above the waterline.

The pile grows before our eyes until the last keg is cut from the rope.

It's time for us to go. Heading in to the unknown, I'm a bit scared, but having thought Lysette might lose her nerve at the last moment, I've got something ready to say to her.

It's not needed. She takes hold of my arm and says, excitedly:

'Oh, Jack, this is the very beginning of freedom and a new life for me.' She makes an odd gesture with her free hand, pulls a face and adds, 'I mean it's the start of an adventure, isn't it?'

There's no doubt in my mind; she's said more than she intended to, but I make the reply, 'It'll be an adventure, all right, and all being well, a new life waits for both of us at the end of it.'

Billy Hammond's men are already shouldering kegs and packages as he takes me by the arm.

'Are you two going, or not? We can't afford to push our luck, hanging about here.'

'Thanks, Billy,' I say it and I mean it. 'We're going, aren't we Lys?'

She nods and we get our feet wet climbing in to the boat.

'Good luck to you both,' Billy calls out as we sit in the centre of the boat, wrapped in our cloaks.

The rowers put their oars in the water. Six mysterious, dark and silent figures, they begin rowing us towards the ship that's waiting for us somewhere out there.

CHAPTER SIXTEEN
A girl and her secrets

I don't really want to talk about the boat journey.

Six hours! That's how long it took us to cross the Channel. The crew had to throw out nets and do some fishing on the way. They told Lysette in that quick-fire gabble they use, that it was because harbour officials keep an eye on the coming and going of fishing boats, and it wouldn't do to return to Boulogne with an empty hold.

Lysette wasn't very happy. Neither was I when one of the crew offered me some sort of greasy-looking, fried fish to eat in the middle of the night. Couldn't he feel the boat pitching and tossing all over the place?

We can see the distant, flickering lights of Boulogne from the rocky cove they brought us to in their small boat and left us in a hurry. They barely waited long enough to give Lysette instructions on how to get to the house where Billy Hammond's supplier, Gabriel Bonheur, lives.

Dawn's breaking, and the first thing we have to do is walk up a zig-zag path that will bring us to the top of the cliff.

I take the lead, with a very quiet Lysette following behind. Something's up, so I need to speak to her about it. I can't stand seeing her unhappy.

The path's a bit narrow but gives us a lovely view of the sea on a misty morning, if you like that sort of thing.

You've never seen two youngsters look more like runaways than we do, as we stand with our luggage in our hands, outside Bonheur's large, shuttered-window-ed house:

'Qu' est-ce que vous attendez?' A small, bright-faced lady asks when she opens the door in answer to my knock.

'M'sieu Bonheur, madame,' Lysette tells her.

'Ah, oui, mam'selle. Entrez, s'il vous plait,' the little lady, dressed from head to foot in black, says, then adds, *'je suis Madame Ferrier, la maison-gardien.'*

'She's the house-keeper,' Lysette informs me.

Looking like everybody's idea of a grandma, the house keeper guides us down a long hallway that has paintings hung on the walls and half a dozen doors leading off it.

We sit in silence in the large room Madame Ferrier has shown us in to. To break it, I'm about to ask Lysette what's troubling her, when the housekeeper returns with a pot of coffee, two cups not much bigger than thimbles and some soft pastries tied in to knots.

I soon find out why the cups are so small. It's because the coffee's strong enough to make your hair stand on end. Just the sort of stuff I need to help keep me awake after being up all night.

Lysette and I are separated by a low, round table. I take a good look at her face. Everything she's been through lately is showing on it. She puts her cup down and lowers her head:

'Please don't stare at me, Jack. I know I look awful.'

'No, you don't,' I tell her, 'you look beautiful, as usual. Don't be sad, sweetheart. I know it'll be a long time before you stop missing your father. Perhaps you never will stop, but it's bound to get easier for you to put up with. On top of that, although you've run away from your mother, I can tell you're still worried about her; it's only natural. At the moment, all you've got left in your life is me. I know I'm not the pick of the bunch, but I'd die for you, if I had to, wouldn't I.'

'Oh, Jack,' Lysette cries, 'I haven't forgotten how you rescued me and how kind you've always been, but I can't see any future for us, and that's not your fault, it's mine.'

I'm about to ask her what she's talking about, when the door opens and a man's cheerful voice says:

'*Bonjour, mes amis.*'

Sporting a pigtail, one of the biggest swells I've ever seen comes in to the room. For a start, he's wearing a very fancy, full length, purple dressing gown.

Lysette and I stand up.

'Good morning, sir. Are you-?'

'*Oui,* I am that notorious, but nevertheless, most popular resident of Boulogne, *Monsieur Gabriel Bonheur.*' He stops spouting for a moment, as though he's expecting a fanfare of trumpets to announce his arrival, and adds, 'you, I presume, are the young runaways I received messages about.'

'That's right. I'm Jack Dawkins and this is my friend, Lysette Godden.'

It's hard to ignore the fact that one of his ears is missing. Bonheur sees the look on my face:

'As I've told a thousand people on a thousand different occasions, *m'sieu,* I could get myself fitted with a false ear, but I rather like the piratical look not having two of them gives me. Indeed, it was a pirate who cut the missing one off, many years ago, just before I blew his brains out.'

He parks himself in a straight-backed chair right next to Lysette, puts an arm round her shoulders in the most familiar fashion, and says, '*Ah, jeune amour* - two young lovers fleeing the wrath of their parents. *C'est tellement romantique.*'

'Lay off!' I tell him, giving him a hint of the Dodger. 'It's nothing like that. Lysette and I are sweet on each other, that's true; but that's not why we're here.'

Bonheur turns his head to the door and bellows, 'Ferrier! *Plus de cafe et croissants!*'

Then it's back to me; after removing his arm from Lysette's shoulders, that is. 'So you are here, because...?'

I give him the gist of it. 'I lost touch with my parents when I was not much more than a babe. Just by chance, I discovered that, two years ago, they were living in a place called Valenciennes. I've got no papers and I'm not sure what side of the law I'm on at the moment. Lysette's run away from her mother. She's here because she speaks French and is fond of me.'

Bonheur comes up with a version of the silly remark I made just before Lysette and I left England.

'So, while Miss Pretty, here, is running away from *sa mère*, you are running towards yours!'

'*Ce n' est pas une blaque!*' Lysette tells him.

That surprises him. 'Please accept my apologies, mam'selle. Of course it is not a joke as far as you are both concerned. You speak excellent French. It puts me on my mettle to speak perfect English.'

'*Je parle très bien le Francais. Ma mère m'a appris,*' my clever girl tells him.

'Your mother taught you? So you have not always been a rebellious daughter, eh? It was Balliol College, Oxford, in my case. My Anglophile father preferred I go there rather than the Sorbonne, which also had its share of rebels at the time.'

After the housekeeper has come and gone, leaving us with a fresh pot of coffee and some more pastries, Bonheur turns his attention back to me:

'Let's get down to business, shall we? You have money, I presume.'

He's no different from the rest on that score. 'Yes, I have money.'

I can see that he's asking himself how much a young tyke like me can have. 'You have already paid for your crossing, but you will need to exchange your English pounds for francs in order to pay me for your stay here. Do you have gold coin, or paper?'

'Paper.'

'I prefer gold, but never mind; I am unable to give you the best rate, but I will change it for you.'

Thoughts of daylight robbery enter my mind. 'I'll have to trust you on that one, Mr Bonheur. We, Lysette and me, that is, don't want to hang about here too long. Is Valenciennes an easy place to get to?'

'It is a hard, two day journey from here; one hundred and sixty millaire, that's about one hundred miles to you poor, misbegotten, out of date English. Georges Remy is the man to see when you get there. He owns a store in Valenciennes and knows everyone. I will be sending a wagon load of supplies to him next week. If you are prepared to wait until then, you can travel with it. Now that Napoleon is ruling the roost again, he will, no doubt, be making plans to fall on poor, little Belgium, like the proverbial wolf on the fold. As a consequence, there's good money to be made, selling the necessities of life to civilians living in the border towns, who fear they may be caught up in another war. As for you and the charming Lysette,' Bonheur makes a little bow in her direction; then continues, 'I advise you not to travel by public coach. Security is on the increase and if you are found without the necessary travel documents, you will be arrested. Now I must bathe, dress and take myself off to a meeting with some of the town worthies. Boulogne too, must be made ready for war, and we businessmen must be ready to take advantage of it. If you need anything while I'm away, ask Ferrier for it. *Bonjour, mes enfants.*'

As soon as he's out of the door, I step round the table and sit in his chair. Lysette takes my hand, and that's really all I need to keep me happy. Then she goes and spoils it by saying:

'Whether we find your parents or not, have you thought about what will become of us afterwards?'

My answer comes quick. 'Whatever happens, we'll stick together and live one day at a time, Lys.'

I'm taken aback when she suddenly sounds angry. 'I hate it when you call me Lys. It sounds so cheap. My name is Lysette; and as for sticking together; what will you do when you run out of money, Jack? You have no education, no skills and no trade, so how do you expect to earn a living, or do you intend to return to robbing and stealing?'

She's scaring me now. 'I haven't thought very far ahead yet, Lysette, but I won't go wrong and I'll take care of you, somehow.'

As stubborn as can be, she says, 'My father and I had such great plans for our future. He agreed that I should lead a life less ordinary and I still intend to do that.'

On she goes. 'The world is such an exciting place, is it not? In nature alone, there are so many marvels to witness. Everything fascinates, from a tiny spider in a cobweb to the mighty African elephant. There are great deserts and mountains, wild, unexplored countries - mysterious islands.'

I don't know what's brought this on. All I can do is agree with her and wonder what it is she's hiding from me.

CHAPTER SEVENTEEN
A letter from Lysette

Our barrel-topped wagon is rolling along a straight road lined with tall, thin trees pointing at the sky; poplars, Lysette calls them. The country is as flat as Romney Marsh, stretching away from us on all sides.

You can't see the ropes of love that bind me to Lysette, but they're there all right, and I'm not going to let anything bad happen to her if I can help it. Feeling like that about a girl who's not grown up in the head as much as I am, makes me responsible for her. Here's an example of what I mean. Although we haven't kissed much lately, when we do, I stop myself from asking her for a lot more than I'm getting. I know I'm not a saint, but, to use another church word, Lysette is sort of sacred; pure even, and who am I to spoil that?

Properly dressed in a blue gown and bonnet, she's sitting behind me in a rough sort of chair I made for her out of some of Bonheur's sale goods. I'm next to the driver, a man called Jean Farron. Don't ask me anything else about him, because that's all I know. We get on all right with nods, smiles and hand signals.

This is our second long day on the road; stopping every three or four hours to rest and water the horses; a good-looking pair of dappled greys.

It cost me the price of three rooms, stabling and food last night. I didn't make a fuss over paying for Farron, because, although I'm sure Bonheur swindled me when he changed my English money into French, he'd been pretty decent to us for the best part of a week.

What with one thing and another, I'm feeling pretty worn out, although I have fluttery feelings of excitement every now and again because we're getting closer to Valenciennes and my parents.

Just before we left his house, Bonheur reminded me that he was sure Georges Remy would put me in touch with my father. We are delivering supplies to his store, so I won't have to search the town for him.

All those, impossible to climb, barriers that once separated me from my mother and father, seem to be disappearing. The funny thing is, it makes me afraid of what will happen when I do catch up with them. They might not want to have anything to do with me after the way I've lived. I don't know what I'll do if they throw me out on my ear. I swallow that and turn to face Lysette:

'I'm glad you've got rid of the smock and those boots, sweet-heart. You look so pretty sitting there, I could eat you.'

Although I mean it, I really only say it to help cheer her up.

'You'll always be my loving friend, won't you, Jack?' she says, reaching out to me.

There she goes with that 'friend' word again. She keeps saying that. I'm afraid to ask her why. When you've been in the gutter and had next to nothing, then something precious drops in your lap, you're always afraid you might lose it.

It doesn't take much to work out why Valenciennes is buzzing with excitement. It's not because we've arrived, that's for sure! No, it's down to everybody panicking because war is coming their way; today, tomorrow, next week- sometime soon.

Even I can understand what they mean when people go on about 'Napoleon's *Nouveau Grande Armee*'. The greedy trouble-maker intends to swallow Belgium in one gulp, just as a starter, like; then he'll invade England for his main course. I'm not sure what country he's going to eat for a pud. The trouble with greedy pigs like him is, no matter how much of the world they gobble up, they're always hungry for more. One thing's certain, though; if he does try to eat up good, old England, the first bite he takes will give him the biggest belly-ache he's ever had!

Farron steers the horses expertly along the crowded streets; the French do like to promenade in the evening, don't they? Finally we arrive outside of a double-fronted general store. *'Emporia Remy'* is written above its doors.

The evening weather's not exactly warm, but I am. Nearer and nearer draws the time!

I step down from the wagon and help Lysette do the same.

A young fellow, sporting a mop of black hair and wearing a leather apron, comes out of the shop.

'Georges Remy?'

I ask the quick question before Farron has the chance to open his mouth.

'Non, monsieur, Monsieur Remy est absent. Il est à Bruxelles. Je suis Luis Bisset.'

Although I've already understood most of what was said, Lysette translates. 'Georges Remy is away in Brussels, Jack. This man is Luis Bisset.'

'Ask him if he's heard of an Englishman named Dawkins, living hereabouts, Lysette.'

She obliges. *'Connaissez-vous un homme nomme-Dawkins, monsieur?'*

Bisset frowns, scratches his head, screws up his face and replies, *'Dawkins? Non, mam'selle. Je suis désolé.'*

'He's sorry, Jack, he doesn't.'

The excitement in me dies away. I'm empty inside and on top of that, I think I'm going down with something. Ah well-.

Farron starts talking to Bisset, making it obvious he's got a job to do and wants to get on with unloading Georges Remy's order.

I butt in with:

'When will Remy be back, *M'sieu Bisset?'*

There you are, he knows enough English to answer. 'He will return in a few days, *m'sieu.'*

I thank him politely. 'Mercy.'

Pretty soon now I'm going to have to take a deep breath and ask Lysette what's going on inside her head. She's keeping more and more distance between us. There's not much left of the knight and his fair lady. Thinking about protection reminds me that I still have the pistol I bought from Dick Jenner, a lifetime ago. It's wrapped in a shirt in my bag.

After those thoughts come and go in an instant; the mind is a marvellous thing, isn't it? I hear myself telling Lysette to:

'Ask Monsieur Bisset where we can stay for the night without breaking the bank.'

Bisset points us to a hotel just down the street from the store.

The manager of the overpriced place has never heard of a man named Dawkins, either. Thoughts of my being on a wild goose chase elbow their way in to my brain box.

To save some francs; I ask Lysette if she would mind if we shared a room, like brother and sister.

'I'm sorry, Jack. I trust you completely, but I couldn't spend a night in the same room as you. It's asking too much of me.'

She's right, of course. Never mind; although my money's running low, it should last us a while yet.

More worrying to me is the way she turns her head, only offering me a cheek to kiss as I say good night to her outside of her room.

'Good night, Jack,' she says, quiet like, 'thank you for dinner. The quiche was very nice wasn't it? I'm sorry about all the trouble I've caused you. Please forgive me.'

I tell her there's nothing to forgive. 'Get some rest and don't worry about anything. Tomorrow, we'll start asking some more people if they know anyone by the name of Dawkins. If they don't, we'll just have to wait until this Remy character returns.

When we do find them, my ma and pa are going to love you almost as much as I do.'

She gives me the smallest of smiles and closes her bedroom door.

Talk about being lonely and worried after that! I'd like to punch a hole in that door, just to let her know how I feel. On top of everything else, I've got a terrible headache and I'm sweating for no reason at all. Ain't life blooming marvellous? You're up, you're down, you're spun around.

It's about seven o'clock in the morning. Wanting an early start, I knocked on her door a few minutes ago. Not getting an answer, I risked peeking inside. Her room was empty, so I came down here believing I would find her already drinking coffee. She wasn't, isn't and won't be; because when, after a struggle with the language, I asked the maid who came to serve me, if she knew where Lysette was; excuse my French.

'*Où est mon amie, Lysette?*'

Young and pretty and looking as though she's part Chinese, the waitress managed to understand, giggled, then told me, '*Elle n'est pas ici, m'sieu.*'

The girl sees my darkening face and finds a bit of English tucked away somewhere in her head.

'Letter for you. I get.'

She got, and I'm reading it now. The fact that Lysette's written it in big letters a child could understand, does nothing to ease my hurt.

My dearest Jack,

I knew almost from the start a day like this would come. I have played you false and I'm very sorry. I cannot possibly explain everything to you in a short note. I can only write this much. I know you love me, but you must not fear for me. A boy named Hugo Mercier is taking me to a house owned by his family. They are very wealthy.

Hugo fell in love with me when he visited London with his father last year. He is eighteen. I will be sixteen on May 2nd. I intend to marry him soon after that and live the sort of free life my father promised I would, and not the one my mother wants. I know I have twisted the truth in the most awful way, but I absolutely refuse to be a slave to convention and spend my life trapped in an English manor house; one of a circle of twittering ladies, gossiping and doing needle-point. Hugo is an adventurer and, like me, a free-thinker. He has promised that we will travel the world together and visit strange lands that few European women have ever seen or dreamt of seeing. I will be able to study their culture and their flora and fauna; record them in sketches and paintings and write books about them. The more time we spent together, Jack, the more my love for you began to grow, but I refuse to give in to it, because I have no wish to live the life of a washer-woman or a parlour maid by marrying you. You will not understand any of this, but I hope the day will come when you feel that you can forgive me. Goodbye and God bless you.

Lysette

I'm sorry, but, halfway through reading the thing, I let out the sort of noise an animal in pain makes. It brings the maid in to the room:

'*M'sieu?*'

'Cognac,' I say. 'A big one. You know, a grandee brandy, or whatever you call it.'

'*Oui, m'sieu.*' She curtsies and disappears through the door she came in by.

I don't care that four men, eating their breakfast at a table by the window, are staring at me. I'd tell them where to go if I had the words. As it is, the glare I give them is enough to make them look down at the food on their plates.

Gulping down the brandy makes me sit up straight and cough until the tears run. The big clock on the wall tells me it's now seven thirty. I still haven't bought a pocket watch.

What a great fool I am! 'You will always be my loving friend, won't you, Jack?'

Lysette has said that to me more than once. She's torn me apart, but I'll catch up with her! It'll take more than a goodbye note to satisfy me. A great fool? I'm a double-dyed one. There I was at Bonheur's, and on the way here, telling myself how grown up I am, compared to Lysette. I don't feel very grown up now I know she's been using me for her own purposes. How could she do it to me?

I'm not feeling well. The sweating wore off last night, but it's come back again.

I rip Lysette's letter in to shreds.

It's not the time of day for a beginner like me to knock back hard spirits. I was feeling sick enough before I swallowed the stuff on an empty stomach.

My mind's still going nineteen to the dozen.

I've been so cock-sure of myself. My lovely, innocent Lysette needed an experienced young jackanapes like me to look after her. She managed to pull the wool over my eyes, good and proper, didn't she; making me more of a jackass than a jackanapes. Laugh? I could do the other thing, but I'm not going to, not yet, anyway. Not until I see her and have it out with her.

What to do? What to do? I don't know; I'm floored, flattened and floundering. Breathe deep, Jack. My head's swimming. Eat some of that bread, at least the butter's good. Chew, swallow it down then drink some hot coffee. Right, oh, that's a bit better; now call that China girl over and see if she knows when and how Lysette left here:

'Excuse moi, miss, I mean, mam'selle.'

'Oui, m'sieu?'

She is sweet. Now then; how to ask her? I point at the clock, take up a pair of pretend reins, point at the maid and make galloping noises. 'What time did mon ami, Lysette Godden departez le hotel?' I ask.

My performance only confuses her. *Je ne comprends pas, m'sieu.*

One of the four gallants sitting by the window gets to his feet and comes to my table. He likes to dress pretty, does this one. Silk hose, knee breeches, a bow for his pigtail and half the colours of the rainbow in his coat, shirt and cravat:

'May I be of assistance to you, young sir?' he asks.

Knowing that, compared to him, I look as though I've been pulled through a hawthorn hedge backwards, I stand up and give the man a slight bow:

'Yes, sir, you can. I'm trying to find out what time my friend, Lysette Godden, left here this morning, and where she went.'

'I don't need to ask the girl, sir,' my volunteer helper says. 'My companions and I witnessed a very pretty girl depart from here late last evening. She was dressed in blue; might that be her?

'Yes, that was her.'

The young man, made smooth-faced by good living, says, 'I do hope you have no romantic attachment to the young charmer, because she was collected by a Frenchman, not much older than yourself, and driven off in a coach that looked as though it once belonged to one of the Bourbon kings. I fear the only good news for you is that, at the girl's insistence, her escort paid your hotel bill for you.'

My voice seems to be coming from a great distance as I ask, 'You don't happen to know what road they took, do you, sir?'

'Maubeuge,' he says. I distinctly heard the young man say they would go to his father's house in Maubeuge. A place I would not take a lady to, now that armies are on the march. Prussians, Austrians, Russians and the intrepid British, of course, are preparing to fight, and Maubeuge may become besieged.'

I ask a silly question. 'You gentlemen are all British?'

'We most certainly are. My companions and I are like four Moses in Midian; sojourners in a foreign land; here to witness what will surely be the final and greatest battle between those two giants of war, Bonaparte and Wellington. Unfortunately for us, neither of them has as yet picked their ground. It's a damned nuisance not knowing where we'll have to race to in order to see the battle. It might be miles away. I say, come and meet my friends and travelling companions, why don't you?'

I'm lifeless as he steers me to where the other three are sitting.

'Here's something for your journal, Percy,' he says to the one whose straining waistcoat buttons look as though they might fly from his fat stomach at any moment. 'This young Romeo has lost his Juliet. The little hussy's run off with Benvolio and he's about to set off in hot pursuit.'

'You are, aren't you, young sir?' he asks, looking at me in kindly fashion.

All right, I'm a living, human being again, so I introduce myself. 'My name's Jack Dawkins, and, yes, I am going after her. How far off is the place you mentioned?'

'Maubeuge is no more than twenty-five miles from here, wouldn't you agree, gentlemen?'

His three friends do agree.

Percy says. 'Introductions all round, then?'

'Of course.' My helper holds out his hand for me to shake. 'Let's be informal, shall we? I'm Stephen. Percy is the one we like to think of as our campaign strategist, he loves his maps and things. Beside him sits Maxwell. He's as tall as the rest of us when he's sitting down, but is even shorter than Nelson was, when he's standing in his cotton socks; hence his high-heeled boots. Finally, there's young Albert; affectionately known to us as 'Our Bert'.'

I'm on the receiving end of handshakes and greetings from all of them. They are very friendly, considering they inhabit a completely different world than I do.

'I propose,' Stephen says to his friends, 'that we embark at once for Maubeuge and take our new-found friend with us. We've decided, have we not, that Bonaparte will home in on Brussels, but the Duke of Wellington will not allow him to get nearer to it than twenty miles? So let's get nearer to it ourselves, and at the same time, help this obviously impoverished young fellow catch up with his true love. Although I fear that if the young lady in question has chosen luxury over l'amour, luxury will win the day. T'was ever thus. Before we depart, let's have a cheer for good old England, men!'

'Huzzah!'

With pedestrians stopping to look at them through the window, all four of them raise clenched fists and cheer.

'Huzzah!'

CHAPTER EIGHTEEN
Four gallants and two free-thinkers

Something's wrong with me. I'm in this private coach with the four young swells who are conversing about which of them has the finest telescope, who knows most about camera obscuras, where and how to gain the best vantage point when battle commences and what supplies to get in for a night camp. All this, while at the same time offering me wine, blue veined cheese, cold meats, French bread and goodness knows what else. As for me, I can't even see clearly. The world's drifting away. Get hold of yourself, Dawkins!

Before we set out for Maubeuge, I thought it best that I tell all four of them that I don't come from their world. I'm a paid up member of the lower orders. They simply brushed that aside:

Percy said, firmly. 'The main thing is, you're British, old chap; besides which, you are a remarkably polite young fellow and we like you.'

Maxwell agreed. 'One must never forget the old adage, *When Adam delved and Eve span, who was then the gentleman?*'

'Hear, hear!' cried the others.

'While we are on the journey, you may like to regale us with the story of how you came to be here,' Stephen suggested.

During my telling of it, Maxwell interrupts me several times by repeating the word, 'extraordinary' as I run through everything from when, as a six-year-old, I was cut adrift in London, to saving Lysette from Madeley and how the search for my parents has brought me here.

'Such courage!' Percy says.

'Stout of heart,' Maxwell agrees.

'Bravo, Jack, old lad. You are British to the core!' Albert applauds. 'To think the worst I had to put up with when I was a young 'un, was an occasional thrashing at Eton.'

'Jack's story makes me realise how little we know about the lives of the masses,' Stephen says. 'By and large, we choose to ignore them. When we view the forthcoming battle, gentlemen, I suggest our thoughts and prayers should be directed at the common soldier. In the main, it will be due to his courage, fortitude and sacrifice that we will owe victory.'

After that, I start to fade away.

I'm not exactly asleep, but Stephen has to give me a shake to let me know the coach has stopped in Maubeuge.

'Will you be able to find your rival, here, Jack?' Stephen asks me as I collect my bag and step down from the coach.

My legs are shaky.

'The rich are easy to find,' I tell him. 'It's the poor who get lost in the crowd. I want to thank all four of you for your kindness. You gentlemen have made me realise that I shouldn't tar all the wealthy with the same brush. I hope you enjoy the battle when it happens.'

'Enjoy' is not quite the word I would use, Jack, but watching the future of Europe being settled by two great armies will be the biggest spectacle since ancient times. Look here, if you ever find yourself near Alton in Hampshire, do come and find me at Wainscott House. The name's Perry-Jones. Stephen Perry-Jones. In London, you can find any one of us at White's Club.'

The thought of trying to talk my way in to that place raises a flicker of a smile somewhere inside me.

Stephen, Percy, Maxwell and Albert; all rich and a bit crazy but uncommonly fine men, shout good luck to me as I walk away, trying to remain upright in my weariness.

'Win the hand of your fair lady, young fellow!' Percy shouts.

Off they go. So patriotic, they've come all this way, coach, coachman and all, to witness what they assume will result in a British victory.

'Mercier's house?' I ask an old man leaning against a tree by a bridge that crosses a river. So far, others I've asked have mostly shrugged their shoulders and pretended they didn't understand my question. Perhaps it's because I'm Engleesh!

'*Comment?*' this one says, looking down his nose at me.

I twist it round and repeat the question. '*Maison Mercier, m'sieu. Directions, s'il vous plaît.*'

'*Ah, mais oui, m'sieu,*' the old boy says, getting quite excited. '*Allons-y.*'

I follow him as he walks a few steps on to the bridge and points down the river. '*Est-ce que tu vois le grand maison?*'

Yes, I can see the big house. It's right by the river, but why am I feeling dizzy? '*Merci, m'sieu.*'

He shrugs his shoulders, a move that seems to be a habit with the French. '*Ce n'est rien, m'sieu.*'

I have to cross the river to gain the street that runs past the front of that mansion. The river's not that wide, but getting to the other side of it seems to be taking me forever. What's up with me? My legs are wobbling. Walk, damn you!

The world's tilting. I'm on the ground. There's a rushing noise in my head...

It's dark; oh, my eyes are closed and I don't want to open them. I feel too weak and tired to do even that. I'm warm and almost floating. Perhaps I'm dead and perhaps you can still hear people talking about you when you are, because I can hear a man's voice; French accent:

'The doctor says he's suffering from mental exhaustion. He must have bed rest. It is not surprising after all the terrible ordeals you told me he has suffered during the last few months. All things considered, he's shown remarkable resilience for a fifteen-year-old boy.'

'My leaving him must have been the last straw, Hugo. He loves me, I know that. Please take care of him for me.'

All right, so I'm not dead. That's Lysette. These sheets are so fine and white. I struggle as best I can to sit up. I'm suddenly overcome with helpless anger at the thought that I might have actually gone toes up without knowing anything about it! If it's going to happen, we deserve fair warning, don't we?

Here she is, on her knees and looking at my face. When she speaks to me, I turn my head away:

'Thank goodness you've come back to us after sleeping for a night and a day, Jack.'

'Don't you say another word,' I tell her. 'Just clear off and leave me alone before I do something desperate.'

I hear a sigh and a rustle and when I look, she's gone.

Why the blue blazes do I want to cry like a blasted baby? Jack Dawkins doesn't do that, does he?

Now there's a young man, dressed to the nines, looking down at me:

'My name is Hugo Mercier,' he says. 'Please don't feel too sad, Jack... may I call you Jack? You have suffered much, and Lysette and I have added to that suffering. We are both...'

'Listen, Frenchie,' I lift my head from the pillow and bark at him, 'Lysette doesn't love you, you know. She loves me.'

'Of course I know she doesn't love me, at least not yet,' he replies in perfect English, 'but neither does she love you in the accepted sense of the word. She likes you well enough, just as she does me. As for myself, I simply adore her, just as you do. It's an unusual situation we find ourselves in, but Lysette is an unusual girl. She wishes to throw off the trammels that restrict women, and live as full a life as any man worth his salt. Sometimes, love means letting go, Jack. I want you to think about that. Lysette and I are of like minds and she will come to love me. I'm sure of it. Try to be kind to her while you are here, won't you? She is, as I say, very fond of you, but unfortunately, while you have nothing to offer her, I can provide her with everything she wants. By the way, the man who gave you directions to this house went to the trouble of informing us that you had collapsed in the street.'

He stops talking and waits for me to reply. When I don't, he sucks his top lip and says, 'I can see that you are worn out, so rest now and we'll talk again when you have recovered some of your strength. If you need anything while you are here under my father's roof, you only have to ask for it.'

I still have nothing to say to him.

After he's gone, I lie there, wondering where the lavvy is and staring at the ceiling. Its swirling, white decoration reminds me of the frosting on a wedding cake. I don't want to be reminded of wedding cakes, so I close my eyes and drift away.

When I wake up, or come to; I'm not sure which, the room is lit by oil lamps with little, glass chimneys sticking out of them. Idly, I wonder why the heat of the flame doesn't break them.

Not having noticed she's there, Lysette startles me by saying:

'I have some warm broth for you, Jack. Please try it. It will make you feel better.'

I sit up. 'It'll take more than that,' I tell her.

Looking as beautiful as ever, she's pulled up a cushioned chair and is sitting hard by me, wearing what looks like a silk jacket. Its metal buttons, done up from top to bottom, remind me of an army uniform. I've never seen anything like it on a woman.

I can't resist opening my mouth to accept the spoonful of broth she puts to my lips. It's warm, beefy and tastes so good I take a second and a third.

'I'm sorry you chose to come here, Jack,' Lysette says, almost in a whisper, 'but now that you have, you must allow me to talk to you so that I can try and make you understand.'

'I already understand,' I tell her, wondering who put me in a nightshirt. 'I came here on a fool's errand, thinking I could win you back. But you were never really mine in the first place, were you? I think I knew that all along. I just didn't want to own up to myself about it. You know what your trouble is, Lys? You care more about money than you do about love. Anyway, how did this Hugo geezer know where and when to collect you? That was so crafty of you, I still find it hard to believe you're capable of it.'

Lysette, looking as though my blows have struck home, screws up her face and licks her lips. I used to be in love with the tip of that tongue. Oh, give me mercy, can't you? I still am in love with it, and with every other part of her.

'I have so much to explain to you,' she says, 'although I know you won't understand my motives.'

'Go on, then,' I tell her. 'Explain away. My feeble brain will do its best to keep up.'

'Are you feeling strong enough to listen to me?' she asks.

She knows I'm drowning in sorrow and bitterness. 'You can always stop if I drop off again, can't you,' I tell her.

She breathes deep, just like I do in times of trouble. 'I told you some half-truths about what happened when you brought me back to Shippenden. Mother did have plans for me, though. With father dead, she was going to send me to a ladies seminary where I would learn the social graces and eventually become a pretty ornament to be shown off at dinner parties by a rich husband. You had already decided to look for your parents in France, so I took advantage of that and came with you. Hugo and I quickly found out that we think alike when he came with his father to stay at our house in London, last year. Daddy was *M'sieu Mercier's* business lawyer in England.'

I interrupt her by asking, 'Remember when we first kissed in a looker's hut on Romney Marsh? I thought you truly loved me, then.'

'You are a very brave boy, Jack, and considering where you come from, quite the romantic young gentlemen. Yes, I kissed you and allowed you to kiss me because girls have feelings and desires, just as boys do. I was waiting for father to fulfil his promise to take me travelling to Egypt and the Holy Land, then allow me to marry Hugo when we returned. He would have hated it if I'd simply become someone's possession. Hugo loves me and he's the sort of husband who is quite prepared to give me what I want, which is to plough my own furrow and make an impact on the world. Where are all the female writers, doctors, artists, inventors, explorers and scientists, Jack? There's a mere scattering of them. I am following Mary Wollstonecraft's example and striking a blow for freedom on behalf of women, everywhere!'

'Follow whoever you like, Lys, but you're hardly a woman yet. You're just a girl with big ideas. I love you, all right, but it's all head and no heart with you, isn't it? And you still haven't said how your French gent came to be in Val... whatever the place was called, to meet you.'

'I do have a heart, Jack, but I refuse to conform and become enslaved. Once you and I arrived in Boulogne, my first idea was to try and spare you too much hurt, by travelling as soon as I could, to Rheims. As I had only a little money, I intended to promise my carrier a rich reward if he delivered me safely to Mercier's chateau. I changed my mind once I knew the day we would be arriving in Valenciennes. I found a few francs in a drawer in my room at Bonheur's house and wrote a letter to Hugo in Rheims. The housekeeper sent it off for me. Hugo came to Valenciennes. His man servant found me easily enough by asking for me at various hotels.'

It's difficult for me to look in to Lysette's eyes, but I manage it:

'No wonder you didn't want to share a room with me the night you ran off. I don't suppose you mind sharing a room with this fancy dress dullard, though. You've been deceitful from start to finish, while I've been straight with you. I'd like to call you all sorts of names, but I can't bring myself to do it, Lysette, not the way I feel about you.'

She almost stamps her little foot. 'I am not sharing a room with Hugo and he is too much the gentleman to ask me to. That is one convention we are both observing. We are still young, Jack, but while you are simply surviving from one day to the next, I have already decided on my future. How can I not feel something for you after everything you've done for me? But we are totally incompatible, so if you really love me, you'll give me your blessing and allow me to lead the sort of life I've decided upon.'

'Have you ever thought I might make something of myself one day?' I ask her. 'If you stick with me, somehow or other, I'll find a way to give you everything you want.'

She shakes her head. 'I refuse to wait ten or twenty years for something that might not happen. Hugo and I have written to my mother. She will hate me for throwing off the yoke of conformity, but she can have her heart's desire, as well, if she accepts the situation. Hugo's father will give her an apartment in Paris, invest money in her family's millinery business and provide her with an annual allowance, sufficient for her to frequent the best places, and perhaps catch a husband for herself. She will only get this if she consents to my marrying Hugo. Knowing her as I do, it is a fait accompli.'

I don't want to listen to her anymore, so I put my head on my pillows and close my eyes, saying, 'You don't sound at all like the sweet girl who teased me and gave me riding lessons. You're as hard as can be.'

'Not hard, Jack,' she says, 'just determined to avoid the fate of most of my sex in the western world. Poor women work and die after a lifetime of what is nothing short of slavery, while rich men acquire thoroughbred, well-trained women to dust off and put on display when they are needed. I'm going to be neither; and if it means sacrificing my feelings for you, so be it.'

Hearing Lysette's soft steps as she walks away, I open my eyes but have a moment's difficulty in getting them to work properly before I can see her retreating form.

A shock runs through me. Below the silky jacket that just about covers her nether regions, she is wearing what appears to be an equally silky pair of wide-legged trousers! It takes me a while to get over it, I can tell you.

Full of a sense of loneliness you would have thought I'd have got used to by now, I slip out of bed in the middle of the night and totter to a window. Someone has closed the drapes, so I open them wide enough to allow me to look at the moonlit river flowing past the end of the garden. Upstream, I can see the bridge I just about managed to walk across.

Do you know something? Although I hid it at the time, I feel the same now as I did after the judge passed sentence on me. I'd reached the bottom of a black pit then, but had that little something inside me, I've mentioned it before, telling me, come on, Jack, you'll climb out of this. It took the luck of the devil that time, but I managed to do it, didn't I? What can be done once can be done again, with or without luck. Who needs it? I manage a half-hearted grin at my reflection in the window. At least a prisoner of love like I am, doesn't have any locked doors or barred windows to cope with. They are left wide open and unlocked. On top of that, after he's slipped free, nobody's going to come looking, because they're glad to see the back of him! - silly midnight thoughts!

My scatterbrain suddenly remembers that I ought to get a letter off to Brownlow, somehow; just to let him know I intend to keep my word and return to him. I hadn't thought of that when I was telling Lysette I'd get on in the world. I hope, when I find my mother and father, they are in a position to help me. If they're not, or are unwilling to, I'll have to suffer six more years of bondage before I can even make a start.

Suddenly cold, I go back to the best bed I've ever slept in, so far.

I'm sitting by the window, wrapped in a blanket this morning, when there's a knock on my door. It doesn't take much to guess who it is.

'Enter,' I tell them in a put on, high-born tone.

'Good morning, Jack,' they chorus.

Lysette is properly dressed, thank goodness.

'Hugo has had your clothes laundered for you,' she says, placing them neatly on a side table. 'What would you like for breakfast?'

'Clothes washed by a laundry maid and breakfast cooked by a skivvy?'

She knows what I'm getting at.

'Oh, Jack,' she says, I can't control or change the whole world, just my own life.'

'Lysette and I are free-thinkers, Jack,' natty Hugo tells me. 'We admire writers such as Rousseau, your William Blake and Lord Byron, among others. As a matter of fact, I've taken to writing poetry myself; this one is in the style of Herrick.'

He thinks for a moment then, striking a pose, begins:

'When ere the bitter wind of loneliness
Doth blow,
I oft recall the vow of love,
Thee trow...'

He stops his preposterous, early-morning versifying. 'Oh, terribly sorry; that's inappropriate under the circumstances.'

I ask Lysette, 'Does all this free thinking mean you can run around the house wearing pantaloons, like a you know what in a knocking shop?'

She laughs at me and uses that word 'conventional' again. 'My dear Jack, I designed the ensemble myself. The trousers are based upon artists' impressions of clothing said to be worn by mythical Amazon women for the freedom they provided.'

'Whatever they're based on, they are downright rude,' I tell her. 'You should be ashamed of yourself.'

Giving Hugo a look that proves I'm already feeling stronger, I ask him, 'Was wearing them scandalous things your idea? I'll do for you one day if you're taking advantage of the silly notions she has.'

'As my father's son, Jack, I give you my word that Lysette, because I love and respect her, is completely safe with me. Proprieties are being observed and Lysette makes her own decisions, which is only right. She is a remarkably gifted and precocious girl.'

Handsome Hugo, blast his eyes, looks so straight and steady at me, I can't help believing him and, although it goes against the grain, liking him, too.

'How is it you speak better English than I do?' I ask him.

'Without going in to too much detail, Jack, I had a British governess and private tutors of the highest order. Now then, Dr Dupont will be calling to see you before lunch. You appear to be much improved. If he agrees you are well enough, perhaps you could leave us tomorrow. Lysette and I want to be in Rheims in time to celebrate her birthday in the presence of her future father-in-law. We must go soon, anyway, before war breaks out. Maubeuge could quite easily become besieged.'

'War is a stupid, futile game, brought about by men who don't have to take part in it,' Lysette says.

I reckon that's only a half-truth, myself; but what do I know, compared to a pair of freethinkers?

CHAPTER NINETEEN
Return to Valenciennes

They stay away from me for most of the day; only popping in when Dr Dupont arrives to see me.

'*Comment notre jeune aventurier se sent il?*'

'The doctor asks how you are feeling today, Jack,' Lysette explains.

'I can work it out for myself,' I tell her. 'Say I'm feeling grandee.'

'Jack, please...' I can read her mind. She wants me to act as though everything's still the way it used to be with us. Well, I can't.

'Look, you're doing me a favour,' I tell her. 'Keeping clear of me as much as you can is a good idea. You smashed me to pieces, didn't you - made a good job of it, too. Well, I've put up with worse. I've stood in the shadow of the gallows before now. I didn't swoon like a girl then, so I think I'll be able to put myself back together and get over your low punch; but you being near me, like you are now, won't help me do it.'

Dupont, Hugo and Lysette, look from one to the other, then Lysette surprises me by stepping forward and putting her arms round me:

'My poor, poor Jack; my friend, my life saver; please forgive me and be happy. I can't stand to see you like this.'

I want to hold her, but what good is that going to do me? As it is, I can smell her hair and feel her body against mine.

'The best thing I can do is clear out today,' I tell her, taking hold of her arms and gently pushing her away.

Hugo pipes up with, 'Please stay with us for one more night, Jack. You need rest.' He then gabbles so fast at Dupont, all I can catch is 'condition' and 'voyager'.

'*Pas avant demain,*' the doctor replies.

Hugo translates, 'Not before tomorrow, Jack.'

'I'm a free-thinker as well, in my own way,' I tell him. 'Where's the bag I had when I dozed off by that bridge? I'm out of here.'

'All right; go if you must.' Hugo looks disappointed, but I think he'll be pleased to get rid of me. 'Come downstairs and I'll arrange for my coachman to take you to a hotel. I will pay *l'addition* for you-the bill, no matter how long you stay. Please feel free to return here at any time, day or night.'

'Thanks,' I say, 'I won't cost you anything, because I'm going back to Valenciennes to find the man who may know something about my parents. Let's hope they don't turn their backs on me when I find them.'

'If you are determined to leave, we will wait downstairs for you,' Hugo says.

I wash and dress myself in my freshly laundered clothes. What's left of my money has been put back in the pocket where I'd left it. I pick up my bag and traipse, stony-faced down a curving staircase to the hallway. Dr Dupont is waiting there, ready to hand me a bottle of something or other.

'*Pour la force,*' he says, holding up three fingers, which I think means I've got to drink some of the stuff three times a day.

I thank him. '*Merci*, doctor.'

This is the moment.

Hugo and Lysette are holding hands and looking as though they are mourners at a funeral as I open the door to the outside world. My brain is racing away like a galloping horse, taking me in a single second from the first moment I saw Lysette, to an unknown future. Damn it! Any future I have will be spoiled rotten if I leave here with my tail between my legs. I turn and face them, clearing my throat before I can speak:

'Well, you two. I hope you have a good and happy life together. You're a decent type, Hugo. Thanks for looking after me. I won't need your coachman. I can do with a walk and some fresh air. Take good care of the best girl in the world, for me, won't you. I'll never forget you, Lysette, you know that, don't you. Look after yourself on your travels. It's a dangerous world, or so I've been told.'

This time she throws her arms around my neck. 'And I'll never forget you, Jack. Never! Find your mother and father and have a long and happy life, my sweet boy.'

I wish she hadn't done that. I'm glad she done that.

With a lump in my throat, I'm out of that door like a shot, before they notice how upset I am.

I head for the bridge, just one of many people; men, women and children, going about their business. I wonder what troubles they've got. Hardly anybody's life seems to run smooth.

It feels like a Sunday. The air's warm and the trees are in leaf. Breath deep, again, Jack. It helps take the pain away.

On the bridge, I stop and look down at the fast-flowing river, then toss Dupont's medicine in to it; trying to get rid of at least one memory.

Even though the ache of losing Lysette is strong inside me, I think I'll always be glad I left her with my head held high, more or less.

Having no idea where I'm going, I cross the bridge and head for a church. There's always life round a church.

I'm not wrong. I enter a small, run down cafe and order a coffee, a grandee one, of course. Perhaps the waiter will be able to tell me how to get to Valenciennes. There may be a coach or an omnibus going that way. I don't fancy walking twenty odd miles.

When I open the leather bag carrying my spares I find there's a draw-string pouch perched right on top of my clothing. It's almost full of gold and silver French pieces. There's a note, as well. It's from Lysette.

Dear Jack,

Hugo and I hope this money helps sustain you while you search for your parents. Wherever I am and whatever I do, or become, you will always be my Roland and I will keep you close to my heart. God bless you, Lysette

They've given me what amounts to about a thousand francs. First off, I want to throw them in the river, where they can keep the medicine company. I manage to avoid doing that. I've been stupid enough already. Chucking money away when I need it won't change anything.

My imitation of a man riding a horse, together with pointing to the street and saying 'Valenciennes' several times, works on the cafe owner.

'*Ah, oui, m'sieu. Un moment s'il vous plait.*'

He goes outside, bellows 'Alphonse!' then comes back in again.

Two minutes later, a middle aged man with a red kerchief knotted round his head, enters the place. The cafe owner is leaning on the counter.

'*Il veut arriver à Valenciennes,*' he tells Alphonse.

'*A-t-il eu de l'argent?*'

Guessing that he's asking the same old question you always get when you want something done, I hold up a French gold piece. '*Oui, m'sieu,* I've got the money.'

'*Tres bon,*' he says, taking the coin from between my fingers and biting it.

The man grins. '*Valenciennes, immediament, no?*'

'*Oui,*' I say, and leaving some small coins on the table, probably too many, I follow him outside and down the road to his yard.

I'm in a one-horse, two-wheeled, two-seater, hooded cart on the road to Valenciennes.

Alphonse, a happy man if ever there was one, is allowing the horse to go along at its own sweet pace while he sings a marching song, repeating over and over again:

'*Aux armes, aux armes,*' and something that sounds like, 'March on, march on!'

Every now and again we have to pull in to the side of the road to allow columns of soldiers, loaded down with muskets and back packs, to pass us, four abreast. Apart from the dignified officers on their prancing horses, they are certainly 'marching on' with red, white and blue flags, and regimental banners flying.

I join in with Alphonse when he stands up in the cart, cheering, and waving at the soldiers. It helps take my mind off, you know who.

There are more and bigger flags hung on the walls of Valenciennes.

As we pass beneath a great stone arch and enter the town, someone looking very much like a policeman carrying a musket, grabs our horse's bridle. On guard, Jack!

He looks first at Alphonse:

'Papiers,' he snaps.

I grab my bag, stand up and jump from the cart. The old instincts are still with me. Run, Jack!

I can hear the officer shouting. I bet he's un-slung that musket. Well, he's too slow. Down this alley, Jackie boy! Turn left. Here's another one, and another. Keep going flat out. Whoa, you're on a main street now, so walk normal.

That looks like the square we passed when we came up from Boulogne. If it is, Georges Remy's store can't be far off.

Well, blow me down. There it is, on the other side of the road; and there's that young lad we spoke to. I can't remember what his name is.

I cross over to him and ask in fractured French:

'*Excusez moi, m'sieu. Est Georges Remy 'ere?*'

I can tell he recognises me. He nods; leans through the open door of the 'Emporia' and shouts '*M'sieu Remy- Engleesh!*'

I'm getting somewhere at last! In another two minutes I might know where my mother is; my father as well with any luck.

The hair on the head of the bandy-legged man who comes to the door, looks like it's just had to put up with a good scratch. It's all over the place. He's about forty years old and I'm glad to see I'm not the only one in the world whose ears stick out.

'English?' he asks.

'Yes, sir,' I answer. 'My name's Jack Dawkins. I was told you can put me in touch with my parents. They are supposed to live hereabouts.'

After a short silence, he says. 'Come in to my office, will you. I might be able to help you. *Luis, prendre soin des choses.*'

Luis. That's what the young man's name is. Luis Bisset.

Remy escorts me to a door behind the counter. It leads to a store room stacked high on all sides with crates and boxes.

Remy closes the door:

'Take a seat.'

There are four chairs by a card table, so I take up his offer and sit on one of them.

Remy, hands on hips, looks down at me and says, rather loudly:

'I'm sorry to have to tell you that Mr Dawkins and his wife left Valenciennes many months ago. I believe they returned to England.'

I knew it! Round and round I go, getting nowhere fast!

Then the dramatics begin; and if you ask me, it's a good job I am who I am. I can't imagine someone like grocer's boy Bisset, or an apprentice, or even a free thinker keeping himself in check when Remy lowers his voice from almost a shout, to a grating whisper, and continues:

'Say nothing. Lose yourself for two days. Come back here after dark...' he puts two fingers to his lips when he thinks I'm about to speak, which I'm not; then says, 'there's a rear entrance to this store, use that when you return, it will be unlocked.'

I've had the training, haven't I; so while I'm dying to ask him what the devil's going on, Remy's whispering takes me right back to Fagin. His watchword had been, 'Always keep it quiet when you're making plans, Dodger, my dear, and never forget that walls have ears and windows have eyes.'

There are no windows, but Remy must think these walls have bats ears so, hard as it is, I keep my mouth shut.

He gets his voice back. 'I'm sorry I cannot help you further, Mr Dawkins, sir. You have come a long way for nothing.'

Before we re-enter the store, he mutters, 'Don't forget. After dark, day after tomorrow, back entrance. Keep low 'til then.'

All right, all right. You ain't dealing with an amateur here. I got it the first time.

'Goodbye, sir,' Remy says to me, as I make my way on to the street.

Sorry if I'm repeating myself, but is anything ever straight forward for me? What possible secret is Georges Remy holding for me? If pa's as lucky as I am, I expect he's in gaol or on the run, or maybe he's managed to get himself hanged. Then again, perhaps when Remy said he and my mother have returned to England, the law's caught up with them and they've gone back in chains, or to give themselves up. If it's something like that, I don't know why Remy didn't come right out with it.

Even though I can afford it, I can't bring myself to book in at the hotel Lysette and I stayed in when we first arrived here, so keeping an eye open for uniforms, I walk in the opposite direction until I come to a river crossing. Seeing that doesn't do me any good either. Everything reminds me of her.

One of my well-known wild thoughts pops in to my brain. I've got two whole days to spare. Plenty of time to go and see her! Oh, no there's not. She's gone to Rheims, hasn't she? I wonder where that is?

Here's a dingy joint. It's the sort of place you'd enjoy staying in if you're partial to dust and don't mind sleeping with your boots under your pillow to stop them from being lifted in the night. There's lots of privacy, too. Nobody can see in through those dirty windows. This'll do me. The place suits my mood.

I sleep in the dump, eat in cheap cafes, walk the back streets and keep myself to myself for the next two days; carrying my bag with me wherever I go. Yesterday, I came across a shop where, for next to nothing, I bought a map of France. In the evening, I sprawl out on a mattress that's not far short of the one I had in Newgate, and study it. Now I know where I am and where Lysette is. She's over a hundred miles away.

Excitement takes over from my gloom as I make my way, in the dark, along the lane that passes the back of Remy's store. I cleaned and re-loaded my pistol before leaving my lodgings. For one thing, I'm carrying a lot of money and I don't like back alleys in strange towns on a dark night. For another, I don't know why *Monsieur Whispering Georges Remy* acted so mysterious. I expect to find that out in the next few minutes. If it turns out to be something nasty, I want to be ready for it.

There's nobody about as I slip along the lane, feeling just like the Artful Dodger of old. Remember him? I do, and it sort of makes me shiver.

Here's a pair of solid double-doors with 'Georges Remy' painted on them in white. It shows up nicely in the dark.

They're not locked.

In I go. There's a wagon, and standing by it with their reins down, are two of the best looking riding-horses you could ever wish for. Up close, I can see that their black saddle blankets have fancy, gold crests on them. They don't belong in a place like this, so Remy must have visitors. Are they waiting for me? Is that why he asked me to come back here tonight - for what purpose? They wouldn't send two mounted officers to arrest a young cove like me just because I'm travelling without papers, would they?

Mind how you go, Jack. Life's full of surprises, none of them good, so the law might be waiting for you in there. The only way to find out is to do a bit of what I used to do best.

I tip toe across the yard to a door.

Nobody can slip through one of them like I can. Within three seconds I'm in the store room and crouched behind a stack of boxes.

There they are, two men dressed like lords in cut-away coats and wearing riding britches, so tight, I wouldn't be seen dead in them. Nice boots, though; some 'below stairs' boot boy must have spent half a day polishing them up.

They're not after me. It's Remy who's in trouble. The points of the Frenchie's sabres are touching the floor, but their pistols are aimed right at him. The biggest dandy of the two is doing all the talking.

'Well, *M'sieu Georges Remy*,' he says, 'or would you prefer me to call you, Major Dawkins?'

I hope they didn't hear me gasp. That's an almighty shock. Major Dawkins? Not true. Remy can't really be my father, can he?

'My name's for my friends,' Remy is saying.

The mouthy Frenchman interrupts him. 'Speaking in your mother tongue, I'll begin by introducing you to my loyal friend and colleague, Majeur Henri Chaumont. And I, as if you don't already know it, am Capitaine-Colonel Phillipe D'Abray.'

Hiding behind the pile of boxes, I wonder how a man can be a captain and a colonel at the same time. It's another daft idea thought up by the French, I expect.

Remy, I won't have it that he's my pa until he tells me himself, makes a slight movement, causing the so called, captain-colonel, to stiffen and order him to stand still.

'Be patient with me, major, I have one or two questions to ask before we execute you as a spy.'

Execute! Spy! Don't I ever get a minute's peace? What can I do to stop that happening? Remy might actually be my pa. I might get one of them with my pistol, but what about the other one?

Hang on; the Frenchie is talking about me, now.

'Your assistant, Luis Bisset, is a patriot. I'm sure he is telling the truth when he says that he has no idea what has become of a certain young man who twice called to see you. I don't suppose you're prepared to tell me where he is? Having arrived direct from your man in Boulogne, he is of great interest to me. You English must be scraping the bottom of the barrel, using him as a message carrier.'

Remy stays as cool as you like. 'I'd never seen or heard of the young fellow until a few days ago. He wanted a job, but having nothing to offer him I sent him on his way.'

'Did you indeed,' D'Abray confirms that, among other things, he's a sneerer. 'Never mind, he will be found. I have a great deal of influence in this city. The police and troops on patrol have all been alerted. Young as he appears to be, his body can still be hung from the walls of the citadel as a warning to others.'

That's fine. Thanks very much. Perhaps one day I'll find a country where they don't want to hang me.

When I try to move one of the cases an inch or two, so that I can get a better view, the stack next to it frightens the life out of me by wobbling. I get away with it, and can now see D'Abray take a very pretty watch from a pocket in his waistcoat. It reminds me that I still haven't got round to buying one for myself, a watch I mean, not a waistcoat.

D'Abray is still going on. 'Now then, before your execution, I want you to die knowing that the Duke of Wellington still has - let me see,' he glances at his watch, 'nearly fourteen hours left to live.'

Sounding as though he's tired of listening to what I'd call guff, Chaumont manages to get a word in:

'Let's kill the man and go, Philippe. We're wasting time here, and you like the sound of your own voice too much.'

No, keep talking, D'Abray, or take a step backwards.

'Allow me to enjoy my moment of triumph, Henri,' mouth almighty says. 'I'm feeling very pleased with myself.'

This man likes to torture people; make them sweat and beg. He's just a well off version of that turnkey, Ryan. Well, hello there, Ryan! I haven't given you a thought for many a long day.

At last, the two Frenchmen do what I've been hoping they'd do. Being a bit too close for comfort to Remy, they decide to step back a couple of paces before shooting him. Sikes once told me that it takes a bold man, or a maniac, to shoot a man, close up, or stick the knife in.

I put my shoulder against the packing cases and down they go, right on top of the Frenchies. Both their pistols go off at the same time, making a deafening noise. Remy's all right, though; through the smoke, I see him swing an almighty punch that knocks D'Abray flat on his back.

I pick up something round and hard, wrapped in canvas. I've no idea what it is but, holding it aloft, I jump a wooden crate and smash it down on Chaumont's head, just as he's about to stand up. He decides not to.

Remy bends and places his hands on his knees.

'That was too damned close, Jack, my boy. What kept you?'

Then he laughs. After facing certain death, the man laughs.

'I jest,' he says. 'As a matter of fact, I was fearful you might turn up and get killed, yourself.'

'Pa?'

I'm almost lifted off the ground as my father throws his arms round me.

He's not whispering now. 'That's right, boy. I simply can't be-lieve you're here. You disappear for ten years then arrive just in time to save your father's life! It makes one wonder if moments like these are pre-ordained. Whether they are, or not, I thank God for the miracle that brought it about. Now let me have another look at you.'

He releases me and steps back, leaving me feeling numb. It's as though I've been turned to stone. Forget Remy. There is no Remy. This man is my father, but he's a stranger to me.

Making an effort to speak, I manage to ask:

'Where's mother?'

'Your mother is fine, Jack. Things being what they are, she is on her way from Brussels to London with your brother and sister.'

She's on her way to London!? Oh, no! Hang on, what did he say? I've got a brother and sister? Well, fancy that!

CHAPTER TWENTY
A ride for life

'Listen, Jack,' my father says; yes, it feels funny using the word, but it's the only one I've got for him, 'this is a big shock for both of us. We've got a lot to say to each other and a thousand questions to ask and answer. Thank heaven you're alive and here with me, but we've got to get ourselves to Brussels, and that might not be too easy. Are you with me, son?'

I manage to tell him, 'I'm with you, all right.'

'Good man,' he says. 'Let's deal with these two first.'

For a moment I believe he means to kill them, so I breathe easy when he asks me to bring him the coil of rope that's hanging on a wall.

When I hand it to him, my father says:

'I would like to put paid to these two, Jack, but killing someone on a battlefield is a whole lot different to shooting them when they're lying helpless on the floor. That's not my style.'

I'm glad to hear him say it. 'I'll tie mine up,' I tell him. 'I've had a bit of experience.'

He shoots me a glance. 'Have you, indeed? All right then; go ahead.'

D'Abray and Chaumont are returning to the land of the living by the time we finish binding them hand and foot.

D'Abray tries to sit up, but with yards of rope round him, finds he can't.

My father's punch has damaged his jaw, but as he looks up at us and we look down at him, he still manages to put on his sneering act:

'Your efforts will be in vain: Wellington is a dead man and there's nothing you can do about it. As for us,' he attempts to nod in the direction of Chaumont, 'you will receive no sympathy from the authorities here. If you go to them, you will be arrested as spies. I can assure you of that.'

'There's many a slip,' father tells him. 'Come on, Jack, let's get going. We'll talk on the way.'

He looks around the store room and sees the cloth covering the little table where I'd sat two days ago. Grabbing it up, he rips it in two.

D'Abray is defiant until he's silenced by the gag. Then it's Chaumont's turn to have half a table cloth shoved in his mouth.

'I don't want them shouting their silly heads off and waking the neighbours,' pa says. 'We're lucky those shots didn't bring people running. I suppose the packing cases and boxes make this place almost sound proof, but I'm not taking any chances.'

He stoops and picks up the fallen pistols. 'There's plenty of powder and shot in that store cupboard. I'll re-load these. I've an idea we may need them.'

'I've got a pistol, Pa,' I tell him. 'I dropped it over there somewhere, when I shoved that pile of boxes over.'

That gets me another look from him. 'You carry a pistol, do you? I can't wait to hear what you've been up to for the last ten years.'

'Surviving, Pa. I've been surviving.'

While I find mine, he loads those pistols in the lamplight, although it looks to me as though he could do it with his eyes shut. Then he picks up one of the sabres and cuts the air with it a couple of times:

'A nice piece of Toledo steel,' he says, 'now let's get to those horses my visitors came on. Once we get going, I want to hear how you found me, when I couldn't find you.'

As we go out the rear door, the first of the many questions I want to ask my father, is:

'How did you manage not to let on who you are, when I first came to see you, Pa?'

He drops a hand on my shoulder. 'I had no choice, my boy. I've been one of Wellington's special agents for over two years and done nothing very useful. Now, all of a sudden, everything's happened at once. Bonaparte's heading our way and you turn up. I've taken one chance too many, in order to gain confirmation that D'Abray has paid someone to assassinate the duke. I planned to leave for Brussels tonight, taking you along with me. But we are in a race, now, Jack. Wellington's arrived in Brussels sooner than expected. He's been in London, consulting with our allies. Chaumont was right, D'Abray talks too much. Hearing rumours, I risked bribing a servant who works in his household, to keep his ears and eyes open. The poor fellow was careless. He got caught and gave me up to save his own skin. Can't say I blame him, really. D'Abray could have had me killed in all manner of ways, but being the type of fellow he is, he just couldn't resist coming here to tell me all about it before he put paid to me himself.'

In the dark of the yard, the horses are stamping and raking their hooves on the cobbles.

'Can you ride?' my father asks.

'A little,' I tell him, 'but not one of these gallopers.'

My mind's off again, this time to a beautiful girl and a pony in a paddock on Romney Marsh.

My father bends to check the horses' saddle girths, 'We've got seventy miles to travel, Jack, and not much time to do it in.'

Sliding the sabre in to its sheath, he adds, 'so you'd better get up behind me. Hang on tight; we'll ride the first one in to the ground then switch to the other one, all right?'

I'm a bit doubtful about the 'hanging on' bit, but I'm not going to let him know that, so I say, 'That's fine, Pa. Let's get going.'

I sit behind my father's broad back. Being so close to him makes me realise how much I'd missed when I was a child. No riding on Daddy's shoulders for me, no birthday treats; no larks in the park...

He keeps the horse under a tight rein as it trots down the dark lane. The second of the thoroughbreds follows, its neck stretched by the rope connecting its halter to the saddle girth at father's knee.

His leather belt is all I've got to hang on to as he digs his heels in to the horse, encouraging it to move faster.

I put my mouth to his ear and ask him:

'Are we going to make it? Seventy miles is a long way for a horse to do in one go, ain't it?'

He talks to me over his shoulder. 'It'll depend on the roads and the animals; but we've got a good chance. According to what D'Abray said, we still have twelve hours or more. By the way, if anything happens to me, and you manage to get through, 'Oranges and Lemons' is the password we're using this week. It'll get you past any of Wellington's check points. Tell them you're the son of Major James Dawkins, of the 7th Hussars.'

Without any warning, he brings the horse to a halt. The other one is a friendly brute. The minute we stop, it begins nuzzling me. You big, soft thing, I haven't got an apple or a carrot.

Lysette! No, I haven't forgotten you. I'm here on the outskirts of Valenciennes, sitting behind my father on the back of a downright nasty Frenchman's horse. We're trying to get to Brussels before someone murders the Duke of Wellington; nothing much to tell, really.

My father interrupts my rambling thoughts:

'There's a bridge up ahead.'

He steers the horses to the shelter of a high wall that edges the road, then tells me, 'There are some armed men hanging about on it. Step down for a minute, Jack, while I take a closer look. Hang on tight to those bridles while I'm gone.'

We dismount. My father, no, I'm still not used to saying it yet, pulls a pistol from his belt and moves off towards the bridge, which is lit from end to end by lanterns.

He's back within a few minutes, moving quiet, just like I do.

'I was right,' he says. 'There are four of them. They're armed, but only two are soldiers. The other two are probably D'Abray's servants, earning themselves some drinking money.'

'What are we going to do about them?'

I ask him that question with a sinking feeling, because I realise we'll probably have to do something desperate.

'Shall I get my pistol out? I've got three or four reloads for it.'

'We won't need that, son. We're going to give them a little surprise.' He flashes a broad grin at me. 'Come on. Mount up.'

He sounds as though he's actually enjoying himself. 'Steady on, Pa,' I say to him. 'Don't go doing anything rash.'

'Mount up,' he repeats, swinging himself in to the saddle and reaching an arm down for me. I give a sort of groan and allow myself to be hauled up behind him.

I prefer doing things on the quiet, myself, but my father obviously doesn't:

'Here we go, Jack, me boy,' he tells me. 'You just hang on and keep your head down.'

I'm thinking, never mind my head, Pa, you keep your voice down, or they'll hear us!

With its steel blade flashing in the half-light, he pulls D'Abray's sabre from its scabbard, turns his head and grins at me again. 'I haven't done anything like this since the charge at Orthes!' he says.

He kicks the horse in to a gallop and keeps on kicking its flanks while I hang on as best I can. Whatever trouble we are heading for is hidden from my view by my father's shoulders.

It doesn't help my nerves. I like to see what's coming at me or what I'm getting in to.

The spare horse seems to think it's taking part in a race, because it's pulling slightly ahead of us; daft thing.

The hair on the back of my neck prickles when father starts yelling at the top of his voice. We're on the bridge! There are two loud explosions. Musket fire! I close my eyes then feel my father's right arm move very violently. A cry of pain rings out above the sounds of his roaring voice and shouts of alarm. I blink and get a brief glimpse of a man leaping at our spare mount. He falls away and is lost to my sight. A pistol is fired, then there's a sudden change in the racket made by our galloping horses.

We're off the bridge and careering onwards! My father is laughing.

'Too easy, Jack!' He shouts over his shoulder. 'Now you know a little about what a charge on horseback feels like. That one won't go down in the 7th's history book, but imagine what it's like to do that with three hundred comrades alongside you, all going flat out, sabres at the ready-the enemy waiting. It's bloody but glorious as well. Anyway, let's press on before they get organised back there, shall we?'

After a lot of hard pounding on a paved road, the horses begin to flag.

'We've been pushing them too hard,' Pa says. 'This horse is done in. We'll have to walk for a bit then change to the other one.'

I slide to the ground. 'My backside's red raw,' I inform him, feeling the area in question with both hands.

He chuckles. 'It'll soon toughen up at this rate.'

We walk the horses... and talk.

After my father tells me how word of his sister's death and my disappearance had reached them, and how he and my mother mourned for me as the war dragged on in Spain and Portugal, I skip ten years of my life and simply say that I found him because

I ran in to the man whose life he'd saved in some mountains I couldn't remember the name of.

Pa says, 'Colour Sergeant Butler? He's a good man and a doughty fighter.'

It's nearly daylight now and although the sun's not yet up there are a lot of labourers in the fields on both sides of the road. Father takes a long look at them and tells me:

'Bonaparte and his Grand Army, or not, these people still have to go about their normal business and earn a crust. That's the way of the world, I suppose. I gather that you came to me through Bonheur. As you may have guessed, we used his nefarious business to transport agents and urgent messages to and fro. We never paid him to work for us; just left him to make money smuggling goods. Farron must have found Bonheur out, so he'll have to shut up shop, now.'

Feeling weary again, I say, 'He sent me to you but never told me that you are my father. Just said Georges Remy would put me in touch with you. It must have been his idea of a joke.'

'What he should have done is keep you and the girl in Boulogne and send word to me about you. It's not his fault everything's shot to pieces. That's due to my own carelessness and not spotting that Farron is a French agent. I'm finished in France, and the clock's ticking, Jack. We'd better ride!'

I look over my shoulder at the long, straight road we've travelled.

'I think I see some horsemen way back there, Pa. Look!'

He looks. 'I can't see who's they are, yet, but as I said; let's ride!'

We climb aboard the fresher of the two horses and set off at speed. I don't feel safe anymore. My fingers ache from hanging on and my legs are dangling free. I risk a backwards glance.

'There are four of them, Pa, and they're catching us up. The front runner looks like that frog who did all the talking.'

My father is bent over the neck of our galloping horse. 'Do you mean D'Abray?'

'Looks like it.'

'Damnation!'

The road seems to be unrolling beneath our horse's flying hooves. Looking this way and that, hoping to find a wood we can hide in, or a side turning we can take, I notice that the workers scattered about in the fields, are standing and watching us going along, pell-mell.

'I think another one of them riders is that Farron,' I shout a bit louder than necessary.

'I could kick myself,' my father says. 'I don't know why I volunteered for this job. I'm no good at it. It takes more than being fluent in French and Italian to make a successful spy.'

I'm not having my father run himself down. 'Don't talk like that, Pa. Ain't we rushing to try and save Wellington's life because you found out he's going to be killed? I think that's pretty good spying, myself.'

I'm still trying hard to hang on, but I'm losing my grip on my father's belt.

There's a set of farm buildings up ahead.

Those are my last thoughts before my fingers slip and I fall from the galloping horse. Why couldn't I make a soft landing on a pile of mud? There's plenty of it lying around. No such luck. I hit the gravelled surface hard.

I'm not out, but my left arm hurts like fury.

My father has wrestled the horses to a halt. I'm dizzy with pain, and the shock of the fall, but I can see his legs moving quickly towards me.

I squirm round, somehow. There are the four horsemen bearing down on us.

My father kneels beside me, takes one of the pistols from his belt and resting the barrel on his forearm, takes a brief sighting and pulls the trigger. The sound of the shot and the wail of a wounded man come at the same moment. The sight of the second pistol being pointed at them scares the life out of the riders, who are now only about ten yards from us. D'Abray, Chaumont and Farron jump their horses over a ditch and in to the fields to their left, while the unknown rider changes direction and disappears along the rear of the farm buildings.

Our own dumb animals decide to join their friends in the field and follow them over the ditch, trampling all over the cabbage plants.

Pa pulls me to my feet. 'Come on, Jack!'

'Sorry, father. I think I've broke my arm!'

At least one of us remains calm; it isn't me! 'We'll see to that in a minute, son,' he says. 'Let's get in to one of those buildings. We need to fort up.'

He half carries, half drags me through an archway and in to a yard surrounded on three sides by low, brick built cattle sheds. Their steep roofs almost reach the ground.

'In here.' He pushes at the top half of a split door.

Holding on to me with one hand, he draws a bolt back on the lower door, shoving it open with his knee.

Someone shouts something and there's the sharp crack of a pistol being fired. The ball pings and whines off brickwork as we stumble our way inside the building.

Father slams the lower door shut as I ease myself onto a pile of sweet-smelling hay.

Now what?

Knelt by the door, my father looks at me and says, quite calmly, 'We're in something of a fix, Jack. You might have warned me things like this happen when you're around. It must be you, because I've led a peaceful life for over two years now, spying being a quiet sort of occupation.'

'You're right, Pa,' I tell him as I nurse my arm. 'I think somebody's got it in for me. I haven't had a bit of peace since Brownlow and Oliver got me out of Newgate, nigh on four months ago.'

That surprises him. 'What do you mean, "Newgate", and who are Brownlow and Oliver, when they're at home?'

I ignore that, but tell him, 'On top of everything else that's happened to me, I've just lost the finest, most beautiful girl in the world to a high and mighty young Frenchman. I don't mind telling you that it's killed me inside. I really love her.'

'That was the girl you had on your arm when you first came to the store, was it?'

'That's right. She turned out to have some queer ideas about the way she wants to live her life. I couldn't give her that; not right now.'

My father doesn't laugh, he simply says, 'I lost my first sweetheart to a midshipman. He's a commodore now, with a soft job at the Admiralty!'

I like my father; he's all right.

He gives me a watered-down version of his grin. 'Tell me more about yourself later. For the moment, we need to keep our minds on the job in hand. I've only got one shot. The rest of the powder and ball is on the nag, but D'Abray doesn't know that, does he.'

I knew all along I should have taken my pistol out of my bag. That's out there, as well. My pockets are full of money, but that's no use in a fight.

CHAPTER TWENTY-ONE
There are definitely more things in heaven and earth, Horatio

The view I have from the bed of hay I'm sitting on, allows me to see D'Abray and Farron bend their heads as they ride through the arched entrance to the farmyard.

'Stay where you are or I'll shoot!' My father tells them, allowing them to see the barrel of his pistol as he crouches by the door.

'Give it up, *m'sieu*,' D'Abray calls back. 'You have lost the race. We can keep you here for hours.'

Pa curses; it's the first time I've heard him do it, and I groan; which is fast becoming a habit with me. 'I wonder where that third rider is hiding himself?' He murmurs to himself.

Clattering roof tiles give us both a quick answer. I tell father that which he already knows.

'He's up there, waiting to blow our heads off if we put them outside the door.'

Apart from a broom, a couple of rakes and a broad shovel, there's nothing to defend ourselves with in this cow shed.

Then a group of farm workers walk through the archway. They get our full attention. The first of them is dressed in knee high boots, breeches and a short jacket. He looks as though he might own the place. I like the fact that he's carrying a gun on his shoulder. Those following him are the poorly dressed, 'we do all the work round here', types. One of them is carrying a pole, strung from one end to the other with the corpses of small birds.

Still making a fuss about my arm, I join father by the door.

'*Dites-moi se key pass?*' the man with the gun asks D'Abray; or at least, that what it sounds like to me. Perhaps you can work it out; to my mind it's something like, 'What's going on round here?'

We both strain to hear what's being said. D'Abray's using words that sound like 'fugitives' and 'justice'.

Pa takes a chance and stands up:

'Don't believe him, *m'sieu!*' he bellows. 'We are two British citizens and we must get to Brussels immediately. Do you understand?'

'I understand, m'sieu, and I think you can come out without fear,' the boss farmer calls back.

My father offers me a helping hand. 'Come on, boy. We're still alive and kicking.'

'I don't know about kicking; my legs are all right, but I think my arm's busted.'

Under the watchful eyes of everyone, including the man on the cow shed roof, waving his pistol about, we cross the cobbled yard.

There's more like a dozen interested workmen crowding in now, wanting to find out what the shooting was all about.

'Good morning to you, sir.' The farmer greets us in English. 'I am Bertrand Pindal, and this is my property.'

My father shakes him by the hand. *'Pardon, m'sieu.* My son and I are in the middle of an extreme emergency. A murder is going to take place in Brussels in about three hours, and we are trying to get there in order to prevent it.'

D'Abray interrupts. 'He is lying, Pindal. As I've already told you, these two are fugitives, escaped from Valenciennes. Thieves and murderers; they have killed a local storekeeper. I insist they return with us.'

'Where are your papers and proof of authority, *m'sieu?*' Pindal demands of him. 'You are in Belgium, not France.'

D'Abray doesn't like that. 'Belgium is part of the French Empire, Pindal, and very soon, *l'empereur* will be here to confirm it.'

This was obviously a sore point with Pindal. 'Twenty years under the heel of the French has been long enough for us, *m'sieu*. Napoleon's time will soon be over and we shall be a free nation again.'

D'Abray's face grows even darker. Heart-thumping time is here again, because he raises his pistol. Somebody's going to die in a minute.

'If you will not hand them over to me, I shall take them by force.'

'I think not,' Pindal says, with quiet confidence. 'I suggest you look around.'

Ah, well, the pistol's lowered. Nothing happened.

From his high perch on his high horse, D'Abray takes a look at the men crowding in on both him and Farron. He takes particular interest in the scythes and sickles that some are holding. Knives and tined hayforks get his attention, as well. They would do a lot worse than ruin his nice riding outfit if they rained down on him.

Pindal gives him some unfriendly advice:

'You had better get your man off that roof, collect the wounded one lying in my field and return yourselves to Valenciennes. I will personally escort the English to Brussels.'

D'Abray acts like a dog that's had his bone pinched from him by a bigger one; the bone it buried a week ago and had been looking forward to chewing on. 'When Napoleon is victorious, I shall make a point of coming for you, Pindal, and next time I'll come in force.'

He raises his voice and calls to the man squatting awkwardly on the roof of the cow shed, 'Emile! Nous allons!'

Emile slides, then jumps from the roof and walks towards us, shoving a pistol in to his belt.

'Your horse is on the road,' D'Abray snaps at him as though it's all been his fault, then swings his own animal about. Yanking on the reins, he spurs it from the yard.

I feel sorry for the horse.

Farron follows suit and Emile receives a back slapping from the jeering workers, who raise a cheer after D'Abray and Farron recover the wounded Chaumont and begin their slow ride back to Valenciennes.

D'Abray manages to have the last word. Turning in his saddle, he shouts:

'Good luck, then, Major Dawkins. Get yourself to Brussels; much good may it do you.'

Still, it's not a complete loss for him. The pair of horses we used to get us this far, fall in behind the group and follow it, taking my bag with them. Blasted cheek!

All sorts of things occur to me at the wrong moment. Now I'm thinking that while horses, sheep and cattle stick together, cats are not scared to live on their own. Not knowing why that is, reminds me of how much I've got to learn. Perhaps the time will come when nobody's trying to get rid of me for one reason or another. I'll be able to do it, then.

My father thanks the Belgian. 'You've done us a great service. Knowing that you are with us, I can tell you in the strictest confidence, that there is going to be an attempt to assassinate the Duke of Wellington, this very morning. I have no other details.'

I can see that Pindal is truly shocked. '*Mon Dieu*! Then we must get you to his headquarters immediately. Let us not delay. I have a light carriage and first class horses to pull it.'

In no time at all, we are bowling along in an open carriage, pulled by a pair of fresh horses, driven by Pindal himself.

My arm is feeling better. I'm sorry if I made a fuss about nothing. It wasn't broken, after all.

I sprawl on a seat in what Pindal calls a landau, watching the countryside slip by.

My father, I blink at him now and again, then think, yes he's still there, is sitting opposite me. I've noticed he's got a habit of scraping his fingers through his hair. I suppose that's why it looked a mess when I first met him as Remy. I can understand why he's doing it right now. He's worried sick that we're going to be too late to save Wellington's life, and with it, the war.

As we draw near the city, we meet columns of marching infantry, lancers prancing along the highway and when we pass a troop of hussars, my father can't stop admiring them. He has memories.

'Oranges and Lemons' get us through two check points.

Now we are coming in to Brussels; a city that sprawls and shines bright under the morning sun.

Pindal slows the carriage and says,

'When he is in Brussels, the duke likes to take a walk in the park every morning; usually with a lady on each arm; or so I've been told. Murder is a simple act, is it not? The assassin merely walks up to his victim and uses a pistol, or springs on him, stabbing him to death with a dagger as he passes by. Escaping afterwards is the difficult thing.'

'Thanks, Pindal,' father says, 'but Wellington's only just arrived here. I don't think he'll be too concerned about taking walks, as yet. It's worth checking, though, before we go to his HQ. Stop at the entrance to the park, will you? People will be swarming like flies to catch a glimpse of him, if he's in there.'

We're travelling along a broad avenue, its pavements teeming with well-dressed pedestrians. Parasols, bonnets and beautiful gowns float along by the side of elegant, well-cut coats and shiny top hats. A military band is playing somewhere in the distance.

It's a Friday. Hasn't anybody got any work to do?

My father says:

'People are behaving normally and going about their business, aren't they, Jack. If Wellington's been killed this morning, we'd know about it. The place would be in an uproar.'

Pindal halts the carriage by a huge pair of wrought iron gates.

'Here is the park, gentlemen. I will wait for you. *Bon Chance.*'

My father and I don't step down from the carriage, all sedate like, we leap from it and run at full-speed in to the park.

Footpaths go off in four directions from a large fountain spouting water in the centre of a round pond. A carriage drive winds its way through clumps of trees.

Where do we start?

There are plenty of uniforms, and gentlemen escorting ladies dressed in all their finery, parading up and down.

My father stops a pair of British officers by stepping in front of them. Their hands go straight to their sword hilts. I can't blame them. We do look like a couple of ruffians. Father is unshaven, his hair is all over the place and we are both travel-stained.

He asks the big question:

'Do either of you two gentlemen know if his lordship, the Duke of Wellington, is in the park? I must see him on urgent business.'

'What do two no-accounts like you want with his lordship?' One of them asks.

'Stand to attention when you speak to a superior officer, blast your eyes!' my father roars at him. Even I'm startled.

'I'm Major James Dawkins of the 7th Hussars. Now, is his lordship in the park, or not?'

'Sorry, sir,' the officers say. 'You did not introduce...'

Father interrupts the protests. 'I haven't got time for all that. Answer my question, lieutenant, or do you expect me to search the whole, damn park for him?'

'As it happens, sir,' the younger of the two, says, 'his lordship has already taken his morning turn with the ladies, and is by now on his way to his hotel headquarters. We saw the great man ourselves didn't we, Lucas? He was helping Lady Frances in to her carriage, half an hour ago.'

'Quite right, Harry.'

'All right, thank you, gentlemen,' my father says to them, calm as you like now. 'With a battle afoot, you're entitled to your peaceful stroll. Good luck to you both.'

'Thank you, sir,' they chorus.

We hurry back to where Pindal is waiting by the carriage.

Father tells him, 'Wellington's left the park and all's well.'

I rub my sore arm. 'We've been tricked. There never was a plan to murder Wellington. Those Frenchies were just after you, and they'd have got you if I hadn't turned up.'

'If that's true,' he replies, 'why did D'Abray come after us?'

I've no answer to that question, but ask him another one, instead. 'What are we going to do now, then?'

'We'll get ourselves to Wellington's headquarters. It's in Rue Montagne du Parc, not far from here.'

Before we have time to climb back in to the landau, our attention is caught by the sound of a large number of raised voices. Further along the pavement, crowds of people are beginning to cheer and applaud. The sound and the applause creeps towards us. Suddenly, there's the man we are looking for. I know it's him. He's sitting upright in an open carriage being pulled by a pair of magnificent horses. It's true then about that nose. It's an eagle's beak!

He doesn't look very happy. You'd think he would be, with everybody waving and cheering him, the way they are. His plain, blue coat looks drab compared to the uniform of the officer sitting next to him with his arm in a sling.

'That's him, isn't it, pa? That's the duke.' We all ask silly questions sometimes, don't we?

My father doesn't answer. All he says is, 'Swithin!'

'Are you all right?' I ask him. 'What are you looking like that for?'

He doesn't answer that, either, just says to Pindal, 'Can you turn the carriage round and follow us, *m'sieu*? Jack and I will go after the duke's carriage on foot.'

Pindal is a very obliging man. 'Certainly, major, I will be close behind you.'

'What's up, Pa?' I ask, as we try to keep pace with Wellington's carriage; which isn't so easy when you're trying to force your way through crowds of nuisances standing in your way.

'There certainly are more things in heaven and earth, Horatio,' my father says. 'The man dressed as an artillery colonel, sitting up there as bold as brass with the duke, is Captain Randall Swithin. He's the good for nothing officer who deserted my regiment after he rode down my sister, Molly, killing her and leaving you to fend for yourself. Although it's like something one of those blood and gore gothic playwrights dream up, it isn't. This is really happening, Jack, and Swithin is capable of anything. I would go as far to say that he's one of the few Britishers capable of assassinating Wellington. He would kill the king if there was money in it for him. We've got to be careful how we handle this, if we can handle it at all, that is. I believe he has a pistol hidden in that sling, and it's pointing straight at the duke.'

As I push my way past people, I'm asking myself, why couldn't it be, that all we had to do today was simply go to the duke's HQ, find him there and give him fair warning? Look at that baker's shop over there! Its window is full of pies and cakes and things. Sorry, I can't stop. I've got to help save his lordship!

All the way along that road, mobs of people stop dead in their tracks in order to cheer. I hear one old lady, waving a parasol, call him, 'The Saviour of Europe.' I wish she'd get out of our way. We're trying to be the saviour of Wellington.

His carriage is pulling ahead of us, but we're near enough to see it turn left, leaving my father and me on the wrong side of the road.

We are in the middle of that road, dodging vehicles, when Pindal's landau draws abreast of us.

'I'm with you, *mes amis*,' he says, hauling on the reins. 'Get in.'

We do, but there's no sign of Wellington's carriage when we make the same left turn.

It's a quieter, narrower street, lined on both sides with great mansions.

My father says:

'Swithin may have taken the duke in to one of these big houses, Jack. Let's get out and walk. You take one side of the road and I'll take the other. Are you still with us, *M'sieu Pindal*?'

'To the end, *m'sieu*,' Pindal replies; and I think it's decent of him to say so.

I poke my nose through three sets of ornate gates before I see Wellington's coach. My father is on the other side of the road, but he can see it as well.

The Duke of Wellington, and I can hardly believe I'm here looking at him, is standing at the door of the house and Swithin is right behind him, jabbing him in the back with a pistol.

He's shouting at the driver. He's on his knees, looking inside the coach:

'You've got twenty seconds to find that key, Briggs. If you don't, I swear I'll shoot you instead of this one here.'

'Don't bother to wait twenty seconds on my behalf, sir,' Wellington says, as polite as can be. 'Shoot him then take your chances with me in a bout of bare-knuckle.'

'Shut up!' Swithin says.

'Got it!' Briggs calls out.

It's a nice throw by him, and a good catch on Swithin's part.

Pindal and my father stand next to me. I think all three of us are aware that Wellington will be a dead man once Swithin gets him in to that house, as he will if we show ourselves.

'Looks like it's down to me again,' I sigh, then stroll through the gates and up the short drive.

CHAPTER TWENTY-TWO
Swithin can't shoot straight; my father can

The coachman is picking his teeth with a knife now, and Swithin has finally got the front door of the house open. Two saddle horses are eating the lawn when I call out, cheerfully:

'Good morning, gentlemen.'

'What are you doing in 'ere?' The coachman wants to know. A rank cockney if I've ever heard one, he tells me to, 'clear orf!'

'I hope I'm not interrupting anything,' I say to him. 'I just thought you might like to know that Boney's dead.'

His answer to that is, 'What?'

'Yeah,' I say, keeping one eye on Swithin and the duke. 'He's dead all right. They say he fell off his horse. The whole town's going wild. They'll be ringing the church bells soon, I expect.'

Swithin says, 'Don't just stand there, Briggs. Get him!'

I straightway add his name to the list of nasty characters I keep stored in my head; not in any alphabetical order, you understand; just in the order they crop up.

The coachman, who appears to be a bit low in the brain stakes, tells Swithin, 'But he sez Napoleon's dead, sir. That means we won't get paid.'

Swithin steps away from the door, still covering the shadowy figure of Wellington with the pistol. 'Don't make a move, your lordship, or you'll die now instead of inside the house, out of sight and out of mind long enough for me to disappear.'

For all the concern he shows, Wellington could be at a garden party. 'If what this ragamuffin says, is true, your goose is cooked, sir; done to a turn.'

'Here, what's going on?' I can act surprised when I want to.

Swithin screams at the coach driver. 'I told you to get him, Briggs! Use your knife on him, man!'

Briggs is a bit of a slow coach man - get it?

By the time he's pulled his knife from his boot, my father and Pindal are standing in the gateway with their pistols in their hands.

Swithin gapes at pa, trying to remember - then does.

'You!'

I step out of the line of fire, looking at the most surprised man in history. There goes Briggs. He's making a dash round the side of the house, and there goes Pindal after him.

Father is looking mighty fierce, pointing a brace of pistols at Swithin.

'Yeah, it's me, Captain James Dawkins, 'cept I've been promoted major; and you're done for, Swithin. You know my shooting. It hasn't changed.'

Swithin thrusts his pistol hard against the duke's throat. 'The pride of old England will be a dead man if you pull a trigger on me, Dawkins.'

My father doesn't seem to care about that. 'Kill him, if you must; but you'll die along with him.'

As my amazing father advances on him, Swithin swears something awful and forces the duke in to the open doorway.

The sound of a pistol shot, coming from the back of the house, decides everything, just as Swithin is about to close the door on us. Shoving the duke back down the steps, almost knocking us over, he stands there for a few seconds, cool as you like.

'With your two pistols between me and my horse, it seems as though I may need mine for whoever's barring the back way out of here, Major Dawkins, sir.'

Seeing my father take aim at him, he slams the door shut, and we hear bolts being rammed home.

I go forward and help Wellington to his feet. Yes I do, honest.

Here's the legend standing right in front of me. He doesn't seem to approve of me, or Pa. I can't think why; we've just saved his bacon.

'Are you all right, your lordship?' My father asks him.

'I'm fine, major. What do you mean by telling that impostor to shoot me if he wanted to?'

Pa ignores that; taking the steps leading to the front door, two at a time, he turns and says, 'Take my advice, your lordship, and stay out of harm's way behind that carriage of yours. Everything else will have to wait. I want that man. I owe him.'

'Oh, you do, do you?' Wellington shouts, 'Well, so do I. It's five thousand for you if you bring him back, dead or alive. Go and get him, sir!'

I don't know what to say to a duke, so I join my father, just as he's using a pistol butt to smash a window beside the door.

With the glass gone, the space is just large enough for me to squeeze through. I don't ask questions, or permission; I just do it.

My feet hit the floor of the entrance hall, crunching broken glass. As I let my father in, a door opens at the far end of the hallway. Pa raises a pistol, and Bertrand Pindal walks in.

'Major?'

'Was that your shot we heard, *m'sieu?*' father asks him.

'Yes, I'm afraid I was forced to shoot Wellington's driver. He came running at me with a knife.'

He doesn't seem too upset about it. Nobody seems to care much about anything like that round here. I suppose it's the same when you're fighting a war. You get used to death and destruction in the end.

My father asks Pindal, 'What about Swithin, the officer who was next to the duke in his carriage?'

'I did not see him, major.'

'Then he must still be in here. You'd better re-load that pistol of yours. You stay here, Jack, or go and keep his lordship company. Swithin is trapped in this house. *M'sieu Pindal* and

I are going to find him. We'll arrest him, if we can. Let a court martial deal with him. Coming, Pindal?'

Leaving me to sit on the bottom step of the great, curving staircase that goes up, and up again, my father and the loyal Pindal, begin searching the ground floor.

While they are doing that, the Duke of Wellington comes in to the hall, crosses its tiled floor and sits down right next to me on the stairs. How much stranger can my life get?

'What's happening, young man? I haven't got all day, you know. I've over a hundred thousand troops to worry about.'

'Well, your highness, your coach driver's been shot. He's dead, I think. If Pindal can hit small birds in flight, he couldn't miss a cockney. Now they, that is, Pindal and my father, are searching the house for Swithin, because he must still be here, unless he's climbed out of a window, or something. Swithin's an old enemy of my family, you know. He killed my Aunt Molly, which turned me in to the Artful Dodger. I'd just lost my girl, Lysette, to a rich Frenchie when I found my father in Valenciennes, when all this started happening. Do you know him, your honour?' My father, I mean.'

'Of course I know him. I appointed him after my chief of spies recommended him to me. He's as tough as iron and speaks French like a Frenchman.'

My father and Pindal return to the hallway.

'He must be hiding somewhere up there,' pa says, pointing up the stairwell.

'In case I'm wrong, Pindal, would you give protection to his lordship and my son? Keep a careful watch; Swithin is ruthless and might try and finish the job he's getting paid for.'

He excuses himself, brushes past the duke and begins to climb the stairs. We all watch him like hawks. I don't know about the other two, but I'm thinking, if Swithin comes on to that first-floor landing, it will be down to whoever shoots first.

Pindal puts his back against a wall so that he can see right up the stairwell. I join him as Wellington stands up and bellows up the stairs:

'Flush him out, man. I'm in a hurry!'

Perhaps he's got in to the habit of shouting a lot because it's noisy on battlefields.

From where I'm standing, the second flight of stairs looks as though it's much narrower than the first. Although I can only see the lower half of his body, I can tell that my father has almost reached the top landing.

Two pistols flash and bang, making my flesh tingle. And there's Swithin. My father's struggling with him and Pindal is running up the stairs. I want to be doing the same, but I can't. I've got a duke gripping my arm. It's the bruised one, as it happens, so I wish he'd ease up a bit.

My father's back is hard against the banister rail and I can hear Swithin snarling, 'Dawkins, you have a nasty habit of getting in my way. First it was your trollop of a sister and now it's you!'

'Get him, Pa! Don't be bested by him!'

Now Swithin's back is against that rail. It must be breaking up, because parts of it are on their way down. Pieces of moulded wood hit the floor, close to where we're standing.

Pindal's arrived up there, but Swithin's started to take the quick way down.

A loud crack, a shout of absolute terror and - well, it's a thirty feet fall on to quarried tiles that have a pretty pattern on them.

He's lying on the floor now, all twisted up and holding tight to a short length of banister. A good example of a man clutching at straws, I suppose. A pool of blood is forming round his head.

Tearing my eyes away from it, I look up and watch my father and Pindal as they walk slowly down the stairs.

I don't think I'll ever forget the sound Swithin's head made when it hit those tiles.

Wellington takes charge. First off, he tells my father what a terrible pistol shooter he is.

'You both were,' he says, nodding at Swithin's body.

Duke or not, my father doesn't hesitate to correct him. 'Being above me on the landing, Swithin got the angle wrong when he fired, your lordship; but if you care to examine his body, you'll discover that my ball struck home. I've seen it before today. A man mortally wounded in battle will fight on for a moment or two.'

'You've seen that have you?' the duke says, 'well, so have I. Now let's go outside and sort out who's who in this tiresome interruption to my busy day.'

No chance of an apology, then.

When I get outside, I'm surprised to find the sun's still shining and the birds are still singing their hearts out. They couldn't care less who's trying to kill who, could they?

'I haven't got time to stand on ceremony,' Wellington tells us when we reach his coach. 'I will deal with you first; *M'sieu... Pindal*, is it not?'

'Yes, your lordship. I am Bertrand Pindal, a landowner from Brugelette.'

The duke inclines his head. 'Thank you for your help in this nasty little affair. I now require you to give me your word as a gentleman that you will not speak of it to anyone. Are you willing to give it? I have good reason to ask it of you.'

'I give it most freely, your lordship. I understand the need for secrecy in such matters.'

'Good man. That saves me from locking you up!' Wellington nods his head in approval. 'In that case, I reward you with those stallions the assassins intended to make their escape on.'

'That is very generous of you, your lordship.'

Generous? They ain't his to give!

'Call them the spoils of war.' Wellington tells him.

Pindal, who I've now added to my short list of people I don't mind rubbing shoulders with, shakes Wellington's hand. 'I suspect you have much to do, your lordship. You will be making plans to give Napoleon a warm reception, no doubt, so I shall leave you and return to my vegetable patch. It has all been most invigorating.'

He turns to me and my father. 'If you ever have need of me again, gentlemen, you know where to find me.'

Those are his parting words. He collects the horses and with a nod in our direction, guides them round the curving drive to where his landau awaits.

It ain't half peaceful all of a sudden!

I'm getting that familiar 'worn out' feeling, and I'm hungry. I can't remember the last time I put food in my mouth. The only place I can find to rest my head is in the duke's coach. That will do. I'm not fussy.

The seats are very well padded. I could be asleep in two minutes, except...the duke is telling my father to tidy himself up, or he'll never pass muster as his coachman, 'and hide that scruff of a son. Throw a rug over him, or something. This ain't a gypsy caravan, you know.'

Well, of all the ungrateful - have a go at him, Pa!

Instead of doing that, my father asks him a question. 'What about the bodies of Swithin and his driver, your lordship?'

'Leave them where they lie! They won't face a firing squad, but they won't have a military funeral, either. Leave them to me. I'll see to it that their bodies disappear. Come along, Major Dawkins, oh, let's make it Colonel Dawkins, shall we? Whatever your rank, let's be away from here. By the way, you should have sent that son of yours to a better school. He uses a form of the English language that requires an interpreter. If you speak his tongue, I would be obliged if you would advise him to remain on the floor of the coach and keep his head under that rug. You know the way, sir; so whip up those horses.'

CHAPTER TWENTY-THREE
My father saves the treasury five thousand pounds

All I can see during the journey are Wellington's boots, but I can hear the people applaud and cheer him.

I'm allowed to get out from under the rug when we arrive at a grand hotel on the Rue Montagne du Parc.

Its lobby is swarming with officers. They surround their commander the second he steps through the door.

He raises a hand:

'Please take yourself off to the hotel's board room, gentlemen, we must now regard it as being our war room. Wait for me there. I have a little business to conduct with Colonel Dawkins and his son. I jest not, this is indeed Colonel James Dawkins. Unfortunately he has mislaid his uniform.'

Off they go, speaking quietly together and making backward glances at us.

'Come to my rooms and tell all,' Wellington says.

I take a back seat in a room that gives my heartstrings a tug. Its ceiling is decorated in the same manner as those in Hugo's house in Maubeuge.

Wellington has a lot to say:

'Swithin had a sort of desperate courage, colonel. He had the nerve to approach me just as I was mounting my carriage, after my early morning walk. I didn't notice I had a different coachman. I mean, who in the world looks at their coachman? Swithin introduced himself as Colonel - Colonel, oh, I forget what the damn fellow called himself; it was Ramsbotham, or some such name. First of all, he told me he brought urgent word from an agent in Valenciennes. I assumed he meant you, of course. Then he threatened me with that pistol and before I knew it, he was riding along in the carriage with me. The sheer gall of the man! He said I'd been invited to attend my farewell party at a house especially rented for the occasion. I was to be the only guest and a refusal would offend. He was kind enough to inform me that it was nothing personal. Money was his only motive. After killing me, he was going to ride straight for the French lines. Oh, yes, we had quite a nice chat during the drive; albeit a little bit one sided; because I didn't take to the fellow, you know. Whoever it was that recruited him, and you say his name is D'Abray, was rewarding him with an estate in some French colony in the East. Swithin was quite frank, too. He told me how he'd gambled away his inheritance and deserted the army. He must have been the world's worst gambler, or the most reckless. The coachman was some wretched deserter he picked out of the gutter.'

Yes, here I am, Jack Dawkins, a guttersnipe myself, not so long ago, listening to the Duke of Wellington give forth; he's another one of those talkers I keep meeting. If he ever gives up standing on hills watching his men get shot, stabbed and blown to pieces, he'll make a good politician. He's got good manners, though; being well brought up, he's thanking my father.

'I congratulate you on uncovering the plot, colonel. You have saved much more than my life. I'll see to it that this D'Abray fellow meets with a nasty accident. I'm afraid I can't allow you to win public accolades for what you and your son have done. Keeping the episode secret is of the utmost importance. I can't appear before all of my scattered forces, and if word gets out that someone has attempted to kill me, the gossip mongers will soon start spreading the word that I'm dead. You know how that sort of thing works. The morale of my troops is of the greatest import right now, and I've been led to believe that they'd miss me if I was gone. I'm about to engage my old enemy in a battle of wits that will decide the fate of Europe for perhaps a hundred years. If I'm not victorious, you will have only saved my worthless hide; but if I defeat Bonaparte,' the duke leans forward and prods my father on his chest, 'you will have been instrumental in altering the course of history. That's quite a thought, eh? Furthermore, I'll not bring shame upon my army by letting it be known that one of its officers was a traitor and a would-be assassin.'

My father wants to say something in return, and so do I, as a matter of fact, but a raised hand and a certain look on Wellington's face, is enough to make both of us keep our mouths shut.

'So, this is how it will be,' Wellington continues, 'you, sir, are no use as an agent anymore, at least, not in France; although our beloved Secretary of War, Lord Palmerston, will, no doubt find a use for you elsewhere in the world. In the meantime, you may re-join your regiment for the grand finale. The forthcoming battle will cost us dear, I know, but I intend to finish Napoleon for good. He'll make no more come-backs. Regarding your son, although he'll be permitted to go out and about with an escort, I am going to keep him incommunicado until after the inevitable battle has taken place. One cannot trust a lad of his age to keep silent about such a mighty matter.'

I begin my protest with, 'Sir...!' but get no further than that. The duke is holding up his hand again. 'Colonel Dawkins, in an unguarded moment I rashly promised you five thousand if you put paid to Swithin, but I'm damned if I know whether I meant pounds or guineas. Let's call it pounds, shall we? That'll save the treasury two hundred and fifty.'

This time Pa does manage to speak. 'You can save the treasury five thousand pounds, your lordship. I acted out of duty, not for financial reward.'

Wellington likes that. 'Then please allow me to award your son five hundred pounds for his diversionary tactics at the house. One of you deserves to make something out of this affair and, as far as courage and quick thinking goes, your boy is a chip off the old block.'

That's another thing. Money keeps falling in to my hands, lately. I don't want to think about them, but the gold and silver coins from Lysette and Hugo were worth about two hundred in English. I've still got most of it. Now another five hundred's coming my way. Let's see; a thousand off Webster, two hundred off you know who and now another five hundred, that's er… just a minute while I work it out, yes, that's a hundred and seventy pounds compensation for every year I've been adrift!

The duke brings the meeting to a close.

'That's it then, gentlemen. My delay in arriving here this morning will add to my reputation as a ladies man. It's the only explanation my staff officers find acceptable. They are always prepared to believe the hints of seduction and amours that abound, but kidnapping and attempted murder? Never! Now, come with me, if you please.'

We follow his upright figure out of the room and along the hotel corridor until he opens one of the many doors lining it.

There they all are, waiting for him in their nice, bright uniforms.

'Your lordship!' They chorus.

His lordship's still not ready for them. 'Please be patient, gentlemen. Is my old friend, Dougie Duggan here?'

Duggan, an ageing cavalry officer steps forward, eager to serve.

Wellington shakes his hand. 'Allow me to introduce you to young Mr Dawkins, Dougie. He has performed a valuable service for his country, so I have chosen you to take good care of him. Provide him with everything he needs, and that includes bringing a barber to him in his hotel room. There's fuzz on his chin, so he might enjoy being shaved for the first time, as well as having his haircut. Now then, please take note of this. He is not to communicate with anyone, do you understand? Assign two reliable young officers to watchdog him night and day.'

'Yes, your lordship,' replies the puzzled Duggan, but what about my duty to my regiment? A battle is coming, sir.'

'I know it is, Dougie; but I want to be able to visit you at your lovely home in the Cotswolds when it's over, not stand over your stricken remains on the field of blood.'

The duke fixes his beady eye on my father. 'Major, I beg your pardon, sir, I mean, Colonel Dawkins, you may say your farewells to your son before rejoining your regiment. You can have him back after I have dealt with my opponent - what's his name again? I can't quite place it, you know.'

'Why, it's Napoleon Bonaparte, your lordship!' his officers chorus, then laugh heartily.

'So 'tis,' Wellington declares; laughing along with them. 'Tell me, gentlemen, what is the latest news regarding our old sparring partner?'

Wellington has got the whole pack of them in a jolly mood. His officers gather round him, waiting to hear how he intends to play the game.

Colonel Duggan buttonholes one of them. He looks as young as me. My father refers to him as being a 'cornet'. He's ordered to conduct us to my rooms on the third floor of the hotel and remain with me if I decide to leave it for any reason.

The sitting-room windows of the luxury suite of rooms I'm in, look out on the park; very nice. At my father's request, the young officer arranges for a selection of hot food to be delivered to us. After that, pa grits his teeth and confirms the sad truth:

'Wherever the 7th Hussars are, Jack, I've been ordered to go to them. All my kit is in the Brussels house that Mary, your mother, and your brother and sister lived in while I was away in Valenciennes. I decided they should return to London, because Bonaparte's army could well sweep through here, despite our best efforts to stop it. I certainly didn't want them to be in Brussels if that happened. The best laid plans, and all that. Now then, we have much to talk about and one night to do it in.'

I agree with that. 'I'm still trying to understand how all this came about, pa. I struggled and struggled while I was on my own, but that already seems like a bad dream. You're here, I'll see mother soon, and the man who started our torment is no more. How can it happen, Pa? It's like God's suddenly paid some attention to us.'

My father understands everything. 'It doesn't pay to ponder on the imponderables, Jack. Let's just show our gratitude by leading the best life we can. Now then, what's all this talk of Newgate?'

Ever since Pa left to join his regiment I've been going out and about, buying everything I want, except for a pocket watch, that is, and walking in the park with Cornet Ralph Bailey. He's a happy-go-lucky fellow, so we get on all right. I've lost count of the days and nights I've been living in the hotel. It's like being kept in a sort of luxury Newgate where your every wish is granted, twenty four hours a day. Ryan wouldn't like it at all.

The rain's lashing down the windows this afternoon and there's distant thunder. At least, it sounds like thunder. I'm a bit stirred up because when Colonel Duggan called in to check on me and my guard this morning, he let drop that it's started.

There's a great battle taking place out there somewhere, and my father's in the middle of it. I won't lose him, will I?

Suddenly, although I don't much like the idea of being shot at and slashed with swords, I want to be there. I could lose my self among the thousands of men and horses plunging about in the smoke and rain, and learn for myself what being in a battle is like.

I say as much to Cornet Bailey:

'Can you get hold of a couple of horses, Ralph? The fight is not so far off. We can get there, if you're game.'

'Of course I'm game, Jack,' he says, 'but one has to obey orders in the army. That's a soldier's first duty, whatever his rank is. Look, come up to the roof of the hotel and I'll show you something. I was up there earlier, before I relieved Forsyth.'

There's a narrow walkway, all the way round the hotel's sloping, tiled roof. The rain is making it dangerously wet, but the view to the south-west takes my mind off that:

'Do you know how far that is?' I ask Bailey, staring at the black as black and blood-red horizon, while listening to the distant ghostly noise of a battle taking place. Way over there, a thousand fireflies seem to be flickering-and-flickering.

'That's about ten miles off, Jack,' Bailey says. 'Man, I wish we were there! Can you imagine it? Put both sides together and you've got something like two hundred thousand men, all fighting like wildcats to win the day; and what's more, every manjack of them is involved in his own private battle with his own private enemy. One falls and another takes his place.'

While my imagination works on that, I say to him, 'We might as well go down. There's no sense in getting soaked. Thanks for bringing me up here, Ralph, but I won't be able to sleep tonight. Will you?'

'I think not,' he says.

The bells are ringing out their victory message and my father has survived! I didn't see what sort of state he was in at the end of the battle, of course, but he turned up here looking immaculate in his colonel's uniform. He's strangely worked up, though:

'We cut off a squadron of French cuirassiers and charged 'em about a dozen times, Jack. We wiped the lot of them out in the end, except for a couple of officers who got taken prisoner. That was only in our small corner of the battlefield. I can't describe it. Nobody could. Every other fight I've been in pales into insignificance.'

He can't seem to stop walking up and down the length of the room, smacking a fist in to his other hand, over and over again.

I suggest that he sits himself down. 'You've had a hard time of it, father.'

'What?' he says, 'sit down? All right, I will.'

He doesn't, though; he just carries on doing what he's doing. 'I lost a lot of friends, Jack, a lot of friends; but you and I are going home!'

I never saw the Duke of Wellington again, but before we left Brussels, a banker's draft for five hundred pounds was placed in my hot, little hand.

Father has told me his plans for the future. He intends to resign his commission, sell up and move lock, stock and barrel to Boston in America. That seems a bit sudden to me.

Dover! And I wasn't sick once while crossing the channel.

It's a long haul to London with nothing much to do but sit in the coach, exchanging the occasional word with my father. Thoughts of Lysette, never very far away, begin to creep in to my mind. The only thing that seems to have kept her at bay lately has been action and physical danger. As soon as things go quiet, there she is.

A hackney cab takes us all the way from Southwark to father's house in Putney.

I don't mind admitting that my heart is in my mouth when he leaves his luggage on the front step; opens the door and walks me right in.

A maid, standing in the hallway, curtsey's and says:

'Good evening, sir. Welcome home.'

'Thank you, Maud.'

Then a lady opens a side door and steps in to the hall. Father, looking absolutely delighted, smiles and says, 'Jack, my boy, allow me to introduce you to your mother.'

It's the end of a chapter, isn't it!

CHAPTER TWENTY-FOUR
There are mothers and there are others

My mother and I don't rush in to each other's arms. Strangers, we stand stock still, ten feet apart in the quiet hallway.

'I'll act as my own porter and carry these bags up,' my father says, taking hold of our luggage. 'That'll leave you two to get to know one another. We'll have our own hugs and kisses later, Mary.'

Picking up our bags, he begins to climb the stairs, stops for a moment and looks down at us. 'There was no time for awkwardness when we first met as father and son was there, Jack.'

I come back with, 'You're right, Pa. I suppose we ought to have thanked those two pistol-packing Frenchies for breaking the ice for us.'

He laughs and continues on his way.

After that, my mother seems to be able to walk towards me. I get my own feet moving, as well.

'Hello, Jack,' she says.

I can only manage, 'Mother.'

She's a handsome woman; beautiful even, with her fair hair hanging in ringlets and her face stubbornly set, as though she's determined to control her feelings, come what may. The blue of her high-waisted, long-sleeved gown, perfectly matches the colour of her wide-awake eyes.

This meeting isn't going to be as easy as I thought it would be. I'm feeling guilty about the sins of the Artful Dodger. Hang on. That's a nice try, but I can't off-load my wrong doings on to him, can I. We're one and the same person.

It's possible my mother might be feeling guilty, too; but unlike me, she has nothing to be ashamed of, nothing at all. She didn't just cast me aside, un-wanted. She left me safe with my Aunt Molly while she went off to the wars with father. What happened to me afterwards is not her fault.

I know how hard it was for her to leave me, because I can now remember everything about our parting; the hustle and bustle surrounding us, the way she cried, took me back from Molly, kissed me again and told me to be a good boy, while an impatient coach driver asked her not to take all day about it.

Skittish Maud opens a door, sticks her head out and asks:

'Where would madam like me to serve the coffee?'

'Just put it in the conservatory, will you,' my mother replies. 'I'll take care of serving it.'

'Yes, ma'am.'

As the maid closes the door, my mother says, 'We'll be more at ease in the conservatory, Jack. The atmosphere out there is far less formal than in the sitting room. Do you like coffee?'

Although I feel like downing something stronger, now's not the time to say so.

'Yes, mother. I would like some coffee.'

The conservatory is full of cane furniture covered in cushions. Flowers growing out of pots, fill the air with their perfume.

Looking through the glass panels, I can see boatyards lining the banks of the River Thames and glimpse sails moving with the flow of the water, which probably smells a lot sweeter up this way than it will by the time it runs past Limehouse.

You would go and think of that place, wouldn't you, Jack. What's the point in day dreaming about her? You've found your mother and father, ain't that enough for you?

Sitting opposite me, with her back against the outside world, my mother looks right in to my eyes. She's weighing me up. I hope she can't see all the bad things I've had to do, or thought I had to. Hold your breath, Jack. Start talking.

'I've dreamt about this moment for ages, mother, and there were plenty of times when I thought that's all it ever would be; a dream.'

She leans towards me. I can sense she's longing to place a hand on me, her son, but she can't quite bring herself to do it, yet. 'Not a day's gone by without me thinking about you, Jack. I've been in mourning for you for ten years.'

It's time to confess. 'Before you think of taking me back, mother, you ought to know that I've done things...'

That's as far as I get before she holds up a hand.

'Stop right there, Jack. I'm not a fool. I'm an army officer's wife who has seen life from the very top to the very bottom. Heaven alone knows how you've managed to keep yourself alive until now, but for the time being, I prefer not to hear details of your past. Not knowing whether he would survive the great battle he has just taken part in, your father wrote to me from Brussels. That letter answered my prayers because it brought me news of you. It also caused me to pray that my husband, your father, would be spared. The very fact that you stumbled upon Colour Sergeant Butler, the man whose life your father saved, is a miracle in itself. A long time ago, a poet observed that there is no armour against fate. It is a true saying, but fate can sometimes work in our favour, Jack.'

If I can't confess anything else, I'll confess my ignorance. 'Excuse me for interrupting you, mother, but that's just one of the things that's worrying me.'

'What, fate?' she asks. 'There's little point in you or anyone else worrying about that.'

'No, mother, it's not that, it's the way you mentioned a poet, casual-like. I expect you can name a dozen, and quote from their works; well, I can't even name one of them. Although I can read and write a bit, and know my sums, I've been living in a world where finding the means to eat was mostly all that mattered, so

I don't know a thing about poets, books, what's out there in the world or in the heavens above.

My mother smiles at me for the first time. 'Gaining knowledge is easy enough, if one has the will, the wit and the opportunity to do it. In his letter, your father wrote that you are intelligent, courageous and a son to be proud of. I trust his judgment, but I hope your father's right about you, and you come up to scratch, young man, because I can be quite a Tartar when roused!'

She laughs then. 'I thought it time we introduced a little levity in to these proceedings, Jack. That's the best I can do at the moment, I'm afraid. I know there's much more to talk about, but we can't possibly cover everything at once, so let's drink our coffee before it gets cold. I can't abide cold coffee.'

Not quite strangers anymore, we sit and drink our coffee.

Offering me an oatmeal biscuit, my mother says:

'It will take a little while for us to grow as close as a mother and son should be, Jack, but having dealt with many a soldier boy and their wives and families over the years, I have become a good judge of character myself. That's why I already know that we are going to get on famously. It may help the process if I tell you that you were born to me on Christmas Day in the year 1799. You were almost Christened, Joseph, but it was decided at the last minute to name you Jack, after your father's own grandfather, Jack Dawkins, who made his fortune in India. Now please don't feel embarrassed when I also tell you that when I came home from Corunna, I was heavily pregnant with Michael, and Grace was born a year later. Your father and I wanted a large family, but after searching high and low for you, I finally lost hope and fell in to a state of despair. Blaming myself for losing you, haunted me so much and for so long, I was unable to conceive any more children.'

'Oh, mother...'

Up goes her hand again. 'It wasn't your fault, Jack, and thanks to your grit and determination, you are back with your family.

Michael and Grace are treasures, but your arrival has increased our bounty, ten-fold.'

Slowly and deliberately, she puts her coffee cup down, leans across the small table and kisses me on the cheek. 'Welcome home, my son.'

I'm happy.

After an evening of quiet celebration and the best night's sleep, ever, I woke up this morning, knowing my mother is everything I've always hoped she would be; a wise and kind woman with a ready smile. She's not the soft and silly sort. I saw her give Michael a clip round the ear for being cheeky to Maud last night.

I reckon the word 'mother' is just about the best there is, don't you?

Talking about 'silly', some of the things we get up to when we're on our own, can be silly, can't they. Take me, for example. Out of sheer joy, I'm lying on my bed, kicking my legs in the air like a two year old, when Grace and Michael come bursting in to the room.

'What are you doing, Jack?' Grace asks me.

'My morning exercises,' I tell her. 'I always do exercises before I get up.'

'Are you really our brother?' she asks.

Michael pipes up. 'Course he is, you daft thing. His ears stick out, just like yours do. I'm lucky; I've got mummy's ears!'

Grace makes a fuss about that. 'My ears don't stick out hardly at all. I'm going to tell mummy you were rude!'

Oh, I love it; normal children having a normal life.

At breakfast this morning, my father announced what I already knew. He intends to move to Boston, Massachusetts, and establish a trading business there as soon as he's free from the army. Mother already knew, because the only questions came from Grace and Michael; mostly comic ones from Grace; such as:

'If the ship sinks, might we get swallowed up by a whale, daddy?'

Sitting at the table, looking from one to the other, I felt part of them; flesh, blood, bone and all.

Remembering what Wellington told my father about the secretary of war finding him a job elsewhere, I knew full well that he's not taking us off to America for the good of our health. He's got a job to do for England. That's a secret I'll be keeping.

The man I already respect above all others, kissed my mother on the cheek, stood up and said to me:

'Well, sir, it's high time I freed you from bondage. Let's begin the process by visiting your benefactor, shall we?'

'Yes, do that first of all,' my mother said, taking my hand. 'Then Jack can be truly ours again.'

A mother's kiss had come my way.

I'm in a cab at the moment, sitting next to my father, on our way to see Mr Brownlow. I'm hoping Oliver will be there, as well.

Pa is telling me that he intends to teach me how to run a business and how he has found a buyer for his house, but you know what it's like with me; I'm travelling along familiar roads, so the memories are rolling in.

I'm heading for Brownlow's, all right, but in my mind, I've got Lysette's head in my lap and young Desmond is asking me:

'Is she going to die, Mr Jack?'

Where are you now, my beautiful Lysette?

'Where are you now, boy?'

It's my father. 'You have a bad habit of drifting off when people are talking to you, don't you, Jack.'

I apologise. 'I'm sorry, sir, I mean, father. I've got too many memories about this area.'

We stand together outside Brownlow's house.

'Nice place,' father observes.

'It is,' I agree, 'but my legs don't seem to want to carry me up those steps.'

He puts his arm round my shoulders. 'Memories, again, Jack? Come on, let's face them together and blow them in to next Christmas!'

It's Mrs Bedwin who opens the door in answer to father's knock.

'Good morning to you,' he says. 'I am Colonel Dawkins, Jack's father. Is Mr Brownlow at home?'

Mrs Bedwin can't hide her thoughts as she looks at a man who is every inch an officer. 'You're Jack's father, sir? Well bless me. I can hardly believe it.'

My father digs in to a pocket and pulls out a few calling cards. 'Please give one of these to Mr Brownlow, madam.'

'Of course, sir; right away, sir.'

What's up with the woman? She's gone red in the face, her eyebrows are going up and down and her mouth is twitching as though she doing her best not to laugh.

'Oliver is in the garden,' she says to me. 'I'm sure Mr Brownlow won't mind if you go through and see him.'

Up and down go her eyebrows again.

'That's right, Jack,' my father says. 'Go and see your friend while I have a talk with Brownlow.'

I know the way, don't I?

Looking through the glass doors leading to the garden, I understand why Mrs Bedwin was failing to keep a straight face. I can see them playing 'catch ball' together.

See who? You ask.

Well, I'll tell you. It's Master Oliver Twist Brownlow Esquire, and Miss Lysette Godden, or is she already Madame Mercier?

My world tilts.

Before I know it, I'm standing on the lawn. Oliver is right in front of me:

'You've come at last, Jack! You knew he would, didn't you, Lysette?'

My angel speaks as I reach out a hand towards her. 'Dearest Jack. Please don't touch me yet. I... I think I'll faint away if you do.'

'Sit down, why don't you?' Oliver says. 'I'll bring you some lemonade.'

We do as he suggests and sit side-by-side on a bench seat. But we can't stay sitting, can we? Up we get, nervous as kittens and feeling an urgent need to walk, run... do something!

We settle for walking the length of the garden. Short of sprouting wings and flying away, we have no other choice.

With Lysette by my side, it's heart-thumping time for me again. Dry throat, can't swallow. Ring them bells. None of this shows on my face as I break the silence between us:

'All right, Lysette. Nothing's changed as far as I'm concerned, but to be honest, I would have preferred not finding you visiting Mr Brownlow, right now. It's bad timing on both our parts. Your being here is going to put me through the mill again. I haven't got over the last time, yet. Don't expect I ever will. Anyway, where's Hugo?'

She speaks quickly. 'I'm here on my own, Jack. I knew you would keep your word with Mr Brownlow and report yourself to him, but I've waited days and days for you to come here.'

Waited days and days for me? Is another small miracle about to happen?

I turn on her. 'Don't you dare raise me up, then drop me again, Lysette. I can only stand so much. What exactly does bring you here?'

I don't have to wait long for an answer. She pours out the words I want to hear.

'You do, Jack. You've brought me here. I went to Rheims with Hugo and met his father at his grand chateau. They gave me a wonderful birthday party, but it all meant nothing to me. I was lonely with Hugo, and lonely among two hundred guests; lonely in a great house standing in hundreds of acres. I was out horse-riding, lonely and alone, when I realised how wilful I'd been in pursuit of the life I want to lead. I was lonely for you, Jack. You were so gallant when you said goodbye to me in Maubeuge, and, oh, I love you so much. I've come back to ask you if you can find it in your heart to forgive me for what I did to you.'

It takes me a minute to breathe really deep then let the air out of my lungs before I can say, 'As far as I'm concerned, there's nothing to forgive. We love each other. We've been separated for a little while, now we are back together again, just like we should be.'

Having reached the end of the garden, we're brought up short by a green and leafy hedgerow.

I turn towards Lysette and place my hands on her shoulders, pulling her a little closer to me.

Looking at her face, so pretty, it's enough to break my forgiving heart. I want to kiss her, but control myself, somehow. Instead, I ask:

'How do things stand with Hugo and your ambition to travel; study nature, draw and paint. Stuff like that?'

She moves closer to me. There's no doubt in my mind. She's waiting for me to kiss her.

'You make me feel ashamed, Jack. You are so steadfast and true; a gentle, parfait knight; my Roland.' Her hand caresses my face. '*Monsieur Mercier* was extremely angry about me leaving. He resorted to calling me some very unpleasant names, but Hugo was kind and understanding. He even travelled to Dieppe with me and made sure I had a safe passage home. As for the rest, I still want to make my mark in the world, as a woman.

Perhaps I shall achieve my ambitions... with you by my side, God willing. Mother has washed her hands of me, so while I continue to study the things I'm interested in, I intend to get myself a job teaching French and other subjects to the children of wealthy parents.'

I can't put it off any longer. We don't have to move very much before our lips meet. It's a gentle, gentle kiss. My goodness, how the sweetness of it makes my heart sing with joy!

We draw apart-just a little; wanting to stay in touch, if you know what I mean. 'Shiver my timbers!' as I once heard a seaman remark. It springs to mind because my 'timbers' are shivering!

Stowing my base desires away, I say to Lysette:

'I've a lot to tell you, sweetheart. For one thing, I've found my family.'

Her face lights up. 'Oh, Jack. That's wonderful.'

'It is, isn't it,' I agree. 'They are not poor, either. My father's in the house with Mr Brownlow, right now, getting me free from those legal ties. We'll both be free, free-thinkers, then, won't we. By the way, on that score, I'm not going to have any girl of mine flaunting herself in pantaloons!'

'Oh, Jack,' she laughs, 'I'm so glad you're still the same stick in the mud boy you were at Shippenden Farm.'

Thoughts of Shippenden bring an instant change of mood in her. The poor girl's feelings are all over the place as she says, 'You've found your family and I've lost mine.'

The sun's shining all over the place as well. We begin walking back up the garden. Oliver is plonking a jug and some glasses on a table by the seat Lysette and I had found we couldn't sit still on.

I cup my hand under her elbow, telling her:

'I'm really sorry about your mother and father. Anything that hurts you hurts me.'

When she murmurs something in return, I stop walking, hold her in my arms and kiss her again. This time, it's as though we're melting in to one another.

I'll wake up in a minute.

The girl I love is holding on to me; I've found my mother and father; I'm clean, well dressed, and have honest money in my pocket. Sing alleluia, Jack! God loves you after all. Do you know something? I'd live the last ten years all over again, just for this moment.

We're a bit too busy to hear the approach of Mr Brownlow and my father, until:

'Ahem,' Brownlow clears his throat and Lysette and I stand away from each other:

'Well, Jack,' my father says, 'having discussed your situation with Mr Brownlow, and bearing in mind the we are going to live in America, quite soon, he has assured me that Mr Justice Stareleigh will release you from bondage and tear up the documents relating to your case.'

'America?' Lysette cries out and collapses on to the bench. 'You're going to America, Jack?'

A complication? I am surprised. Everything normally goes so smooth for me!

'I haven't had the chance to tell you, yet, Lysette. Father; this is Miss Lysette Godden, and we love each other.'

'I can see that,' he replies in a matter of fact way. 'Mr Brownlow has told me all about the girl and her murdered father. He's also told me how shocked he was when Miss Godden's mother disowned her in his presence, last week. According to Mrs Godden, by running away to France with you, her daughter has put herself so far beyond the pale, no man of any standing in society would dream of marrying her. In my humble opinion, Mrs Godden's mercenary ambitions and heartless attitude puts her beyond the pale as a mother.'

What a man my father is! He simplifies everything by kneeling beside Lysette and saying:

'I'm used to making quick decisions and smiting the enemy, Miss Godden. Based on what Mr Brownlow has told me about you, and following my own instincts, I say that I don't believe for a moment there's anything remotely scandalous about you. If you're agreeable to the idea, you'd best come home with Jack and me. There'll be a few rules laid down as far as you two are concerned, but Jack being a born gentleman and you a principled young lady, I'm sure they will prove to be unnecessary. My wife needs help with Jack's unruly siblings, both here and now, and on the other side of the Atlantic Ocean, if you are game for an adventure. Poor pay, two ghastly children to teach and take care of, and a sound beating every other Thursday. What say you? Shall we shake on it?'

While Lysette smiles and takes hold of one of his hands, I'm shaking the other and saying, 'Thank you, father. Thank you very much.'

Epilogue

Although it's two months since the Battle of Waterloo took place, it's still on everybody's lips. I've been kept too busy helping my mother and father, by running errands all over London, delivering letters, ordering packing cases and stuff, to think about it very much. Lysette is doing the job my father offered her, so she's had her hands full, as well; taking care of my young brother and sister, Michael and Grace. Their names sound kind of holy, don't you think? Well, believe me, they ain't no such thing! You wouldn't believe the kind of mischief those two can get up to if they get half a chance.

It's high summer now, and those two young 'uns are almost fenced in by yours truly and our Ma and Pa, as we stand together, half-hid by our luggage, waiting for a coach at the Spaniard's Inn on Hampstead Heath.

I'm listening to the noisy approach of a coach and six, when something marvellous happens to me. Lysette emerges from the Ladies only to re-join us after doing whatever ladies do in those places. I take one look at her and, hello there ! my mind slides me back to a place called Gravesend and I'm falling into this girl's eyes for about a thousand years!

I'm not gone for that long, though. Lysette brings me back to Hampstead by squeezing my hand. We're bound for Liverpool and the ship that will take us to Boston.

   I'm almost as excited about it as my young brother and sister are. Lysette has already suggested to me that, once her charges have grown a little, I can go off with her to 'explore the wilderness, making notes and sketches of all the flora and fauna we come across'.

I'll have to think about that. I'm not too keen on going in to the great unknown. I like the known.

Mr Brownlow and Oliver are here to see us off.

'I had my doubts about you at times, Jack,' Brownlow says, as he shakes my hand, 'but you came through in the end. I can do nothing less than congratulate you.'

Oliver wants to have a private word with me. 'So, now you are off to America and, no doubt, further adventures, Jack.'

He looks at me, all-forlorn. 'Won't you think of me sometimes? I shall never forget you, you know.'

'I saved you once, and you set me free twice, Ollie, so of course I'll think of you and who knows, you might come and find me out there, one day.'

It's time for me to join my angel and my family on the coach, so Mr Brownlow shakes my hand for the second time and wishes me 'Bon Voyage'.

The waving goes on until we turn a corner in the road.

Braced by Michael on one side of me and Grace on the other, I relax on the upholstered seat.

Father is sitting opposite us, with my mother and Lysette.

I still haven't got used to simply looking at the three of them. I could do it all day long.

Pa stretches his legs out, and says:

'I've heard there's money to be made in transporting goods to far-flung outposts in the Americas, Mary.'

A glance at my mother's face tells me we both know that my father will be obliged to get out and about in order to do his secret work for England.

I pipe up with, 'I don't like the idea of you travelling on your own out there, pa. You'd better take me along with you. Someone told me the country's full of savages who like nothing better than to skin you alive and eat your liver if they catch you.'

'Eat your liver!' Grace squeals. 'How horrid!'

'Yummy,' Michael says, rubbing his stomach.

As we racket north, my mother reaches across and puts her hand on my knee:

'My dear Jack,' she says, 'You did what you had to do in order to stay alive, but knowing you've always been an honest boy at heart, makes me feel so proud of you.'

I've been waiting for a moment like this. 'An honest boy, mother, I don't know about that.'

I unclench my fist and conjure up my best Artful Dodger grin as they all gape at me. 'There's no need to look so worried,' I tell them. 'This is just a little keepsake to remind me of the life I used to lead.'

I'm holding Mr Brownlow's pocket watch in the palm of my hand.

THE END

GLOSSARY

A-Z

Arcadian: describing a beautiful, secluded rural area.

Autolycus: self-proclaimed King of Thieves in Greek mythology.

Belle Sauvage: 15th-century coaching-inn on Ludgate Hill, London.

Beau Brummel (1778-1840): A male fashion icon of his day.

Cheeryble Twins: characters in 'Nicholas Nickleby' by Charles Dickens (1839)

Crib: the place one lives.

Cully: sarcastic, disrespectful term for a male.

Delved: fished, in this instance.

Dip: a pickpocket.

Ede and Ravenscroft: London tailors, established 1689.

Herrick, Robert: poet (1591-1674)

Hackney Carriage: London's regulated taxi service. The name, Hackney, probably derives from, Achetta, a Sardinian breed of horse.

Hollands: Gin.

Havisham, Miss Cassandra: a character in 'Great Expectations' by Charles Dickens (1861)

Immortal Bard: William Shakespeare.

Jackanapes: an impertinent male person.

Jaggers, Frank: a lawyer in 'Oliver Twist' by Charles Dickens (1838)

Johnson, Dr Samuel (1709-1784): literary giant who, among other achievements, compiled a comprehensive English dictionary.

John Bull: a mythological figure who represents true Englishness.

La Chair Blesse: flesh wound.

Lye Soap: made from wood ash.

Luddite: anti machine-age workers, particularly in the cotton industry.

Men of Kent/Kentish Men: the former are born east of the River Medway, the latter to the west.

Martello Towers: A line of small, defensive forts on England's south and east coast, among many other places. Built after the French revolution, they were named after part of a fortress at Mortella Point, Sardinia.

Moore, Richard: highway robber executed at Newgate on February 22nd 1815

Morpheus: Greek god of dreams and sleep.

Porter: Beer made with malt and hops. The beer-making process meant that it was safer to drink than water.

Prison hulk: de-commissioned warships used as floating prisons.

Quilp, Daniel: evil character in 'The Old Curiosity Shop' by Charles Dickens (1841)

Rum Gagger: a seaman who over-indulged in drinking alcohol.

Sheppard Jack (1702-1724): A notorious pickpocket and burglar, he made a daring escape from Newgate Prison. Hanged at Tyburn, November 1724

Shiv: a term for a knife.

Span: used a spinning wheel.

Stareleigh, Mr Justice: a character in 'The Pickwick Papers' by Charles Dickens (1837)

Strong, Dr: a character in 'David Copperfield' by Charles Dickens (1850)

That's all gammon: a Cockney answer to an unbelievable statement.

Togs and Blunt: clothes and possessions.

Trow: think or believe.

Waterloo, Battle of: With the British and her allies victorious over the French; of the 190,000 troops that took part in the battle on June 18ᵗʰ 1815, approximately 48,000 were killed or wounded, with many more thousands unaccounted for.

Weller, Tony and Sam: father and son in 'The Pickwick Papers' by Charles Dickens (1837)

Wherry: a light rowing-boat used to ferry passengers on rivers.

White's Club: An exclusive club in St James, London. Founded in 1693

Wipe: a handkerchief.

Wollstonecraft, Mary (1759-1797): writer, philosopher and female activist.

In touch with Mr Dickens

I once had an all too brief friendship with a man who'd held a father's hand, whose own father, as a child, had clutched the hand of his father, Charles Dickens. This most tenuous of connections to the illustrious writer was made when I assisted his great grandson, Cedric Charles Dickens (1916-2006), in creating an annual 'Pickwick's Christmas Banquet' in the very Ballroom where Messrs Pickwick, Tupman, Snodgrass, Jingle and Winkle, supposedly overindulged-themselves 'It wasn't the wine,' murmured Mr Snodgrass in a broken voice, 'it was the salmon.'

What joyous events our banquets were and what a truly Dickensian character Cedric was; part Cheeryble, part Fezziwig and part Ebenezer Scrooge after he became reformed and, 'knew how to keep Christmas better than any man.' If Cedric's great grandfather helped to create Christmas as we know it today, he certainly knew how to perpetuate it.

Apart from the fact that everything had to be 'top hole' for the banquets, Cedric only had one other rule. The dishes on our substantial menu had to be made from produce grown or reared in Kent - or fished from its waters; apart, that is, from the cheese. The county had a lot to offer, but very little of that. As Mr Jingle declared in *The Pickwick Papers.* 'Kent, sir? Everybody knows Kent! Apples, cherries, hops - and women!' I hasten to add that the last of these were not on our menu!

After downing a glass or two of Cedric's 'secret recipe' punch; a drink to remember, the great, the good and most certainly the wealthy, dressed in all their Victorian finery; bustles and bonnets, top hats and frock coats, would prepare to tackle a six-course feast in the Georgian Ballroom; its splendour enhanced by festive decorations and a giant Christmas tree with gifts piled high round it, ready for distribution to charities.

But first: wearing the tallest of toques and the longest apron I could lay my hands on, I would weave my way around the excited diners, holding aloft an enormous, bronzed turkey adorned with coloured streamers, holly and citrus peel. Pretending to trip, clumsily save the bird, calling out something like,

'Apologies, ladies and gents; I've roasted the pudding and flambèed the turkey! Drunk a bit too much cooking sherry, don't you know!'

Applause, cries of 'Bravo' and the noise of stamping feet would follow me out of the room. Cedric always approved.

Throughout the evening and between each course, the actor, Gerald Dickens, who would pass for his great, great grandfather in broad daylight, would entertain everyone with his bravura, one-man performance of *A Christmas Carol*

Then, towards the end of the evening, with only flickering candles to light my way, I would tour the room again, this time, holding on high a large Christmas pudding, sufficiently aflame to give a modern Health and Safety inspector a nervous breakdown.

At the end, the guests, about as full of Christmas cheer as one can get, would stand in line, waiting to stir the fruity, aromatic mixture that would become the following year's Christmas pudding.

Then it was on to Rochester's brightly-lit high street; hardly changed since Charles Dickens, himself, strolled there, doffing his hat to the ladies.

Congratulating each other on a job well done, Cedric and I, together with our efficient team would drink a toast to each other in time-honoured fashion.

My last contact with Cedric came after he'd read one of my privately published novels; he commented,

'I could not do better myself, Terry!'

That was good enough for me.

Terry Ward

ACKNOWLEDGEMENTS

I will be forever grateful to James Essinger for his advice and guidance - and for his insistence that I concentrate my mind!

My thanks also to Charlotte Mouncey for her marvellous cover and her careful and meticulous work with the typesetting.

My loving thanks to my wife, Daphne, for her unending patience and to my sons, Gary and Paul, for their support and technical assistance.